CURSED IN BLOOD

Her mother stepped forward, her face resembling nothing human. "You've learned well the ways of men, how to fight and kill." A sorcerous, menacing anger raged in her dark green eyes. "You've stolen all I love—my husband, my son, my dreams for you. My daughter, a witch with power greater than I have ever seen. But you've thrown that away.

"I lay this curse: you will follow a path of violence for the rest of your days, pitting your weapons-skill against endless foes. But only that skill. No more. You've stolen my family from me. I steal your witch-power."

Pain lanced through the girl's head and she reeled. Her mother picked up the fallen sword, set it between her own breasts, braced the hilt against a wall, and lunged forward. Trailing a thick river of blood, she fell across her son's corpse, and crawled to her husband, squeezed his cold hand. "Gods of my coven," the mother cried, "I know you not, woman! Not my daughter! You are a *thing* of fire and—*frost*!"

FROST

Look for these Tor books by Robin W. Bailey

FROST
SKULL GATE
BLOODSONGS

VOLUME
I
OF THE
SAGA OF
FROST

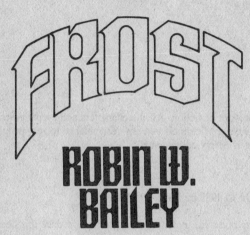

FROST

ROBIN W. BAILEY

TOR

A TOM DOHERTY ASSOCIATES BOOK

FROST

Copyright © 1983 by Robert W. Bailey

First Tor printing: February 1987

A TOR Book

Published by Tom Doherty Associates, Inc.
49 West 24 Street
New York, N.Y. 10010

Cover art by Kevin Eugene Johnson

ISBN: 0-812-53143-4
CAN. ED.: 0-812-53144-2

Printed in the United States of America

0 9 8 7 6 5 4 3 2 1

For Carolyn Cherryh and Wilson Tucker—
Teachers

And for Kate Wilde and Michael Fogal—
Friends

For Diana most of all—
the sweetest Poohawk in the tribe.

Chapter One

FROST REACHED INTO HER SADDLEBAG FOR THE LAST strip of dried meat that made up her hastily drawn provisions. Relaxing in the saddle, she began to chew the tough substance, caring little that it had no taste. A swig of cool liquid from her nearly empty waterskin washed it down without complaint, and she rode on toward Shazad.

With the storm over, the clouds gone, a bright moon shone down through the trees. Once, Frost stopped her horse and gazed skyward for long, questioning moments, for amid the stars there seemed to be a single red eye, staring toward the ground. But a drifting breeze stirred the thick branches and dripping leaves, shaking water into her upturned eyes. When she could see again, the vision was gone. A trick of the moon, no doubt, or her imagination. Her mother had warned her that madness was the fate of murderers.

She cast her eyes about, peering into the darkness. Etai Calan, this wood was called. Forest of the Forgotten. *Forest of the Damned,* she thought.

Glimmering in the moonlight were the demon-things that gave Etai Calan its name; monstrous webs stretched between the huge old trunks, burning with a dew-laden fire that never faded. With elegant, lazy grace they draped among the limbs and branches. Esgarian legends spoke of an ancient, half forgotten race of spider-like creatures that once inhabited the land and used this forest as a museum to display their most beautiful works of art—webs which to this day endured. What had become of that race, no one remembered. No trace of them remained, and no legend or song told of their passing. But the webs were treated with reverence, and when the road was cut through Etai Calan not a strand was disturbed.

Frost was more than glad the path avoided the strange webs. She had no love for spiders, artistic or otherwise. From a safe distance, though, she wondered why they never blew apart in storms like the one she had just come through, and what gave them such an eerie light. The webs grew thicker as she rode deeper into the wood, and a twist in the road brought them close enough to touch.

She stopped her horse and listened. Since darkness had fallen, Etai Calan had been silent. Unnaturally so. Except for the steady fall of her mount's hooves and the dripping water off wet leaves, no other sound touched her ears. The quiet was unsettling, but after awhile she rode on, alert for any hint that she was not the only living thing in the night.

The air came suddenly alive with sound, a soft rythmic flutter at first as if the dark was filled with thousands of wings. The beating grew and grew as a vague shadow passed overhead, hiding the bloated moon from sight. Frost grimaced as the noise assailed her and fought to stay astride her panicking steed. Then, sound and shadow faded in the distance, and the wood was quiet as before.

A chill fell upon the forest. Frost drew her damp cloak closer around her. Magic, she was sure. . . . Had the storm, too, been created and not natural?

Again the shadow passed over the trees. Her mount trembled and tried to rear, and Frost fought to hold him still, cursing the pig-farmer who had sold him to her.

Thick clouds rolled in and blotted out the stars. The moon slowly vanished, taking the last light. Only the glowing webs of Etai Calan showed her the road.

A pungent odor of dead leaves and decayed wood swam in her nostrils borne by a cold wind that played suddenly in the leaves and ceased as suddenly.

From the sky a dense column of vapor fell, and as it touched the ground it flowed outward like water in all directions. Another column, then several more, descended on her right and left, as straight as bars in a cell door. She drew her sword and swung it through the nearest one. A wisp clung to her blade, then trailed away into the air.

She sheathed her weapon with difficulty, wrapping the reins tighter around her free hand as she fought to control her mount.

The smoky columns fell everywhere, increasing in number with each breath. As they met the ground a thick carpet of fog spread over the forest floor. Trees on either side of the path began to fade, obscured by the mist.

A column of fog fell on her thigh and oozed over her knee. Its touch was feathery soft, icy cold. She recoiled, wheeling her horse in a tight circle.

The road was gone, hidden in the heavy mist, yet she leaned close to her horse's neck and whipped him into motion.

Like giant spears the columns fell. Frost leaned away from their touch, weaving her mount through them. It no longer mattered that the road was invisible. She urged the beast faster along, seeking some escape. The air was filling with the vapor, and it burned her lungs with cold fire when she breathed.

Too late she saw the web, had a dark vision of writhing in those glistening strands while a fat spider sucked her blood. With a desperate cry she swerved and was knocked from the saddle by a thick, low branch.

Hard and flat on her back she hit the ground, splashing mud. The rim of a shield, the last piece of armor she had, bit painfully into her spine, causing her to regret the way she wore it strapped over her shoulders. She coughed, struggling for breath through a bruised throat.

Staggering to her feet, she spotted her horse waiting uncertainly in the fog. There was panic in the animal's crazed eyes. It stamped the earth and shook its tangled mane; then suddenly it whirled and galloped out of sight.

She cursed bitterly. Everything she owned was tied to that miserable creature. Everything except her sword, shield and the clothes on her back.

Her father's saddle was gone. Two days before she had carried that saddle for miles, her last legacy, rather than abandon it when her first horse had broken a leg.

She looked around to get bearings. Unslinging the shield, she set it on her right arm. With her left hand she grasped her sword's hilt for reassurance and began to walk.

Afoot there was more time to think rationally. Magical forces were at play in this forest, and she was caught up in them; whether by accident or deliberate design remained to be seen. Weather control was fundamental to anyone with mystic knowledge, yet the suddenness of the cold and the depth of the fog spoke of a powerful, possibly malignant intelligence. And the thunderous beating of wings, of thousands of wings—

She pushed on, stumbling on unseen rocks and roots. Then abruptly, the fog gave way, rolling from her feet so she could see plainly the obstacles in her path. *Guidance,* she realized, for the mist began to open at odd angles leading her in directions she had not intended to go. She stopped to consider— and the mist waited for her.

She was lost for sure, and tired of wandering blindly. Holding her shield high, she went where the path led.

Suddenly, the trail ended. She waited expectantly for the fog to open in some new direction, but it did not.

A robed and hooded figure stepped out of the mist not an arm's length away. Neither face nor hands showed beneath the folds of the shrouding garment. Frost whipped out her sword. The point hovered at the Stranger's throat.

"Another move, and I'll run you through," she threatened with a calm she did not feel.

The Stranger spoke her name. Her real name.

Enraged, she raised her blade to slay, but a power took hold of her left arm, and she found she could not strike, nor could she slam the edge of her shield at the unseen face. A subtle dread crept up her spine, changing her desire to kill to a more defensive attitude. She backed a couple of steps, regarding the figure carefully, warily.

"Speak not that name again, or I swear I'll find some way to gut you, demon or no."

"Very well, Frost. I shall use your chosen name, though it is neither pretty, nor pleasing to the tongue." The voice, a man's, was richly melodic, filled with sweet music, soft, yet strong. He made no move to attack. Still, she kept her sword leveled as a barrier between them.

"How do you know any name to call me by?"

"Your names are as clear in your mind as words on a page to me," he answered. "Every thought you have ever had is writ thereon, and I have seen a little of it."

It was likely. Once, she had such power, however limited, to see another's mind. That this stranger had free access to her private thoughts did not please her. "Why?" she asked.

"There is a task I must pass on to you. My task first, but you must do it for me now."

"Why should I do anything for you?"

The Stranger shrugged. "I could say that you will do it for money, but I have none to give you. I could say that you will do it to save this miserable world and your own life with it, but you will most likely fail and lose both. Or I could say that you will do it because by undertaking the task and confronting the dangers you may, for a little while, escape the nightmares and memories that torture you, and for that reason only I believe you will do as I ask."

Her sword arm trembled, and she struggled to suppress the temper that swelled within her. He knew about the nightmares. He knew it all.

"In plain words, what do you want of me?" she said through clenched teeth. "But I warn you, I'll probably refuse your task. I don't think I like you much."

A hand extended to her. In the palm was a leather-bound book with iron hinges and a lock. The leather was cracked and worn with age. The lock was rusted and of a kind she had never seen before. To judge by the edges, the pages were yellowed and brittle. The thing exuded a musty, molding smell that crept unpleasantly up her nose. Yet, she was attracted to the delicate characters and runes that were carved into the binding. They caught and held her eye. She reached out carefully to touch it.

"You must deliver this to a sorcerer in Chondos."

Frost jerked her hand back. Her grip on the sword tightened. "Do I look like a fool? Chondos is a land ruled by black magic. Sensible men avoid it as they would a plague."

"Because of rumors the Chondites themselves have fostered," the Stranger said. "True, the land is ruled by sorcery, but not all sorcerers are black sorcerers, as you should know. You are a witch yourself."

"No longer," she muttered. "My witch-powers are gone."

The Stranger shook his head. "Your mother's curse only deprived you of certain psychic mechanisms by which you express those powers. The power itself is still within you, though you may never again be able to tap it."

"No matter. I have a sword now."

"In time, you may wish for the return of your skills. The foes you face may not always be human."

"I'm learning," she answered slowly, "that I prefer to see up close who I'm killing. Or what. There's little enough pleasure in this business and none at all if you can't see your enemy's face when he dies."

"You have a strong spirit," the Stranger observed. "It will serve you in good stead through the days and nights to come."

Suddenly, the figure tilted his head as if listening for something. Frost listened, too. The misty air was still and silent.

"They have found me," he announced calmly. "They must not discover you here, too."

"Who has found you?" She listened again. "I hear nothing."

"There is not much time, please. Take the Book and get far away." He held the ancient tome out to her. "Please!" he urged when she hesitated.

"Not so fast. I still want some answers. Just what is this book, and why must it go to Chondos?"

The Stranger glanced skyward again, but Frost still heard nothing but their own short breathing.

"There is little time, so listen carefully." He thrust the Book into her arms, brushing aside the sword she held between them. "This is the Book of the Last Battle."

Her mouth gaped wide. The Book was legendary. No mortal had ever laid eyes on it, but the dark secrets that lay between its covers made it the object of many a mystic quest. Even her mother, Esgaria's most potent sorceress, had attempted to find it and failed. Frost sheathed her blade to examine the Book more closely.

"For uncounted millennia it lay hidden at the heart of a distant mountain," the Stranger explained, "but a Shardahani wizard stumbled by sheer accident upon its resting place."

"A Shardahani?" she interrupted. "They make poor wizards. No imagination."

"Zarad-Krul *was* a poor wizard dabbling in philosophies he

couldn't begin to understand until he found the Book. But in the instant he first became aware of the volume's true nature the Dark Forces he worships also became aware of it. And like humans, they desire it too, for the Book of the Last Battle is said to contain the strategies, the plans and the Words of Power that will be used in the final confrontation of Light against Darkness.

"This Zarad-Krul has become a tool of the Dark Gods. Though he is unable to open the Book now, his masters feed him more knowledge each day in the hope he will find a way to pry it open—or failing that, to summon a Dark One into this plane to learn its secrets. The wizard is not yet strong enough for that, but already his new magic has given him dominion over all of Shardaha. And his power grows. Soon, it will reach the limits of his mortal mind. Already it has made him mad, and he plans to call not one, but many Dark Lords into this world and unleash them on his enemies.

"Nor will the Forces of Light do anything to prevent it. Not willingly. The time is not yet right for the final confrontation. If the Dark Ones are called through, the scales of destiny will be unbalanced, and the hour of the Last Battle will be delayed beyond all foreseeing. If Zarad-Krul can be thwarted it must be by you and me—and, perhaps, one other."

"What other?"

The Stranger lifted his gaze yet again, peering into the mist above his head. "A Chondite sorcerer, a master in the Brotherhood of the Black Arrow. His name is Kregan. Take the Book to him. He will know what to do with it."

"But how did you come by the Book if Zarad-Krul found it first?"

"There's no more time. You must flee now."

Frost set her feet. "Give me the answer first. I don't know if I trust you." But now she heard, faint and far away, the ominous beating of wings.

"I stole it from Zarad-Krul's tower while he slept, but a guardian raised the alarm before I could slip away. I fled with the Book, but his demons pursue me. I've warred against them all night, nearly to exhaustion. Finally, I threw up this fog to hide myself, knowing it would not be enough to save my life. It was a desperate maneuver when I thought I'd lost the gamble, that Zarad-Krul's creatures would kill me and take the Book back to him. But then, I sensed you riding in the wood.''

The sound of the wings drew nearer. Steadily they beat *doom, doom, doom* on the night air, but Frost could see nothing to cause such dreadful cadence.

"Go now," the Stranger begged. "If Zarad-Krul sends his eye, he will find you, too; then all hope will be lost.''

"Come with me. We'll flee together.''

He shook his head. "No, Zarad-Krul knows my aura now. He can find me wherever I run.''

"Then I'll stay and help you fight.''

"No!" he cried. "Your sword will be of no use against these creatures. Flee! Now!''

The air boomed with the frantic pulse of invisible wings. Her instincts told her to run. This was sorcery, and her own mystic powers were gone. She clasped the Book tightly in her shield hand and unsheathed her sword. However useless it might be it was a weapon at least. She turned to go.

"Wait!" shouted the Stranger suddenly before she was far away. "I can give you two weapons to help fight Zarad-Krul.'' He threw off his robe. His body was perfect, and the naked flesh shone with a golden light. Frost had never called a man beautiful before, but this man was that. He wore no other garment, but around his waist on a belt of silver there hung a dagger. He tossed it to her. The sheath containing the blade was also of silver, pure and gleaming.

"This is Demonfang, and it is well named, for a warning comes with it: do not draw it idly from its silver sheath; once removed the dagger must taste blood—either your enemy's or your own.''

"And the second weapon?'' shouted Frost. The beating became a thunderous roar in her ears.

"It will come to you in time and of its own will. Now run as quick as you can.''

"Your name," she cried. "I want to know your name!''

"What does it matter? I am a Tool of Light.''

The noise reached a deafening crescendo, heralding the arrival of Zarad-Krul's minions. Through the fog, thousands upon thousands of tiny shapes fluttered to and fro, searching for the man who gave no name. Frost drew back her sword and swung furiously at the creatures, but they flitted easily away, too small to make decent targets.

Suddenly, the shadow-shapes found the Stranger. He raised his arms to swat them away, flailing frantically at the air. They swarmed over him, settled in his hair, in his eyes. She raised her sword again. If she could not drive away his tormentors, she could at least give him a quick death. But as she stepped forward, he managed to lift an arm in warning and shouted one last, desperate cry.

Twittering shapes engulfed his beautiful body and bore him down. He struggled under the sheer weight of numbers, but it was no use. A few last contortions, and his fight was over.

Obeying his final command, Frost turned and ran into the fog, casting fearful glances over her shoulder. When the fallen form of the Stranger was no more than a vague, formless lump on the misty ground, she threw herself down behind a bush to watch and wait. She felt the Book pressed between her body and the moist earth. Demonfang in its silver sheath lay beside her, its glittering belt looped over her arm.

She watched as the shadowy creatures settled upon the Stranger's still body, afraid that she would be discovered and dealt with in similar fashion. Shortly the wings stopped beating. The fog began to dissipate.

Through long hours she remained unmoving. As the last of the mist lifted, she sucked in her breath, unable quite to believe what she saw. In the pale light of pre-dawn, thousands of butterflies blanketed the Stranger's corpse until no part of it could be seen. Over this, there hovered a rheumy eye, red and swollen and evil. It floated for a time, fixed on the spot where murder had been done. Then it looked up and surveyed the forest in a slow rotation. As it swept in her direction Frost caught just a glimpse of the black pupil and shivered. The eye paused. Though it seemed not to see her, she crawled closer to the bush and hid her face. When she looked up again the eye was gone.

On the Stranger's body the butterflies remained perched, lazily fanning their wings until the first rays of a new sun appeared in the sky. In her hiding place, she dared not move. Then, as if on command, they took to the air, spreading wings in the fresh morning light.

Soundlessly they flew now, and the forest sparkled with colors, rich greens, reds and golds as the delicate insects danced among the leaves.

Never had she seen such rare beauty. They meandered briefly through the trees, then gathering into a great swarm, flew into the northwest, so alluring, so precious their many-hued wings, so perfect in flight. She watched until she could see them no more.

Then, she turned her eyes back to the Stranger, and her stomach heaved. A pile of bones, picked clean, gleamed whitely there. All through the night the butterflies had feasted on his flesh. Not even a drop of blood was left to stain the grass.

Chapter Two

AT MIDDAY, FROST WIPED THE SWEAT FROM HER BROW and cursed the flea-bitten horse that had deserted her. It was a long walk through Etai Calan. Her throat was dry, and she had not seen a stream for hours. Plucking a leaf, she crumpled it and stuffed it in her mouth. The sappy liquid had a foul taste, but at least it was wet.

The vision of the Stranger's grisly skeleton haunted her. Now and then, she took the Book from its resting place inside her tunic, half-tempted to toss it into the bushes and forget about it. Yet, the loathsome death she had witnessed caused her eyes to narrow in a silent vow, and her heart hardened against the wizard Zarad-Krul.

By late afternoon her very bones were tired. Her shield was a heavy stone tied to her back, and her legs, stiff and sore from four days in the saddle, ached painfully. Though she rested frequently, there seemed to be no end to the forest.

Off the road to her left she heard a crackle in the brush. She paused only for a minute, then dismissed it as some animal. After a few short steps, she heard another sound, this time on her right.

Eight men appeared suddenly out of the brush and made a ring around her. Dirt smeared their faces; their hair was shaggy and unkempt. Their clothes were stained with mud and filth. The stink of them polluted the clean freshness of the forest air.

Raiders, she realized. Such men often crawled across the border into Esgaria, attacking farmhouses and small trade caravans. Before a patrol could be mounted to catch them they would lose themselves in the wood and make their way back to Rholaroth to fence their pilfered goods.

Shazad was full of men like these. That city's coffers were gorged on the bounty of her people.

Five of them held swords. One bore a falchion, and two more carried dirks with blades long as her forearm. Her own sword was in her fist, and she crouched low, ready to meet the first attacker.

Instead, one of the raiders grinned broadly, showing yellowed, broken teeth. The grin widened and suddenly he roared with laughter. "God's loins, it's a woman," he bellowed. "We been stalkin' a woman!"

"Well, ye couldn't tell it by 'er clothes," said another.

"Or that sticker she's holdin'," added a third.

They all laughed and began to circle her, throwing taunts and insults. Was she cuttin' flowers for her table? Searchin' for an unfaithful lover? Naw, she'd never had no lovers, so she'd given up bein' a woman an' planned to make it as a man from now on.

The man who had spoken first ended the game with a wave of his hand.

"I'd sure like that shield," said a voice behind her.

"I could sure use a new cloak," said another. "Lost mine in that card game last week. 'Course it was prettier than this one, but I'll make do."

"I want the sword."

"The boots look in fair shape."

Frost made no move. She listened to the voices, the rustle of their clothes, the shuffling of feet, knowing just where each of the raiders stood though she could not see them all.

"Well, what about her?" said the first man, their leader, apparently. "She's pretty enough. What d'ye think we should do with her?"

There was only one thing to do with a woman, someone answered.

Frost went cold. No man had ever touched her as these men meant to. She smelled their dirty bodies and swore that the first to attempt it would pay a high price.

The leader's eyes met hers, and his grin disappeared. His sword flicked, and he made a quick side-step, expecting to get inside her guard and knock her blade away.

Frost sensed his overconfidence. She swung hard, catching his sword near the hilt, sending it flying from his grip.

The man leaped back in surprise, checking his fingers to make sure they were all there. Then, he glared, and she saw the anger that flamed in his face. He seized the sword of the man beside him, shoving him roughly and cursing.

Drawing a deep breath, she shut her eyes for just a moment, remembering the words of her weapons-master. He had prepared her for this, drilled her in absolute darkness, taught her to handle a multiple attack. She heard the sounds of their breathing, felt the tension that filled the air, smelled their sweat. Her sword grip tightened, and she thought of her shield. No use trying to get it free now. Let it protect her back. She took her sword in both hands, bastard style, and adjusted her stance.

"Think y'ere pretty good with that sticker, don't ye, woman? Well, ye just made it a lot tougher on ye than it had to be. Before, we were just gonna have a little fun, but now ye made ol' Vericus mad. Embarrassed 'im a little 'fore his men, so now he's gotta show 'em what happens when people make Vericus mad." His smile came back, and he showed his rotten teeth. "Take that sticker away from her, boys."

A man to Vericus' right moved first. Frost swung her sword in a whistling arc and chopped halfway through him. Vericus bellowed angrily, swung and missed as she struggled to free her blade. Tugging it away, she leaped at him and smashed her knee into his groin. As he doubled over, she pushed him headlong into a tree.

The circle was broken. Frost ran a few steps and turned to face the rest. Two more charged, stepping on their fallen comrades to get at her. She parried the first man's blow and, on the backswing, lopped off the other's sword hand. From the corner of her eye she saw the remaining raiders trying to surround her again.

She was tired from her long walk. Each swing of her weapon seemed slower than the last, and every block sent shivers up her arm. Worse, the hilt of her sword was slick with blood.

A descending blade whistled, and Frost whirled, dodged and parried, panting for breath. The falchion rose again and crashed down. She flung up her sword to intercept it, but so strong was the stroke that she lost her grip. Her sword tumbled into the road.

Her left arm hung limp and aching at her side. Having disarmed her, the falchion hesitated. With a gasp and the last of her fading strength, she slammed her fist against the man's jaw. It had small effect, and he caught her wrist when she tried again.

Held fast, another raider seized her useless arm and twisted it cruelly behind her. She winced and cried out, clenching her eyes against the pain. When she opened them Vericus was grinning over her, his nose close to hers.

He slapped her viciously. She rolled her head aside to avoid the full stinging force, but a trickle of blood ran from her lip.

He gripped her chin, forced her to look where he directed. Two men were dead; one lay moaning on the ground clutching a handless stump.

"Bitch!" he shouted. "You miserable bitch! Y'er gonna pay fer this. Good boys, every one of 'em, and that one with no hand my very own son! You'll wish ye'd laid down an' had it nice an' proper when ye had the chance 'fore I'm through with ye now."

Vericus began to loosen his clothes, lust and hatred burning in his eyes. The others licked their lips, grinning in anticipation.

"Now lay 'er down on the ground an' hold 'er tight. Ye don't have to be none too gentle about it, neither."

Frost smashed her foot against the shin of one of her captors and got a fist in the stomach in return. She struggled, twisting, as her feet were jerked from under her. With a man on each limb they pinned her in the dirt.

Vericus ran filthy hands over her breasts and across her belly. When his fingers brushed something under her garment his face lit up.

"Hey, the bitch as been holdin' out on us, boys!" He shoved his hand roughly under her tunic and pulled out the Book of the Last Battle.

"No!"

The raider captain slapped her mouth before she could make another sound. His fist pressed down on her lips. "Don't ye worry now. Ye're not gonna be doin' much readin' anymore." He threw the Book casually to one of his men. "Keep it. Might bring a copper or two later."

Dirty fingers clawed at her belt, and Vericus leered as her tunic fell open. A flash of pain as his big hand pinched one breast.

"She ain't got much fer tits," commented the raider who knelt on her sword-arm.

"They'll do," Vericus huffed.

Frost stiffened, cursing her helplessness. She shut her eyes again to hold back tears, refused to feel the coarse hands that wandered so freely on her body.

Then, a peculiar distant cry interrupted his pleasure. Vericus looked questioningly at the others. They returned his puzzled gaze and shrugged.

The cry sounded again, unearthly.

Then, Frost felt a vibration in the road against her spine. Pinned as she was, she could still press an ear to the ground.

Hoof-beats, approaching fast. She arched, hoping for a view of the road behind.

A third time she heard the cry. Suddenly, her captors leaped up, reaching for swords, cursing, calling on their gods.

Frost rolled over, stared.

A beast, a stygian nightmare from hell's lowest levels, charged. Tail and mane lashed the air. Where eyes should have been there burned two wild, blazing spots of angry flame, and from its forelock sprouted a giant, twisted spike of gleaming obsidian, long as a man's arm.

Head lowered, the unicorn slammed its horn through the nearest raider. With a triumphant cry it tossed the screaming man over its back into the bushes.

She watched with a stunned eye, then pulled her clothes together, snatched up her own sword. However dangerous the impossible creature might be, there was a score to settle, and she chose the closest of her attackers.

"Turn and die, you pig!"

The man bearing the falchion spun at the sound of her voice. Her sword bit through his mouth, shattering teeth, cleaving bone. Something fell from his lifeless fingers. The

Book of the Last Battle. Frost thanked her own gods and scooped it up, thrust it back under her tunic. In her thirst for vengeance she had nearly forgotten about it.

She was spotted, though. One raider glanced at the unicorn, then at her, his face a pale mask of fear. Clearly, he thought her the easier foe, and with his long dirk he lunged. Her longer blade knocked his aside with an easy slash. Desperately, he struck again. She leaped aside and swung, but the man was nimble as she and dodged her blow. Another exchange, and he managed to circle past her to the open road, broke from the fight and ran, but she followed with quick strides. With a startled cry he toppled in the dirt, hamstrung by a clever stroke. She met his fearful gaze for just a moment, then thrust her point through his throat.

A scream made her turn as the unicorn's deadly hooves crashed down on a raider's skull. The beast reared again and pulped his chest.

She looked around; only Vericus remained.

The bandit captain saw her, too, and snatched a second sword from the hand of a dead cohort. Doubly armed, his eyes flickered from her to the unicorn and back again.

The unicorn pawed the earth and reared, snorting. The great horn, stained crimson, flashed as the creature shook its mane. Yet, it did not charge, and it seemed Vericus had won a short respite.

"Witch!" he shouted hysterically. "My boys—all dead!"

Frost kept her eyes on the unicorn, wary of the animal, but determined to see Vericus die. She moved in slowly, sliding the shield from her back, holding it high on her right arm.

Vericus ranted. "Curse ye! Damn ye to hell, ye an' this demon!"

She stopped then, wondering at the unicorn. Vericus stood between her and the creature. If she killed him would it attack her?

"Ye an' that monster did 'em in, an' now ye think ye got ol' Vericus. Well, ye'll not take me, witch!" He raised one sword and hurled it with all his might straight for her.

She didn't flinch, but casually lifted her own blade and knocked the glittering missile from the air.

But the motion seemed to enrage the unicorn. Kicking up dust, it charged Vericus. Defiantly, the raider drew back to strike at the lowered head.

22

His broad, undefended back to her, Frost acted instantly. Her own sword flashed across the short distance, sank to the hilt between his powerful shoulders.

The unicorn stopped in mid-charge, shaking its huge head.

Wide-eyed, a surprised Vericus touched the point that protruded from his body and sighed disbelievingly. Blood ran down the front of his hairy chest. He rubbed his hands in it and held them up to his eyes. His lips curled back in a curse. "Well, ye killed me too—damn ye witch!" His knees buckled and he fell, sucking for a last breath that never came.

The unicorn paced slowly over and sniffed his bright blood. Then, it looked at Frost and snorted.

She could read nothing in the creature's face. Without her sword she was easy meat if it charged. She glanced around for a weapon to defend herself. Nothing. Her fist closed on the hilt of Demonfang; the dagger was better than nothing at all.

But something about the unicorn seemed different. The fire where its eyes should have been wavered and dimmed. It pranced nervously among the bandits' bodies, stopping frequently to stare at her. Finally, the beast lowered its head and plodded shyly toward her.

She tensed, not quite drawing Demonfang. As if sensing her distrust the unicorn halted. It looked up at her and the flames that were eyes glowed softly.

Her fingers uncurled from the dagger's hilt.

The blood-caked horn slid under her arm as the unicorn nuzzled her hand. Its breath was sweet and warm on her palm.

Cautiously, she stroked the animal between its strange eyes and down the broad face. It trembled beneath her touch as she rubbed the long neck, smoothed the tangled mane, growing bolder with each passing moment.

The long legs were perfect, swift and strong with hooves larger than a normal horse's and shining black like the deadly spike on its brow. The tail swept the ground, so thick and lustrous.

She touched the horn, ran her hand over its length in awe and wonder. With a corner of her cloak she wiped the blood from it until it gleamed in the sunlight.

It confounded her how quickly a bond formed between her and this beast. Such animals existed only in myths, she told herself, or in hell. How could it possibly be standing here licking her fingers?

By chance, then, she brushed the silver hilt of Demonfang, and suddenly she recalled the words of the Stranger in the forest. The second weapon would come to her, he said. Did he mean the unicorn?

Resolutely, she wrapped her hand in the matted mane and leaped onto its back. It took two steps sideways and stood still. She breathed a sigh of relief. She had expected to be thrown, quite probably trampled. Instead, the unicorn seemed so tame it was difficult to remember it had killed two men.

She jumped down long enough to retrieve her sword from the raider captain's body. With a two-handed effort the blade came free, and she wiped it clean on the dead man's sleeve.

Once again she mounted the unicorn. No longer afoot she could make Shazad by nightfall, and at last be out of this damned forest.

"Wait," a voice called weakly. "Please."

She looked back. The man Vericus had called son raised up on one elbow waving a bloody stump where his hand had been.

"Help me," he pleaded.

She peered down on him, suddenly seeing another youth—her own brother. They looked alike, were about the same age, and she had stood over him, too, her sword dripping with his hated blood.

"The only thing I owe you is a blade through your worthless gut."

"You can't leave me here to die!" he sniveled, lifting the stump higher, pointing it accusingly at her. Red fluid squirted on the ground and soaked into the dirt, making dark puddles. It rolled down his arm into his sleeve.

Frost gazed at the pallid face. If the wound were bound and cauterized he might yet live, but she doubted it. She had seen such injuries before among her father's warriors. Almost always the blood turned to poison and the skin went green around the wound. Death was slow and painful.

Not that a raider's death mattered. She had worse sins to answer for. She nudged the unicorn with her heels and started down the road.

"How?" she heard him shriek. "How could this happen? A woman and a horse. I'm killed!"

That made her stop. She twisted in surprise. Was the boy blind or just crazed from despair? To call her steed a common

24

horse. Vericus had seen the unicorn and called it a monster. The others had done the same.

On an impulse, she rode back to him and leaned from the unicorn's back. The raider youth sat up, regarding her with hopeful eyes.

"Maybe I will help you—if you answer a question."

He nodded eagerly.

"What kind of horse am I riding?"

He stared back dumbly and she repeated the question. "Answer, if you want my help."

His mouth warped in a cautious smile. "Well, it's a stallion, a big black."

Several minutes passed while she weighed his words. Then, unsheathing her sword, she plunged it through his heart. A quick death was more than a raider deserved.

The road through Etai Calan wandered northward for many miles. The webs that glittered in the tops of the old trees grew scarce, and soon she saw no more of them. The ancient, moss-covered giants gave way to younger trees as she neared the edge of the wood, and the wind bore a new smell—the smell of civilization.

As the sun sank in the sky, she emerged from the forest and looked across the Gargassi Plain at the gates of Shazad.

She stroked the unicorn's crest, murmuring the name she had chosen for him—Ashur, after the Esgarian God of War. Right now, he was a problem. In the city his peculiar eyes and shining horn would attract far too much attention, and she had no love of crowds. She threw a leg over Ashur's neck and slid to the ground.

Pulling a clump of grass, she held it for her newfound friend to chew. "Will you wait for me?" she whispered. Ashur nibbled the offering.

Watching to see if the creature would follow, she backed a few steps. Ashur raised his head and fixed her with those disconcerting eyes.

"I'll be back," she promised.

That seemed to satisfy him. With a swish of his tail he began to munch more of the sweet grass.

Frost walked toward the gates. The failing light gave the Gargassi Plain a crimson cast. Through squinting eyes she peered at the dying sun and wished it did not remind her of the Eye of Zarad-Krul.

Her footsteps made little clouds of powdery dust. This plain was a legend among her people, for here, three hundred years ago the women of Esgaria, with magic and sorcery, destroyed a Rholarothan army and saved their menfolk from a crushing defeat at the hands of King Gargassi.

The gates of Shazad were never closed. The walls were made only to keep money in, not keep out any who might spend it. There were no guards at the gate, either. Pulling the hood of her cloak over her face, she strode through the low archway into a broad lane. Garbage and refuse littered the streets. She wrinkled her nose at the stench.

But she had arrived at an ideal time; too late for honest folks, and too early for the sleasier crowd. She passed through the streets meeting only a few people. None attempted to speak to her. In Shazad strangers came and went as they pleased, and no one inquired about their business.

At last, she found an inn. A rough-hewn shingle hanging in front proclaimed it the Woeful Widow. An unlikely name, she thought, but she went in, noting three horses tethered near the door. She'd have company whether she wanted it or not, it seemed. She drew the cloak around her.

The waning sunlight traced her shadow on the tavern floor. Four pairs of eyes flickered briefly in her direction, and she smiled secretly. It amused her that they did not recognize her sex.

She took a stool at a long wooden table, unslung her shield and leaned it against the wall near at hand. Though it was clumsy to sit wearing a sword, she managed, pushing it down by her legs under the table.

The innkeeper, a nervous little man, hurried to serve her. Frost noticed how his eyes kept flitting to the three men on the far side of the room by the cold fireplace.

"Your pleasure, sir?"

She kept her voice low. "A room that's safe to sleep in, but first bring me something wet, preferably something with some sting to it; then bring a bite to eat." Two gold *korgots* clinked on the table. The innkeeper swept them up with a quick, furtive motion.

"And tell me," said Frost, "why you call this place the Woeful Widow?"

The innkeeper shot a glance at the three men. "Cause that's

what my missus'll be if customers get too drunk and do me harm." He scuttled away.

Frost rested her chin on her fists and regarded the three men from the concealing shadow of her hood. One seemed quite old. His brown garments were tattered and dusty, and a little hood covered his head. Bent over a bowl of posset he tried his best to eat in peace, but the two younger men who flanked him seemed determined to prevent that.

She studied them closely. Both men were strong and well built with hair of similar color. Brothers, she decided. The tight pants and dark leather jerkins they wore were finely made, proving wealth. Each wore a sword, though she couldn't judge the quality in the dim light. The hilts, however, glimmered with jewels. They'd have to know how to use such trinkets to keep them in this city of thieves, so they were swordsmen, too.

The brothers suddenly broke into rude laughter. One gave the old man a hard slap on the shoulder knocking him from his stool. The second brother turned the bowl of posset upside down, spilling the contents.

Frost watched silently, a coldness growing inside her, as the old man crawled back to his seat. He dragged a finger over the table's surface, scraping what he could of his meal back into the bowl. Patiently, he resumed eating.

The brothers howled, clapped each other on the back, slapped their knees and took the bowl again.

The innkeeper returned with a platter of meat, some raw vegetables and a bottle of strong-tasting liquor. Better fare than she expected. She took a long drink to wash the dust from her throat, and then fell to the meat.

The little owner looked on as she ate, eager to please. Yet, his eyes were ever on the ruffian brothers, and she could smell his fear.

She touched his sleeve and gestured at the three. With a weary sigh, the innkeeper sank down on a stool opposite her. "The oldest sons of the governor, Lord Rholf," he whispered. "That one is Than, the other Chavi. They've tormented the old man mercilessly for the past hour. A shame, too, for he paid good coin."

"Throw them out," Frost suggested.

"The governor's favorite sons?" He shook his head.

She shrugged and returned to her supper, determined to shut out the crude mouthings of Lord Rholf's spoiled offspring. It was none of her affair. The old man meant nothing to her.

But her host bent close to her ear. "Between you and me, I think those two should be whipped. Teach them some proper manners. That old man's done them no wrong."

The insults grew louder, more vulgar. Chavi overturned the bowl again. Than poured a cup of wine on the old man's head. When the innkeeper got up to clean away the spilled posset, Than shoved him back roughly with a curse.

"Keep your nose in your own business if you want to keep it at all." Chavi waved a fist in the smaller man's face, and he slunk back to his stool near Frost.

At last, the old man spoke. "There is no need to harm the proprietor. He has done nothing to you."

The brothers looked at each other in surprise. Chavi seized the old man by the throat and lifted him to his feet. "Trying to tell us what to do, beggar?"

"I didn't think he could talk at all," said Than.

The old man made no response.

"You too good to talk to us?" shouted Chavi, shaking his victim.

"It's not polite to treat the governor's sons that way," Than admonished. "Right, brother?"

Chavi smiled cruelly, and the old man flew over the table, sprawling in a heap near Frost. Than and Chavi came after him. "That's right," Chavi agreed.

This time it was Than who reached for the old man. In his haste and clumsiness, he stumbled against Frost's table, spilling her wine.

She turned a little sideways, placed her foot squarely on Than's butt and shoved him headlong into the wall.

Chavi exploded with mirth at this new entertainment, watching his brother stagger to his feet.

"Horse dung!" Than shouted at Frost, wiping a trickle of blood that rolled into his eye. "You'll pay for that!" His fingers flexed menacingly as he reached for her.

She should have stayed out of it, she reminded herself too late. Rising, she drew her sword.

The old man stepped quietly behind her. Chavi's laughter

died abruptly, but he did not interfere. In his safe corner, the innkeeper nearly fainted.

"So that's how you want it!" Than drew his own sword. "I'll shove this through your gizzard, then!"

Boxed between two tables, she was in no place to fight. With agile grace, she leaped over her own table into open floor space.

Than gestured to his brother. "Let's carve the meddler."

But Chavi shook his head. "He's two full heads shorter than you. You don't need me." His tone was light, mocking. Frost saw the grin on his face.

She glanced at her shield. It rested against the wall, no good to her. In cramped quarters she preferred two-handed techniques.

Her weapons-master would disapprove. *A shield is always an advantage,* he said. But she had proved him fatally wrong the same day her brother had died.

Her cloak was an encumbrance. Her right hand touched the knotted clasp. Cloak and hood fell to the floor, and she kicked them under a table out of the way.

"It's a woman!" cried Than.

Frost was quick to take advantage of his surprise. Her sword darted like a serpent's tongue, striking Than's blade, knocking it from his startled grip. She leaned the point of her sword on his chest, smiling. Twice she'd pulled that trick today.

"That wasn't fair," he protested.

"Fair is for fools." Frost pressed slightly. The point tore his jerkin and pricked the skin. A drop of blood trickled, and he gave a little cry of pain. "Do you think you can find the words to apologize to this old man?"

Than turned scarlet, but said nothing. Frost leaned a little harder. Chavi stood by, hysterical with laughter, taunting his brother.

"Well," she insisted.

Than stuttered. "I . . . I apologize."

She backed slowly, then, seeing the hate that flared in Than's eyes. She had humiliated him, a foolish thing to do unless she also intended to kill him. But she had had enough of death this day.

Than wiped his hand over the tiny wound, smearing a crimson stain on his chest. He stared at his own blood.

For just a moment, Frost diverted her attention, stooped to regain her cloak. It was a move she instantly regretted.

Recovering his sword, Than lunged with a wild bellow. Frost barely dodged. The blow struck the table, shearing off a chunk of wood. Than turned on her again.

"Stupid woman! You should have killed me when you had the chance!"

There was no reason to answer. She knew he was right. Hadn't she been taught never to draw steel unless she meant to use it? Well, it was an error she could correct.

Poised on the balls of her feet, she waited completely still, offering an easy target for a lunge.

Than made the predicted move. His weapon rushed in. Her own flicked out with practiced ease, met it, brushed it aside. She saw his face turn red with anger and excitement. Here was a man who *liked* to kill.

As the fight went on he raved, shouting curses and spewing brave boasts. Like a berserker he charged her, his blade hissing venomously through the air.

Steel rang on steel. Furniture shattered under the impact of sword blows. Tables overturned, stools were kicked aside. Than's rantings could be heard in the next street, but Frost saved her breath for fighting.

She moved lithe as a cat, maneuvering her foe, never remaining in one spot. She tapped the other sword with just enough force to deflect it and never pitted her own strength directly against her opponent's. Still, Than managed by sheer strength alone to smash down her defense. Though her sword took the brunt of the blow a streak of fiery red gashed her shoulder.

"Hah!" he shouted in triumph. "The cow has blood in her after all!"

Flushed with sudden rage, she attacked, swinging and hacking with a ferocity she had not shown. Her blade sang as it lashed through his guard, scoring a deep cut across his stomach. She felt the berserker's fury leave her foe. Fear came into his eyes. But there was no mercy in her now, and her weapon scored once more on his sword arm.

Forgotten in the battle, the old man suddenly called out in warning.

Frost leaped aside without a backward glance. A shadow

and the sound of drawing steel said enough. Chavi's sword sliced the empty space where she had been.

Two foes now, and one was fresh. Sweat poured down her body. The inn was too close for this kind of fight. She danced around Than, keeping the injured fighter between her and the new foe. But both brothers were skilled swordsmen. Though she could handle either alone with a fair chance, together they were overpowering. Frost found her back to the wall.

Death hurtled toward her skull. Desperately, she threw herself forward, making a tight ball of her body. She rolled to the left past Than, careful to keep her sword. Regaining her feet, she swung in a wide arc, putting all her weight and strength into it.

Before Than could react flesh and muscle tore, bone splintered. He crashed to the floor, screaming in shock and agony, his left leg sheared through at the hip.

Chavi stared in disbelief. His brother's blood made a dark pool around his feet, staining his boots.

Frost stood back, welcoming the respite, a chance to breathe. If Chavi abandoned the fight to care for his brother, so would she.

Such was not her luck.

Ceremoniously, Chavi dipped his hand in the bright blood and smeared his face with it. Then, he rubbed it on his own blade and spoke the ritual words of the Rholarothan blood-feud.

"Now, one of us must mingle blood with my fallen brother. You or me."

Frost held her ground and let Chavi make the first move. It began again, but this time there were no curses or meaningless boasts. Only the sounds of swords and the quick, heavy breathing of both fighters filled the room.

Skilled and fast as she was, Frost lacked Chavi's brute power. Her journey and earlier fight with Vericus and his crew worked against her. Much too soon, her arm grew weary. More and more, she felt the shock of each barely thwarted blow. Openings that should have meant death for Chavi closed again before she could take advantage of them. One way or another, it would end soon, and she made a final desperate effort.

Chavi responded with a savage attack. Frost stumbled and

caught herself too late. Unable to avoid it, her blade met Chavi's in a direct test of strength, a contest she had no hope of winning. So powerful was his blow and the shock of it that Frost's arm went numb, and the sword fell from her hand.

Chavi grinned in satisfaction and triumph through the hideous mask of his brother's blood. The sword went up for the fatal stroke.

She watched that ascending blade, seeing her end on its keen edge. Though her left hand was useless her right found Demonfang and jerked it from its silver sheath.

A horrible shrieking rent the air as of souls trapped in burning hell. The anguished noise echoed through the inn, intense and *demanding*.

Horrified, Frost realized the dagger was the source and nearly dropped it. Yet, Demonfang tingled in her hand, and her fingers curled around the hilt.

So close to revenge, Chavi stared, frozen in fear of the sorcerous dagger. She saw his sword waver, his hand tremble.

The Stranger's words rang in her head. *It must taste blood. Either your enemy's or your own.*

Chavi's smooth chest offered itself to her. Her hand drew back, and she realized that, for fear of the blade, Chavi would make no move to save himself. Wide-eyed, he watched entranced as she plunged Demonfang through his heart.

The dagger went abruptly silent. A moment of quiet, then Chavi's mouth opened. The same demonic shrieking issued forth as he crumpled to the floor.

Frost gaped at the little weapon, trying not to panic. It had *made* her kill. And now the blade gleamed with a peculiar sheen even through the blood that stained it.

Her first thought was to fling it away and run. But as the excitement of battle passed so did her fear. A witch's instinct and a warrior's reason took hold. The Stranger had given the dagger for a purpose. Demonfang could not be abandoned. She returned it to its sheath.

Demonfang. A fitting name, she thought.

There was a groan. It seemed Than still lived. The innkeeper knelt by him, trying to staunch the flow of blood with his apron, no doubt from fear of what the governor would do if both sons died in his tavern.

The old man, the original cause of all the trouble, was quickly at her side, handing back her sword, throwing her cloak over her shoulders.

"We'd better leave," he whispered. "They have two more brothers and a father just as bad-tempered. We'll not get away without a chase."

She made for the door, saying a farewell to thoughts of a soft bed. It would be the hard ground for her if she got any sleep this night.

"Wait!" shouted the innkeeper. "The damages . . ."

Darkness had swallowed Shazad. A crowd had gathered in the street to investigate the disturbance. She pulled up her hood, searching for an opening through the mob. People pressed from all sides, assailing her with questions. Yet, no hands were laid on her for she was only a woman and her sword was hidden beneath her cloak. Frost knew she must get away, and quickly.

Then, from up the street came the cries of frightened men and women. The sounds of panic and flight reached the crowd gathered at the Woeful Widow causing them to forget her. A fleeing throng poured around a corner, casting terrified backward glances.

Eyes blazing, Ashur charged around the same corner, ebony horn alive with moonlight and stars, driving the frightened mob before.

The old man whispered, "Don't worry, they see only a wild horse and fear being trampled—nothing more."

The street emptied rapidly as the crowd sought safety from the rampaging animal. Ashur stopped long enough for her to swing up. Leaning close to his neck, she tangled her hands in the mane. The unicorn flew over the cobbled streets, sparks leaping from his hooves. Then, they were through the gates and Shazad faded behind.

Breathless, she looked over her shoulder. The old man followed on a horse she'd seen tethered at the inn.

Down the westward length of the Gargassi Plain they sped in full moonlight. Only slightly faster than a normal horse, Ashur's endurance was supernatural, and the little brown nag that carried the old man strove valiantly to keep the pace. Long into the night they rode without rest.

Over Shazad, a great red eye shimmered briefly, searching the city for the Book of the Last Battle or for an aura only dimly perceived in the Great Forest.

In a small inn it found a lingering trace of that aura clinging to a shield of Esgarian manufacture.

Chapter Three

SNUG IN HER CLOAK, SHE STARED AT THE WILDLY FLICK-ering campfire. A harsh, biting wind snatched away sparks and hot ash, sending them swirling into the night. Her own raven hair lashed her eyes.

She had never felt so weary, yet she could not sleep. Faces haunted her dreams, nightmares tormented her. She looked at the dark stains that spotted her sleeves. Asleep or awake, what did it matter. Visions of death pursued her.

In the distance, her companion stood at the edge of the high plateau where they were camped, keeping watch on the plain below. His tattered garments flapped noisily in the wind, and he hugged himself for warmth.

Perhaps it was some remaining vestige of her witch's instinct that told her they were being pursued. It was too dark to see though, and too cold for the old man to keep watch alone. She called him back to the fire.

"How's the shoulder?" he asked, settling down by the fire's warmth.

She touched the place where Than's sword had cut her and winced. It ached like hell, and she could feel the crusted blood crack when she moved it. "I'll live," she announced, "no doubt to experience worse."

She studied the old man in the uncertain light. He wasn't really so old. Though gray at the temples, his face was just beginning to show the tracks of time. There was still vitality in those dark, deep-set eyes. She looked at his hands. Dirty and rough, but unwrinkled.

"Have you a name?"

He shrugged, peering into the flames. "I've been called many names since I left my homeland, not all of them complimentary. *Old man* will do awhile longer."

A silence broken only by the wailing wind hung between them. The fire began to dim and the last log was added to it.

"I thought Esgarians forbade their women to handle weapons," her companion remarked casually.

She smothered her surprise with an effort. "How do you know I'm Esgarian?"

"You speak the Rholarothan tongue well, and almost without accent." The old man smiled. "But only *almost*."

"For an old man you have keen ears."

A sudden wind fanned the campfire, sweeping smoke and glowing sparks beyond the plateau's edge. The old man shifted away from the flames, moving closer to Frost. She hugged her knees to her chest.

"To repeat, if I may—what makes an Esgarian woman take up the sword, contrary to the laws and customs of her people?"

She turned her eyes away. "It's not something I care to talk about."

"I sense pain in your heart," he said softly. "Talking might ease it a little."

She slammed her fist on the ground, wincing at the jolt to her injured shoulder. "There is no pain," she hissed, "and nothing to speak of, least of all to a stranger."

A shadow passed over the moon, causing her to glance upward. The sky was cloudless.

"The third one I've seen tonight," the old man commented darkly. "By my soul, something searches for us."

She nodded. "I've seen it, too. Some kind of bird, I think."

He shook his head. "More than a bird—an emissary. It will scour the land until it finds what it seeks, then report to its master."

"What do you know of such things? Are you a wizard or sorcerer?" She regretted the note of scorn in her voice, but a man who had permitted himself to be abused by the likes of Lord Rholf's sons was surely innocent of the ways of magic.

"I've traveled a few roads in my lifetime," he answered evenly. "An old man with sharp ears can pick up bits and pieces of knowledge along the way."

His eyes reflected the firelight, and she saw a brief hint of something else there that vanished when he spoke again. "But what of you, Frost? With the limited knowledge that I have I can sense a subtle force locked inside you."

"Once, I was a witch." She bit her tongue as she said it. Why should she open up to this old vagabond? Yet, what harm was done? He knew she was Esgarian, so he probably knew that, like all Esgarian females, she had received some tutoring in the mysteries of Tak, the witch-god. Still, she swore to guard herself more carefully. He was too easy to talk to. "But I have no powers now."

The wind that swept the plateau grew colder. The chill caused her shoulder to ache bitterly, and she moved as close to the fire as she dared.

"I name this place *Cundalacontir*—Cursed by Wind." The old man muttered, gathered his robe close around his ankles.

"Too many people use that word without understanding its full horror."

He regarded her closely. "Is that your secret, Frost? Are you cursed?"

"By my mother's dying breath." She sucked her lip and said no more.

Another shadow dimmed the moon, and Frost looked up to see the bird-thing abruptly swoop. Straight for them it came, pinions beating the air. For long minutes it circled above their camp. Then, with an unearthly cry it flew northward and disappeared in the night.

Furiously, the old man scooped dirt on the fire, extinguishing its light. Frost raced to the plateau's edge and searched the dark plain for any sign of pursuit. Nothing. She hurried back to her new-found comrade.

The wind died and the world became still.

"I'm leaving this place," she declared suddenly. "We're too exposed in all this openness."

"I agree," answered the old man. He gazed sullenly at the

northern sky. "Something's afoot this night, and it seeks for one of us." He turned meaningfully to face her. "I don't know which."

A little way off, Ashur and the old man's brown mare huddled together, munching the scant grass. Frost gave a low whistle. The unicorn ran to her; the mare followed.

"You have a beautiful animal," her companion praised. "In all my days I've never seen such a horse."

Frost smiled secretly. It seemed that to everyone else Ashur was just a horse. But Vericus and the dead raiders had seen Ashur, called him a monster and worse. Only the surviving raider had called him a horse.

Once, her weapons-master had claimed a man's senses were sharpest when he was about to die. Were those words truer than her teacher realized? Maybe, in the face of certain, terrible death even a mortal man could see enchanted forms as they really were.

Why, then, did she see a unicorn? Was it because the Stranger in the forest had given him to her? Or was it because her own end was drawing swiftly near? She had no answer.

When they were mounted they searched for the trail that led down to the plain. As they were about to descend, Frost jerked Ashur to a halt.

"My shield!" she cried. "I left it in Shazad."

"It can't be helped now," the old man answered sternly. "Shazad is too dangerous for you."

She looked back in the direction they had come. "One by one, I've lost the things that belonged to my father: his horse, his saddle and now the shield that bore his sign. My past is being stripped away."

The old man urged his mare down the steep path. "If you want a future, then we'd better ride. There's only danger behind us."

Only danger lies ahead, she thought. *What has man done to be so hated by the gods?*

At the foot of the rocky trail they turned northward and sped across a dead landscape with only the pale moon's waning light to show the way. The constant jostling made her wound ache frightfully and the wind chaffed her face raw, but the pace remained swift and steady.

When at last she signaled to stop, the moon had fallen below the horizon and an eerie twilight lit the sky. Ashur's mane was flecked with lather, and the little mare, near exhaustion, wheezed for breath. Dismounting, they began a slow walk over the bleak countryside.

In the distant north stood the lonely, haunted peak of Drood Mountain.

"A place to be avoided," Frost said ominously. She regarded the mountain pensively. Then, with a deep sigh she turned west toward Chondos.

"Chondos!" the old man whispered when he perceived their course. "What business have you in that dark land?"

"I seek a man," she answered. "If you're afraid, ride away."

He pulled up his hood, concealing his face. "You didn't desert me at the Widow—can I desert you now?"

"A wise man would do so."

He gave no answer, and his steps never faltered.

Just before sunrise a huge, fat crow fluttered through a window into the private chambers of the wizard Zarad-Krul and perched upon the skull of some nameless god's idol. On his throne of black obsidian Zarad-Krul looked up from a ruby-colored ball that rested in his left palm. Rolling its eyes, preening its feathers, the crow shit a pile on the idol's head. Then, the bird hopped to the floor and paced before the dark throne, chittering in a vile tongue.

Zarad-Krul's face twisted in a vague semblance of a smile.

When the sun was high, Frost and the old man at last made camp in a small grove. Water from a cool stream quenched their thirst, but only a handful of sour berries could they find to eat.

She sat wearily in the grass, propped against the trunk of a young tree and watched her companion. Some leaves near the water had caught his interest. Plucking them, he kneeled to wash the dust from his cache.

Gingerly, she touched her shoulder. Her left arm had been useless for hours, and the pain worried her. Some years back she'd seen a man lose an arm. Not a pretty prospect. She forced herself to think of other things.

Pressed against her flesh, the Book was heavy inside her

tunic, and she took it out. The ancient leather binding was warm with the heat of her body as she studied the carven runes upon it, wondering what story they told. She fingered the lock. It looked so old. She tried to insert a finger between the pages, an impossible task. Unsheathing her sword she drew the sharp blade along the cover near the lock. It would take no cut—not even a scratch.

After awhile, she laid the Book on the grass and closed her eyes.

A splash. She looked up to see the old man hurrying toward her, bearing something in his hands. Casually, she shifted her thigh to conceal the Book.

On a frond was smeared a handful of brownish slime from the stream's bank. Bits of grass and crumpled leaves were mixed with it. Placing the concoction carefully on the ground, the old man reached for her sleeve.

She pulled away. "What are you doing?"

Undaunted, he caught the material between his hands. "You're in pain," he said curtly. "I've seen it in your eyes half the night."

No use denying it. She couldn't flex her arm. When she tried to make a fist the fingers only twitched.

With a tug the sleeve came away, exposing the gash. Gentle though he tried to be, tears misted her eyes as he scrubbed away the dried blood. Around the wound the flesh had turned an angry red. Dipping his fingers in the slime, the old man made a plaster. The mud was cool and heavy on her skin.

"This poltice will relieve the pain and draw out any poisons. We were lucky to find the right herbs in this part of the country."

She gave a deep sigh while her entire arm and shoulder was smeared with the strange medicine. In the hot sun it dried quickly, a stiff, soothing cast.

"It smells like wildflowers—very pleasant," she said, sniffing.

"The herbs," he answered and rose to his feet. "Now relax and let the plaster do its work. You need sleep, and I'm taking the watch."

Frost leaned back against the tree, the peculiar odor of the mud filling her senses. Her eyes closed, head dropped to her chest and she slept a dreamless, untroubled sleep.

The sun was below the trees when she awakened. The first pale star winked in the sky. Frost jumped to her feet. The old man had let her sleep too long. In fact, there must have been a drug in that poltice to put her out so quickly. She slammed a fist into her palm.

She expected pain. None came. Amazed, she flexed her arm. Nothing. Her fingers worked normally, too. She rubbed the limb briskly, flaking away the caked mud, exposing her shoulder. A livid scar, but the wound had sealed.

She looked around for her companion, spotted him by the stream, his back to her, staring at the water. She started across the glade.

The Book. She had nearly forgotten. Turning to retrieve it, she stiffened. It was gone. She looked back at the stream, a cold anger creeping into her heart. A soft hiss of steel on leather, her sword was in her hand.

As she came on, the old man rose, turned, faced her. In his hand was the Book of the Last Battle. Saying nothing, his dark eyes locked with hers.

The point of her weapon settled on his chest. "Give it back," she said tersely.

He made no move. "Do you know what this is?"

"Give it back," she repeated, a tremor in her voice. "I don't want to hurt you, but . . ."

"Do you know what you have?" The change in his voice was startling. No longer an old man's voice, but full of strength and urgency, it shook her to her soul.

"I know."

"What?" he shouted. "Say the words, woman—I must know that you know!"

She hesitated, reluctant to speak the name aloud. "The Book of the Last Battle."

His form seemed to swell, then sag. "Gods," he muttered. "Oh gods! What have I stumbled into so blindly?"

No longer was he bent with age. His back straightened; he paced with a sure step. Regarding the small volume with horrible fascination, one fist clenched and unclenched. Last, his eyes shut tight, prayerfully, and when they opened, he held out the Book.

"Take this cursed thing from my hands," he ordered. "And put away that stupid sword."

She grabbed the Book, and the sword went back into its scabbard. "What do you know about this?" she asked. The Book disappeared once more within her tunic.

He paced beside the stream, face lined with agitation and worry. "More than any mortal should. I knew it had come into this world. An acquaintance asked my help in finding it, but we serve different gods, and he wouldn't completely confide in me. I had no choice but to refuse, knowing he would continue to search alone.

"For several days I wondered how he fared, for though it was a fool's quest the very daring of it preyed upon my mind. In a bowl of magic waters I followed his progress, but when he crossed into Shardaha the waters turned black and I could see no more. I knew, then, he was in danger, but I couldn't help him.

"Two more nights the waters remained dark, but on the third I saw a strange vision. Not my friend, but a woman whose face was hidden. From Esgaria she came astride a violent beast from a time long forgotten. In her hands she carried the world; balanced on her shoulders was a great golden scale that tilted first one way, then the other. A witch and a warrior, her hands were stained with murdered blood, yet I could not call her evil.

"Whoever she was, I knew our destinies were linked, else she could not have appeared in my bowl. On the last full moon I left my homeland and journeyed to Shazad where my gods warned me she would appear."

He stopped his pacing, faced her. His eyes, two coals, burned into her. "You are that woman, Frost. I didn't know when you would come—I was prepared to wait months, years, if necessary. I hoped when I first heard your accent at the inn, witnessed your swordplay. I knew for certain when the unicorn charged up the street to carry you away."

Frost blinked. "What did you say?"

"Oh yes," he grinned. "I'm well aware that Ashur is no horse. Like most of my people, I have the gift of *true-sight*. I see things as they really are, not as they appear."

She had other questions about that, but passed over them. "Why did you take the Book?"

"When you fell asleep I saw it hidden beneath your leg. I knew at once what it was."

"Then you can read the runes written on it?"

"I can only recognize them," he answered. "No earthly tongue can speak that language. But tell me how you came by it?"

Sitting upon the grass she related her meeting with the Stranger and told how he had taken the Book from Zarad-Krul. Lastly, she revealed the manner of his death.

"Butterflies," she whispered. The image still burned in her mind, brought a chill to her flesh.

He bowed his head sadly. "Men believe that evil things have evil shapes, that they are ugly and hideous to behold. So they are to those with *true-sight,* but to an ordinary mortal evil takes a beautiful form to confuse and lure the unsuspecting. My friend died a noble death."

"A noble death," echoed Frost, "is no less dead."

"Dwell on it no more," he responded thoughtfully. "But tell me, what man do you seek in Chondos? Few dare to visit that dreaded land."

"A Brother of the Black Arrow," she answered. "A man named Kregan."

Suddenly he shook with harsh, bitter laughter. "Oh gods!" he cried. "Rich beyond imagining! I should have realized." He laughed harder and tore at his robes. "Oh, I've kept this hated guise too long!"

It hardly seemed a time for laughter. She stared, unspeaking, disapproving, wondering what madness had befallen him.

"Oh, laugh with me, Frost, at this one jest. There will be little mirth soon enough, I fear."

She was unmoved. "Why should I laugh?"

His eyes held a rare twinkle. He bent close to mock her stern tone. "I'm Kregan," he said.

Chapter Four

CASTING HIS TATTERED GARMENTS CONTEMPTUOUSLY into the bushes, Kregan's naked, bronzed skin glimmered in the sun's last rays. His body showed great strength; though past his youth, he was not truly old.

Frost had never been so close to a naked man. She stared shamelessly. "Why a disguise?"

Kregan waded into the stream, began to bathe. "Chondites are not well-liked in these parts. It's safer, easier to go about disguised. To most eyes a ragged old man is too harmless and too poor to warrant much attention."

Finishing his bath, he took from the mare's saddlebags fresh, clean clothes; black leggings and boots of soft black leather that reached his knees; a sleeveless tunic of fine ebon silk that laced to the throat; a belt of golden links, the buckle a cleverly wrought arrow-sign of his Brotherhood; lastly, a voluminous cloak, hemmed and bordered with runes in gold thread. Powerful and fearsome he looked.

"I thought you'd stolen the horse," she remarked caustically. "Guess I was wrong."

Kregan laughed. "Did you respect me more as a horse-thief?'' He winked and patted the brown mare affectionately. "I raised Neri from a foal; she'd carry me through the Nine Hells if I asked her, or run herself to death to keep pace with your witch-steed.''

"A fault in your disguise, though,'' she observed. "How could a ragged old man own such a horse?''

He nodded. "Exactly what Lord Rholf's sons wanted to know when I rode up to the inn. Still, it was a long journey from Chondos; I didn't want to leave her behind.''

From the north rose a wind, cold and chill as the winds of Cundalacontir. The sun had deserted the sky; in the northeast dark clouds gathered.

The Book of the Last Battle lay heavy and warm next to her stomach. She clutched it unconsciously as the wind rustled her clothes, feeling the rough binding and carven characters through the material of her tunic.

"Well, you've saved me a long ride to Chondos,'' she said with a sigh. "Now tell me what to do with this.'' She took out the Book.

Kregan's face darkened. "I don't know yet what to do with it.'' His brow wrinkled; a grim mood settled on his features. "Riding to Chondos must still be the plan. There are tools there I will need, and people to help us. If I can do anything with the Book we must take it to Chondos.''

Entering that land was still not a pleasing prospect. Though she trusted this one Chondite, his people had an evil reputation that she could not easily forget. The Stranger in the woodland trusted them, though, and all he had said had come true.

"If there's no other way, then we've wasted enough time,'' she said.

Her friend looked thoughtful, held up an objecting hand. "I would waste just a little more,'' he said soberly. "Our road has been long—your own somewhat longer and bloodier than mine. Should you wish to avail yourself of the stream and its cleansing waters I would not complain.''

Frost smiled at his tactfulness. Indeed, she could smell her own stink; the road dust was thick on her face and her hands. Her garments were splotched with dark stains, dead men's blood. Her hair, tangled and wild from hard riding, was even crusted with blood.

"Not long ago my father would have cut off the lips of any

man who dared say such a thing." She shrugged her shoulders. A sad note crept into her voice. "Well, times change."

"If you're modest, I'll busy myself elsewhere," Kregan offered.

She pulled off a boot. "Modesty is something I left behind," she hesitated, looked over her shoulder to the south, Esgaria, "in a past life."

How could she tell him? How could she tell anyone of her crime?

Her clothes in a pile by the water's edge, Book and sword near at hand, she strode into the stream. The water rippled, caressed her with gentle coolness. With unconscious grace she leaned forward. A cascade of thick, black hair swirled as she immersed herself, rose and began to scrub.

The bath lightened her mood. She stretched face down, letting the water flow over her, feeling the sand and pebbles strewn on the bottom with her fingers and toes.

She scrubbed her clothes, too, washing out the dust, but not the brown stains that spotted the gray fabric. As she worked, she glanced up at Kregan, aware that he had not taken his eyes away since she stripped. He sat near the bank, and it amused her to watch him shift position every few moments. Now he sat with his knees drawn tightly together.

"Maybe this will help," she said, and splashed him.

She pulled on her dripping garments, buckled her sword.

"You shouldn't wear those wet," Kregan said, rising.

She blinked. The late evening twilight could not completely hide the prominent sign of his arousal. "You just want to admire the view a little longer," she chided. "I'll dry out quick enough when we start to ride." As an afterthought, she added, "You can ride that way, can't you?"

Kregan smoothed the front of his tunic and smiled broadly.

She picked up the Book and put it away, called to Ashur. Munching a bit of grass, the unicorn tossed its head and trotted to her side.

"I've a little dried meat in my saddlebag," Kregan said. "We'll eat as we ride."

When they were mounted she took the offered morsel. The meat was heavily salted, but hungry as she was, nothing ever tasted sweeter. They rode slowly, chewing, but when the meal was done, she nudged Ashur with her heels. The unicorn broke into a run; Neri followed, and Frost watched their shadows race before as the bright moon peered over the horizon behind them.

An ominous wall rose on their right—the Creel Mountains. Like giant mercenary soldiers, stiff, rugged, they loomed casting a shadow of fear black as Drood Mountain itself.

Frost felt a creeping between her shoulders, forced it away. She had heard tales of a race that dwelled among those rocky peaks and steep valleys, a tribe so vicious and primitive that even battle-hardened Rholarothan regulars refused to come here. She was grateful they passed only at the foot of the mountains and did not have to travel though them.

There were no mountains in Esgaria, but once she had stood on the high cliffs above the Calendi Sea, a girl of fifteen summers. The salt spray stung her face, the wind whipped her hair as she unleashed the full, terrible strength of her witch-craft. Giant waves crashed on the jagged rocks below; the sea churned, raged.

Not the handiwork of a god commanded by a wizard, nor the result of a sorcerer's symbol, gesture or word of power. A witch—the force was natural, a part of her. She compelled the storm. She alone calmed it.

Never again, though. Her power was gone, her skill stolen away. Now, she had only her sword.

Her brother had learned of her secret obsession, tried to kill her as was his right under an ancient Esgarian law forbidding females to handle men's weapons. His was the blood spilled that night, though, and her mother had cursed her for it.

A brooding melancholy dampened her spirit. To drive away the memories she counted the hoof-beats that echoed in her ears.

Kregan was no longer beside her. She slowed her pace to allow him to catch up. Neri was heavily lathered; her brown hide glistened with sweat. Kregan reined in and slid from the saddle. Fatigue shone on his features.

"I won't kill her, woman," he said calmly enough, stroking the mare lovingly. "Not even to save that damned Book."

She took a deep breath and dropped from Ashur's back. The unicorn was worn, too, dark mane flecked with foam.

"I wouldn't ask that," she answered. "We'll walk awhile."

Her own voice startled her, morose and gloomy, heavy with

exhaustion. She wished her companion would talk, lift this dark mood from her, but he said nothing; only the sounds of their breathing and their footsteps disturbed the silent night.

Then, the unicorn nickered, stopped and sniffed the air. Frost urged him along, but he stopped again and sniffed. Neri stopped, too. The little mare began to stamp and tremble. The fiery eye-spots on Ashur's face flamed suddenly, burned wildly, and the unicorn reared.

Frost grabbed a handful of his mane. Kregan stroked and cooed to Neri.

Gradually, the animals calmed, but now *she* could not relax. The fire in Ashur's hellish eyes shone brighter than ever, casting pools of light upon the ground. She turned to Kregan, but he motioned her to silence, listened, searched in all directions.

She became acutely aware of their exposed position. On the broad plain there was no place to seek cover. Her sword made a soft hiss as it slid free of the sheath.

With no warning, the unicorn reared again, a trumpeting, unearthly cry in its throat. Neri whinnied piteously and jerked her head from side to side until the metal bit bloodied her mouth.

Frost felt a prickling on her neck, turned and screamed.

The Eye of Zarad-Krul loomed over her. Swollen veins full of dark blood laced the rheumy jelly; the foul black pupil, a window into the vilest part of Hell, gleamed with malignant mirth.

As she met its gaze she knew her soul was lost. A numbness spread through her limbs, an icy chill that froze her blood, held her motionless, rooted. She screamed again, but no sound passed her lips. A half-uttered curse, a cry and she knew Kregan would be no help. Nor the animals; they, too, were trapped by the spell that gripped her.

An evil quiet settled on the world.

Then, from the rocky, barren earth blades of grass, emerald serpents, sprouted, grew, coiled around her ankles. Tiny flowers sprang up beneath her feet at a fantastic rate, bloomed with radiant hues, filled the air with a senses-stealing sweetness. Up her thighs the blossoms climbed, into her boots, into her sleeves. A sharp bite, a sting, and petalous mouths sucked her blood.

She shuddered, writhing inside as the flowers kissed her flesh, wormed under her belt, slithered over her breasts. She remembered the sword in her hand, tried to lift it, but her muscles would not respond.

Her throat tightened. A bead of sweat ran into her eye; she could do nothing to relieve the salty pain. A cloying panic swelled within her, though she worked to fight it down.

Concentrating, she filled her mind with visions of bones and grinning butterflies. She imagined her bones mingled with Kregan's in the dirt, two wild daisies blossoming serenely in the eye-sockets of her skull.

She nurtured that thought and, slowly, feeling came into her left hand. Her fingers clenched tighter on the hilt of her sword. Her arm raised an inch—but no more. Zarad-Krul's Eye burned into her, perceiving her plan and thwarting it with a power that nearly numbed her mind. Tears scalded her cheeks; she felt herself slipping into a deep void, knowing she would never return.

Then, Ashur cried out, a sound of helpless agony. The echo of it beat at her brain. The unicorn bellowed again, each time bringing her farther from the abyss the bloated Eye sucked her toward. She focussed her will on the sound, conjured images of the unicorn's suffering, used them to feed the rage and hatred that would weaken Zarad-Krul's spell. *We won't quit, Ashur,* she swore inwardly. *We won't die!*

She strained against the wizard's power. Sweat rolled thickly down her face, neck, arms. The sword quivered in her hand; the point lifted another inch. Her head began to throb; muscles ached as she battled for possession of her own body.

Her eyelids fluttered. With a furious effort she snapped them shut . . .

And the spell shattered. In the instant Zarad-Krul's gaze lost hers her body and will became her own again. A savage snarl curled her lips. The sword flew up in a glittering arc.

Fierce, desperate, she hacked and pulled at the grass and flowers that encased the lower half of her form. Red, mottled circles marked her skin where the vampire plants had touched her. Kregan was nearly lost in the blossoms; only a little of his face was yet exposed. The legs of their mounts were similarly encased, but most of the plants had gone for the animal's throats. Neither Kregan nor Neri moved, transfixed by the

Eye's power, but Ashur tossed his head wildly, though he could not flee.

Perhaps it was the peculiar nature of the unicorn's eyes, or the fact that he was, himself, a creature of magic that made him immune to the Eye's mesmeric spell. Frost had little time to wonder, recalling only the Stranger's words—that the unicorn was a weapon to aid her against Zarad-Krul.

She tore away the last of the vampire plants with a triumphant shout. Shielding her eyes with an uplifted arm, her blade swung up, then down, meeting slight resistance as the steel edge sliced through membranous layers, cleaving the black pupil in half.

Steaming blood and humor splashed on the ground. The vampire blossoms threw themselves into the bilious liquid, thirsting, sucking it up.

Grim with satisfaction, she regarded her handiwork. The Eye reflected shock and pain as the loathsome thing emptied its fluid like a broken egg. The jaundiced ichor spilled from the wound, soaked into the earth, and the transparent husk that remained wobbled obscenely, then collapsed. She watched, revulsion knotting her stomach, as the husk dissolved in foul-smelling vapor, leaving the earth stained with a black dew.

Then, unexpectedly, the raw edge of a psychic scream lanced her brain. When the shock of it passed she smiled cruelly, knowing that in distant Shardaha Zarad-Krul had gone permanently blind in one eye.

Freed from the trance, Kregan ripped at the flowers that clung to his body. His face a mask of fury, he shredded the vines that tangled his ankles, curled around his thighs. Ashur and Neri had already struggled free, and the unicorn diligently trampled the few remaining blossoms, snorting indignantly.

She smiled, but her joy was short-lived. A sound chilled her heart. She glanced skyward, then at Kregan. He heard it, too, the steady flutter of soft wings.

"Your butterflies?" A quiet dread laced his words.

"Ride, man!" she called, leaping astride Ashur. "Like Hell's hot breath was on your neck!"

They flew over the plain; their shadows quested far ahead, misshapen by the rugged terrain. To the right another shadow blotted the stars, a rhythmic thrumming that pursued them, beat their ears.

Kregan cast fearful glances over his shoulder and shouted against the rushing wind.

"If we can last until sunrise they'll leave us alone," she yelled back.

Ashur would not falter; the unicorn's stamina was arcane. It was Neri she worried about. The little mare had a valiant heart but was too tired to keep the pace for long.

Yet, long before the first rays of morning lit the sky the sound began to fade. Frost looked up. Unexplainably, the shadow had turned north. She slowed Ashur's pace, suspecting a trick, but the swarm held to its new course. She motioned Kregan to stop.

"It's a long time till dawn, yet they're turning away."

The Chondite scratched his chin. "Zarad-Krul has exhausted himself tonight," he offered at last. "Without the Eye, his will alone had to guide the insects. Over such a distance that kind of control would be a tremendous strain."

The insect horde disappeared, swallowed up in the dark. Frost and Kregan walked alongside their animals; Neri could be ridden no more that night.

"His madness has taken deep roots," observed the Chondite. "There are many ways to see over the vast reaches, but with an inflated sense of the dramatic, the wizard chose to send an actual part of himself, leaving him vulnerable to physical attack."

"It allowed him to exercise his power, though," she pointed out. "No illusion could have conjured those plants."

"True," he admitted. "That kind of magic required more than just gazing into a scrying crystal from the safety of his tower. Still, he badly underestimated the resourcefulness of his foes. I'm a Chondite sorcerer, and you—something special."

She ignored his wink. "What will he do next?"

Kregan shrugged. "Who can anticipate a madman? But you've won the first round, at least. The wizard is undoubtedly suffering considerable pain from the wound you've dealt him."

"A small skirmish in a larger war," she answered darkly. "And wounded animals are always the most deadly."

A flock of nocturnal birds flew overhead, winging south for the Calendi Sea. She recalled the bird-things at Cundalacontir. Emissaries, Kregan called them. Spies, she realized.

Their trail had been too easy to follow. So eager to reach Chondos, they had given no thought to evading an enemy. Too late to worry, now. Zarad-Krul had already discovered the direction they were travelling and just as surely had recognized Kregan's Chondite garb. It took no great magic to guess their destination.

"How far to Chondos?" she asked.

"Hard to say in this darkness. Another day's ride at a swift pace. Longer if we continue walking."

"I want to make the border by sunset," she told her companion. "Will Neri last?"

"She'll last," he answered confidently, "given a little rest now. But we can't cross the border at just any point we choose. The Cocytus River that separates Rholaroth and Chondos can only be forded at three places."

Frost tilted her head, frowning. "The closest place?"

"A causeway guarded at either side by Zondu in Rholaroth and Erebus in Chondos. The nearest point, but not necessarily the safest, considering how the Zonduns hate all Chondites. The other two points are natural crossings where the raging waters grow calm and shallow enough for a careful man to wade; they lie farther to the north."

"Then we ride to Zondu."

"It will be dangerous for you, too," he warned. "By now Lord Rholf will have our descriptions from that innkeeper, and honor demands he avenge his sons, no matter that they provoked the fight. It's the Rholarothan way; they believe damnation awaits any man who does not avenge his kin."

"What are you saying?" Frost demanded impatiently.

"If word of your fight has reached Zondu we could be riding into a trap. The law would hold you until Rholf came."

"We've ridden very fast with only short rests."

"A determined rider with a string of fresh horses could have been faster."

But there was no choice. When night descended, Zarad-Krul would strike again: Chondos offered possible safety. There, Kregan would find the right sorcerous tools to fight back; he'd have his brotherhood to help. Together, they'd find a hiding place for the Book. Whatever the risk in Zondu, they had to make Chondos by nightfall.

As the first rays of an early sun painted the sky they halted on the edge of a rocky crest. A vast, barren expanse stretched for miles, not quite a desert. No trees or farmhouses dotted the land, no clump of grass grew in the sun-baked earth.

"The Zondaur," Kregan said, indicating the plain with a sweeping gesture.

"The Last Warning," she translated.

Beyond the Zondaur ran the Cocytus, called the River of Lamentations. Its poisonous waters succored no forests, no groves, no tree, flower or blade of grass. No fish swam there, and no creature drank from its muddy banks.

And beyond the river—Chondos. Where men who were not completely human worked vile sorceries. Demons and monsters roamed freely there, feasting on infants' blood, begetting more monsters on the willing bodies of Chondite women.

At least, so the legends told. This much she knew: to sane men Chondos was another name for the Nine Hells.

She swallowed. "Before your friend died in Etai Calan he dismissed the tales of your homeland as mere rumors meant to scare off unwanted intruders."

Kregan raised an eyebrow. "A long time ago a foolish young Rholarothan king named Tordesh refused to believe those tales. He saw Chondos as a land to be conquered, made his own. Talk of sorcerers and demons and ghouls he dismissed as peasant superstition. No living soul had ever been seen on the west bank of the Cocytus. Surely a kingdom of any size at all would have posted border guards. No, he told his people, if anyone lived in Chondos they must be uncivilized barbarians or tribal primitives. They would stand no chance at all against an invading army.

"So deaf to the pleas of his advisors, hungry for conquest, Tordesh began to build a causeway over the raging Cocytus. The two natural fording points were prone to unpredictable flooding; the causeway would insure an open line for his armies and supply caravans."

She listened, fascinated.

"The construction site, a small camp at first, grew quickly into a city as wine merchants, gamblers and honey-scented women crossed the Zondaur to vie for the workers' coins. Soon, the streets were full of prostitutes, murder in every alley, brawls and drunkenness. Almost as a joke they named the city *Zondu,* meaning 'warning.'

"Construction went slow. Each night the swift Cocytus

seemed to wash away the day's progress. But Tordesh pushed his men hard, never sparing the lash when they dared to grumble. Soldiers worked beside common laborers, and if some were swept away, drowned, it was no matter. Lives meant nothing to a king, but the causeway and the conquest of Chondos meant everything.

"At last the broad, gleaming structure was completed. The waters of the Cocytus churned angrily, but Tordesh and his armies could pass over in safety.

"He planned a three-pronged invasion. Tordesh would lead one division over the causeway. Two commanders would each lead other divisions across the two natural points. One would push north, one south, the other straight to the heart of the country. Then, the three would unite to finish off any remaining pockets of resistance.

"The night before the invasion the young king plied his men with wine. Every keg in the city was opened; the streets were purple with grapes' blood. Women were caught, used, sometimes even paid. From the balcony of his private chamber, Tordesh tossed coins to the throng, laughed drunkenly as they scrambled in the mud for his bits of gold. They cried his name, and he proclaimed himself King of Rholaroth and of Chondos, and of all he surveyed.

"Next morning Tordesh sat astride a snow-white horse, his army assembled behind him. On his brow glittered the crown of Rholaroth. The finest robes and richest jewels adorned his body. His father's two-handed great sword hung in a scabbard by his side.

"A wild light shone in his eyes and he assured his men of a quick victory. Scouts had returned over the causeway. No Chondite force opposed them; no slightest sign of resistance could be found. Loudly, he boasted that Chondos would fall without losing a single Rholarothan life.

"He wheeled his horse about. The causeway gate stood open, waiting. Drawing his sword, he lifted it high. The sun glinted on the polished blade, dazzling any who looked upon it, and they took this for an omen of triumph. With a flourish, Tordesh led his singing soldiers through the gate.

"As they rode forward a sound filled the air, the ringing of countless crystal bells. The causeway trembled suddenly. Horses shied, reared in terror, throwing hapless riders. A powerful gale rose up. The waters of the Cocytus heaved; great tossing waves snatched the falling bodies of luckless, un-balanced warriors.

"At the very center of the causeway Tordesh clung stubbornly to his reins and urged his army on.

"The tremors ceased. The river calmed.

"As they watched with fear-filled and uncomprehending eyes, the air began to shift and shimmer. A city like none they had ever dreamed appeared on the opposite bank, shrouded in mist that quickly melted in the morning sunlight. The end of the causeway was swallowed up by the black mouth of a skull-crested gate.

"Twisted, smooth-sided towers reared in warped magnificence, challenging the sky, each crowned with an evil gargoyle. Along spires and rooftops foul, bat-winged demons licked claws and fangs imbrued crimson. An immense wall of black rock encircled the arcane fortress, and atop the palisade the souls of damned men screamed and writhed in sculpted torment.

"Soldiers threw up their hands in despair, covered their eyes from the sight. Moaning and lamentation swelled from the throats of seasoned warriors. Some ran back to the gates of Zondu; some threw themselves desperately into the river, choosing drowning over a worse imagined fate.

"The king's commanders, faces pale with fear, pleaded for the safety of Zondu's walls, but Tordesh was adamant. He strove to rally his troops. Brandishing his great sword, he urged them to advance.

"Though they did not retreat, they would not go on.

"Tordesh taunted them, threatened them. He promised huge sums of gold and silver.

"No one would follow.

" 'It's an illusion!' he cried, exasperated. 'Fools! Cowards all! An illusion!'

"A tall, thin figure appeared on the parapet of the black-walled city, a voluminous cloak about his slight frame. He raised an arm, pointed a long finger, and every soldier felt that cold limb touch their hearts. His liquid voice rolled in every ear.

" 'Turn back, Tordesh! Take your soldiers back to their homes and families. Hell has not yet prepared a place hot enough for your greedy soul!'

"Tordesh reddened with rage. Seeds of madness blossomed

suddenly in his bent mind. 'You and all your city are a mirage!'

"The young king spurred his horse over the causeway, gripping the saddle with his knees, swinging his blade at nonexistent foes, raving, cursing the world.

"On the wall the figure drew from the folds of his cloak a single arrow and a bow of black wood. Every eye watched in horrified silence as the arrow was fitted to the string and drawn slowly back. The feather touched the ear. For a long moment there was no movement. Then, the archer released the string. The deadly missile plunged through the air and buried itself deep in the heart of Tordesh's splendid white horse.

"The unfortunate beast tumbled forward, spilling his unwary rider head over heels. Tordesh gave a cry as his father's sword clattered over the edge, lost in the Cocytus. He struggled to his knees, bruised in a thousand places, his right shoulder smashed. But the worst pain was the humiliation he saw in the eyes of his men.

"Bitterly, he turned and cursed the guardian on the wall.

" 'Turn back, Tordesh,' the archer said. 'Turn away from Hell.'

"Dismayed, the Rholarothan king skulked back to Zondu. His soldiers parted to let him pass, then followed, bowed, broken with defeat.

"Legends claim he shut himself up in his palace and was never seen again. The governing of the nation he left to his commanders, and when he died, shamed and disgraced, not a soul mourned." Kregan licked his lips as he finished his tale.

Frost took a deep breath, let it out slowly. "An interesting story," she said at last.

"A true one," the Chondite answered sullenly. "Whatever my friend told you, Chondos is no place for faint hearts. Many strange things walk that land, things to make your darkest nightmares pale in comparison."

Scarlet heat rose in her cheeks. "Not my nightmares." Embarrassed then, she slapped the unicorn's rump and sped down the ridge over the *Zondaur*.

Chapter Five

A DEEP SUNSET STAINED THE LAND WITH A DARK CRIMson hue. Streamers of iodine and purple clouds laced the sky, wispy fingers that did little to hold back night's progress.

Frost waved a weary hand at the horde of insects that buzzed around her face, in her ears. The plain that fostered no other life was a home for countless varieties of insects: ants, beetles, roaches, but most especially, gnats. Great swarms, they hung like thick curtains over the rocky soil. Man and animal suffered alike. Attracted to the sweat of their bodies, the gnats had bedeviled them all afternoon.

Nothing to do but bear it and try not to breathe too often—or swallow.

"It gets colder with nightfall," Kregan called. "They'll go away, then."

She took no comfort in that. With the coming of darkness she feared a new attack by Zarad-Krul. They had beaten him once, she would not count on such luck a second time.

They had not made good speed. The animals were tired. So was she. Her thighs ached painfully from too much riding, her half numb fingers tangled in Ashur's mane. No rest during the day, they walked and rode alternately, pushing for Chondos.

It was not much farther.

She clutched the Book of the Last Battle inside her tunic as she had several times that day and regarded the sky. The last rays of light retreated; the first star hovered low in the east.

He will come. She gripped the Book with a ferocity that made her knuckles crack. *He will come, and we will not be ready.*

"Give no more thought to the wizard," advised Kregan suddenly. "There stand the walls of Zondu."

Her heart lifted as she stared where her companion pointed, straining to see. Only a patch of deeper darkness on the plain, she marveled that he had seen it at all.

"Not sight," he answered, tapping his nose. "Smell."

She sniffed. There was a subtle difference in the air. Population, industry, the smell of the forge, cook-fires and garbage. The odors lingered on the edge of her senses, becoming a distasteful reek as they drew nearer.

Then a new smell, water.

"The Cocytus," Kregan said, pointing again. She could barely see the dark ribbon that cut through the land. "You can't see the causeway or Erebus beyond. Zondu sits directly in our way."

She sat up straight, straining for a better view of the river. But the night was too thick. Chondos was near; that knowledge sent a shiver up her spine.

She stopped, suddenly nervous, afraid. Zarad-Krul behind her, Chondos before. Her hands trembled and she hid them before Kregan could notice. Between two such forces her own sword seemed small indeed.

She bit her lip, swallowed, then urged Ashur forward.

The wall of Zondu rose over them, tall and broad, scarred with age and by the angry duststorms that seasonally swept the Zondaur. In places, the mortar was crumbled. The huge blocks of stone were chipped and cracked, worn smooth at the corners. The wall's shadow fell over them, deep and brooding and silent.

The great steel-banded gates were closed; no sentry stood guard to open them.

"You said the eastern gates were always open."

Kregan scratched his chin. "They usually are." He looked behind, all around. "I don't like this."

"Neither do I." She turned the unicorn aside, paced him back and forth before the gate. "Can we reach the causeway by skirting the walls?"

The Chondite shook his head. "The walls reach to the water's edge. The causeway proceeds from inside the city."

She took Ashur back a few paces, looked up at the high parapet.

"Ho, up there!" she called, spying no sentry. "Open the gates if you're awake."

The gleam of a helmet above the bastion, of a spearpoint. "Who are you? What do you want in Zondu this time of night?" The voice was gruff, uncivil.

"Honest travelers in need of food and rest," she answered, wishing she could see better.

"By Gath, a woman by the sound of you!" Laughter and muttering—so there were others up there. "I have good eyes, though!" the voice continued with a more menacing tone, "and see your companion wears Chondite garb."

Kregan bristled, snarled. "Then a Chondite I must be, fool." Then smugly, tauntingly, "Now will you open the gate, or shall I pull the wall from under your shiftless feet?" He raised his hand, made a clawing gesture, laughed softly.

Her mouth twisted in a frown. The Chondite's haughty words could as easily have brought a hail of arrows down on them. It was not wise to offend when offense served no purpose.

Scrambling sounds above. Antique chains and pulleys groaned; the gate creaked slowly open.

Kregan turned then, met her stare, coldly aloof. "He swears by Gath," he said of the sentry, "the spider-god of chaos, but it is Chondite sorcery he truly fears."

She had not thought him so arrogant. A curious smile etched his lips; he sat straight, stiff in the saddle. Was it fatigue or the nearness of his homeland that wrought this change in him? She averted her eyes, no answer in his face.

"Don't stop," he whispered when the gate was wide. "Make straight for the causeway on the far side of the city. We'll find rest and food in Erebus."

A slow fire smouldered in her breast; a darkening mood damped it. The same commanding, insolent tone he had used with the sentry. She resented it, felt the heat rise again in her cheeks, but said nothing. He knew she had never planned to stop in Zondu when Chondos lay just over the river.

She pushed through the gate first, obstinately denying Kregan the lead.

Too late, she heard the rasp of steel, the rustle of clothing. A shadow fell across her path—someone on a roof top.

She reached for her sword as Kregan shouted a warning, freed the blade as the shadow dropped on her. Booted feet knocked her to the ground. Stunned, she looked up to see more men rushing from an alley. Another attacker leaped from the roof, swinging his sword. The flat edge bounced on the Chondite's skull. He fell, hit the ground hard and did not move. Someone grabbed her arm, dragged her over the cobbles, and she screamed.

A trumpeting bray. Ebony hooves flashed, and her attacker crumpled with a moan. Blood and brains oozed from his crushed helmet. Bile rose in her throat; her stomach convulsed.

Then, reflexes took over as more hands grabbed her. Her sword gleamed on the street not too far away. She kicked savagely, raked her nails over soft flesh. An arm curled around her neck and she bit down, tasting salty, bitter blood. With teeth and nails, fists and feet, knees and elbows she fought, gaining no respite.

Her foes seemed numberless. Without her sword they quickly bore her down, pinned her. Though she writhed and twisted she could not get free.

Yet, still there were screams, the sounds of fighting. Held fast, she managed a look through the ring of her captors.

Ashur's horn thrust once, twice. Two bodies arched through the air, crashed into a wall, broken and lifeless. The unicorn wailed in triumph and challenge.

But a group of soldiers circled him with ropes and spears and swords. Worse, down the road, Frost saw the gates start to swing shut. If Ashur were trapped in the city he would surely be killed. She squirmed uselessly in the hands that pinned her.

"Run!" she shouted. "Get away!"

A sword hilt crashed on her head. Light exploded behind her eyes, then faded. A yawning darkness sucked at her senses.

"Ashur," she croaked.

For one moment the unicorn's fiery eyes seemed to meet hers. It called to her as it reared, and another man died beneath those baleful hooves. Then, a spear flashed, barely missing the creature.

"Run," she managed weakly, too faint to be heard. "Please!"

A mournful, unearthly note echoed in her ears, Ashur's cry. The horn tossed, the arcane fire of his eyes washed the street with amber light, casting warped shadows. And suddenly, the great beast broke for the gate, pursued by a rain of poorly aimed spears and shouting warriors. The gate-chains groaned. Hooves rang on the cobbles, throwing sparks. With scant time to spare, Ashur sped through and away from the city.

Frost sobbed, hating the tears that scalded her cheeks, and slipped into oblivion.

She woke with a throbbing head, dimly aware of the heavy manacles that bound her wrists. Damp, musty straw, thick with the smell of stale urine, pressed on her face. She wrinkled her nose, tried to sit, but moving brought a wave of nausea. She gave up the effort and waited quietly for her head to clear.

Faint light filtered through a narrow, barred window in the cell door. Beyond, she heard voices, the rattle of dice, a game being played.

She managed to sit, then to stand, a first, hesitant step toward the door. In the dark, she kicked something, tripped and fell with a clatter and scraping of chains. Groping, she found the obstacle—a small stool.

A face appeared in the window. "Hey, she's awake," someone called. More footsteps.

A key grated in the lock. She crouched, took a tighter grip on one of the stool's legs.

Three men filled the room. Two in soldiers' garb held swords ready; the jailor, an obese giant, held a torch and beckoned.

Smirks, grins, lust in the guards' eyes. Suddenly, she realized that a mild blush was all that covered her form. Her clothes and weapons lay on a table in the corridor.

With a frustrated shrug she tossed the stool aside and stepped out of the cell. The guards sheathed their blades and took her by the arms. Selecting a key from his large ring, the jailor removed the manacles.

"She's a nice one," muttered a guard, grinning broadly. "Who would ever know?"

The jailor grunted, an unpleasant bullish noise. "Little woman not for likes of you. Just take her upstairs. Zarabeth's waiting."

The same guard put his face next to hers and whispered what he would do if he had a little time with her. She blushed hotly, clenched her fists, but fought to control her anger. She turned her face, looked him in the eye, smiling.

"You've undoubtedly had plenty of practice—with other guards."

His hand drew back and she braced for a stinging slap, but a huge, meaty paw closed on his wrist and held it in a crushing grip.

"Not to hurt little woman," the jailor warned.

The guard glared, promising retributions to come.

But the jailor's words offered new hope. Whoever wanted her preferred her in one piece. That was some advantage, at least, for she had no qualms about hurting these three if she got the opportunity. She spotted her sword and Demonfang with her clothes on the table, just out of reach.

"Go now," grumbled the jailor, clanking his keys with irritation. "Make Zarabeth mad if you keep her waiting."

Frost saw her chance suddenly as the insulted guard reached out to shove her. His hand brushed an unresisting shoulder as she sank into a deep crouch. Unbalanced, he pitched forward, crying out as she straightened. He tumbled into the other guard; both fell in a heap.

Only the jailor stood between her and her weapons. She hit him hard and low with her shoulder, slamming him back against the wall.

Rejoicing, she reached for the sword.

But even as her fingers touched the hilt a fat hand twisted in her hair. The jailor was not stunned as she had hoped; his obese form had absorbed the impact without harm. With an angry grunt he jerked sharply, snapping her head back, and dragged her from her weapons. The corridor resounded with her outcry as she struggled to free herself from his painful grip, and the cold floor stones scraped her shoulders as he forced her down.

An immense fist hovered over her face, ready to smash.

"No! Don't mark her face!"

A woman's voice, used to command. The jailor looked up to see who ordered him, his own face a mask of fury. Frost could see no one; the voice came from behind her, but she felt the fat man stir and tremble when it spoke. When he looked back down on her, the fury was gone from his features, replaced by a more subtle mixture of fear and cruelty.

"All right, then," he whispered. "Not her face."

His hand covered her breast and began a gentle, teasing massage. Then, steel fingers started to squeeze slowly. An involuntary scream reverberated through the halls. Frost sucked breath and clamped her eyes shut against the incredible jolts of pain. Her knees kicked ineffectually on the giant's back, and her nails raked the flesh on his thick arms. Grinning, he trapped both her wrists with one hand, pinned her with a knee in the stomach.

How long the pain continued she could not say. It seemed forever, and her throat was raw long before the jailor's weight lifted from her.

She strained to sit, her breast afire, tears a freely flowing stain on her cheeks. The two guards, on their feet again, looked on aghast.

"Not mark her face you said." A half-smile flickered on the jailor's ugly face.

An old woman stepped out of the gloom, cursing as she pushed the guards aside. Kneeling down, she placed a consolate arm around Frost's bare shoulders.

"Now get up, dear. You'll know better than to try that again, won't you?"

Frost pushed the frail old arm away and glared at the leering jailor. "I'm going to kill you," she warned, and not even the shaking in her voice could deny her resolution.

He scowled, raised a menacing fist, but with surprising quickness the old woman sprang up and caught his arm. "That's enough!" Authority swelled her voice. "She's for Tumac, and you know his command."

Tumac. She turned the name over in her memory. It meant nothing to her. A man of power, though, to judge by the jailor's reaction.

The old woman turned back to her, then. "And you mind your mouth," she said sternly. "I don't intend to scrape you off the wall if you make Orgolio mad a second time."

The jailor folded his fat arms, regarded her coldly.

"Now get up." She offered Frost a hand and pulled her to her feet. Surprising strength in that small, veined hand. "No serious damage," she pronounced as she examined the tortured breast. "The pain will pass, and soon the greatest joy in Zondu will be yours."

Frost forced a bitter smile. "My greatest joy will be to leave this treacherous city."

"Oh no, dear," she answered curtly. "Just forget about that." Then, she turned to the guards standing just behind her and dealt them each a savage kick on the shins. "Out of my way, you worthless morons! I send you to fetch one girl and she nearly cracks your empty skulls. If I report your disgusting behavior, Tumac will have your heads piked on the front palace gates."

They shuffled aside, begging pardon. The woman strode magnificently by them, unheeding, motioning for Frost to follow. Humiliated, the guards fell in behind.

Frost thought to ask a name.

"I am Zarabeth," came the answer, "keeper of Lord Tumac's seraglio."

They passed through a number of brightly lit halls, encountering no one, then through a number of dark ones with a single torch to show the way. Frost tried to count her steps, the right turns and the left so that she could retrace the course. It was a hopeless task; the way was too long and winding, and the walls were all the same. At last they stopped. An ivory door and two barrel-chested sentries barred the way.

Zarabeth addressed the original guards. "This is as far as you go. Return to your duties and pray that I forget your faces."

The two saluted sharply, spun about and disappeared down the corridor. When the echo of their footsteps had faded, the door sentries bowed and parted. Zarabeth rapped a special knock on the portal and it swung open.

The scents of costly perfumes touched her nostrils. A young girl held the door wide, lowered her eyes in abasement as Zarabeth passed, but met Frost's own gaze with a look of cool superiority.

She paused, took in the pale paints that shaded the girl's face, the kohl smeared, almond-shaped eyes and the thick black hair that hung past the hips. A piece of transparent silk fell over one shoulder to her ankles, fastened at the waist by a chain of delicate golden links from which gems and precious stones dangled on silver threads.

The girl stuck out her tongue.

Frost made a gesture she had seen her father's men use in

dice games or heated quarrels, unsure of its meaning, but loving the blush it brought to the concubine's cheeks. She followed Zarabeth into the chamber.

It was staggering, vast. Slender columns of white marble rose to a domed ceiling which was painted with scenes of passion and lovemaking. The walls were hung with tapestries depicting nude, lovely females at play in gardens or woodlands, pursued by stags, bulls or lusty men. In contrast to the cold stones of the corridors, the floor was thick with fleecy carpets and rich rugs. There were no furnishings other than cushions and pillows piled high and, here and there, a brazier of incense.

Nine more women in various stages of dress looked up as Zarabeth clapped her hands. Behind her, Frost heard the door close.

"See that this woman is bathed and clothed suitably," Zarabeth ordered. "She sits with Tumac tonight."

She watched the different reactions of the concubines. Some were jealous. A few seemed awed. Most at least feigned indifference. Whoever Tumac was, these women were his, though. That meant a high statesman, possibly governor. She lingered on that. *She was for him,* Zarabeth had said. Well, by the three eyes of Tak, she had other ideas.

Casually, she brushed a girl aside and crossed to the door. No knob, only a large keyhole. She cursed, whirled. The one she had pushed—the same one who had admitted them—smiled guilefully and waved a large iron key. Its end was a ring that served as a handle when the lock was turned.

Zarabeth took the key, dropped it down her bosom and folded her arms. No malice showed in her old gray eyes. "You had to try once, and now you've done so. Leave it at that."

She considered taking the key from the old whore. She doubted the other females in the chamber could stop her. Oddly, though, she was developing a liking for Zarabeth, an admiration for her strength and forthrightness.

She decided to bide her time. Other opportunities would come.

The women led her away.

They scrubbed her with stiff brushes. With heavy oils and perfumes they massaged her. Then, her hair was washed, combed dry and more perfumes added to it. Eyes were carefully, tastefully painted, then her lips and cheeks. Zarabeth personally tended her short nails, staining them a shade that matched her eyes.

When her grooming was finished they dressed her in the same transparent veil they all wore.

"This is too much!" she cried, ripping the thin garment to shreds. "I'll not display myself in this lascivious manner. If you want to dress me, then give me clothes."

Zarabeth whispered to a girl. A length of light blue silk was brought to replace the transparent one. Two women fussed as they draped it over her and fastened it with one of their own golden belts.

Zarabeth rose. "No, no dears. Too much of her breast is bare, and Orgolio's finger marks are starting to show."

Livid blue bruises spotted her breast. The garment was removed and arranged over her left shoulder, carefully hiding the mottled flesh.

Frost studied her reflection in a length of polished bronze. Her front and back were covered, but her sides from shoulder to ankle were completely bare. Only the gold belt and dangling jewels kept the cloth in place. It was a shocking, brazen costume, yet she found she did not entirely dislike it.

"You're very lovely, child." Zarabeth paced a small circle, nodded approvingly. She beckoned for one of the women. "Bring my personal chest of jewels."

When the chest was brought and opened, Zarabeth dug deep into the contents, at last removing a thin circlet of twisted silver. One polished moonstone gleamed on the band. She gave the ornament a long, loving look, then drew a deep breath as she placed in on Frost's brow, centering the jewel with ginger care.

"I give this to you."

A murmur raced through the concubines, angry glances and jealous whispers. "Zarabeth!" one dared, "you can't!"

The old woman slapped the dissenter in the mouth until she cowered away. An inner fire lit Zarabeth's eyes. "It's not your place to say what I can or cannot do," she warned. "Don't ever presume it is."

She turned back to Frost. "That was a gift from Tumac's father, given our first night together. I was very young then, and as high-spirited as you." With a wave, she dismissed the others. "It's time for you to go now. Tumac is waiting."

They crossed the chamber to a certain tapestry. Behind it was another door opened by the same iron key. Two guards with pole axes waited on the other side. Frost marveled how they bowed their huge, hulking bodies so low when Zarabeth spoke.

"The new one is ready."

The old courtesan led the way, the guards in the rear respectfully silent. From an unseen cranny two new guards assumed their vacated posts.

Her bare feet made no noise on the cool tiles as they traveled a series of winding passages. There were no windows, and the few doors along the way were closed. Oil lamps blazed on the walls, but she shivered, doubting she could ever find her way alone through such a maze.

Faint strains of music and laughter drifted toward them from behind a set of immense oaken doors. Zarabeth stopped, and one of the guards came forward, seized gleaming brass handles and pushed.

Her mouth went moist as the savory odors of roasted meats surged from the dining hall. Music, sweet and wild, poured into the passage while dancers and tumblers cavorted in the center of the floor. Servants bearing platters of sweatmeats and vegetables scurried among the guests, and wine goblets were constantly refilled by a score of pretty maidens.

She stepped uncertainly inside.

Where did Zondu get such fare in so barren a land? She looked questioningly at Zarabeth, who smiled, took her hand and ushered her through the hall. Straight to the head table and the highest lords and ladies.

One man rose ponderously, ceremoniously as they approached. He gazed down on them. Frost met his gaze, forgetting to bow until Zarabeth slapped her on the stomach.

Short and fat, he wore bright robes and too many rings. His head balanced precariously on a thin neck adorned with chains and precious gems that glittered brilliantly in the dancing light of countless torches. His balding scalp was only partially hidden beneath a golden coronet.

Zarabeth bowed again. "I have prepared her, Lord, as you commanded me."

Tiny white teeth showed in his smile. "My dear," he addressed Frost, "you are quite exquisite. More so than when I saw you first. Oh, don't trouble your memory—you were, ah, sleeping at the time." He motioned to an empty chair at his right hand. "I've saved a place of honor for you."

A winecup smashed on the floor. A young nobleman leaped

to his feet, slamming an angry fist on the board. "Lord Tumac!" All eyes turned to the outraged guest. "She wears your chain—the badge of your concubines!"

Tumac was unruffled. "You don't miss a thing, do you, young Telric?" He took a sip of wine. "Be a good boy and don't make a fuss about it."

The fist pounded the table again. "She's mine! She murdered two of my brothers; the honor of my house demands she die!"

Tumac stepped down from the dais that elevated the main table above the others, came forward and took her hand, kissed it and smiled. "Die? This lovely vision? I couldn't allow that, oh no. Such a waste!" He guided her to the seat by his, dismissing Zarabeth with a gesture. "I confess that I considered giving her to you, but now that I've seen her scrubbed and properly attired I realize that would have been a gross error in judgment."

"She murdered my brothers!"

"And rest assured that I will personally see to her punishment."

Frost didn't miss his sly wink.

"My father will not like this!" Telric screamed.

Tumac fluttered his hands serenely. "There is very little Lord Rholf can do about it. Now sit down and try to enjoy the festivities before you work yourself into a choler."

Telric purpled. "For the last time, Tumac, I ask you—give her up."

Zondu's governor frowned in mild irritation. "I'll put it to the men among you," he addressed his guests. "This lad tells a wild tale of murder done by this beautiful creature." He placed a fleshy, pallid hand on her head, stroked her hair. It was a disgusting truth that he held her fate in his palm at the moment, so she tried not to shrink away. "In fact," he continued, "he claims she killed his brothers using a sword in a common tavern brawl." A big grin lit his features. He lifted her arm and squeezed her bicep playfully. "Now I ask—could this pale, delicate limb slay such two strong swordsmen as old Rholf's sons? Come now, and give me judgment. What say you?"

The feast hall erupted with laughter.

Tumac shrugged, made a helpless pass in the air. "Well, young Telric. You've heard the verdict with your own ears. I can't, in good faith, turn her over to you. But be assured that when I have the time I will investigate your claim and seek the truth of this unpleasant matter. Until then, be at peace and enjoy my wine.''

The son of Lord Rholf swept a blistering gaze over the hall, and the guests grew uncomfortably silent. Then, he spat contemptuously in a platter of steaming meats, spun on his heel and strode from the banquet.

"Convey my greetings to your noble father," Tumac called as the youth disappeared through the doors. Then, confidentially to Frost: "Never did like his father—quite a pompous ass, really.''

She sipped reflectively at the wine he offered and nibbled a piece of fruit, then a slice of meat. Kregan had warned her they would be pursued by Rholf and his family. The Shazadi governor must have found their tracks and guessed their destination; as Kregan had feared, some hard riding and a string of fresh horses had put Telric in Zondu first and given him time to lay a trap for them.

But there was more than one trap to fear this evening it seemed, and more than one trapper.

Instinctively as she thought of Zarad-Krul her hand strayed toward where she kept the Book of the Last Battle. Her fingers brushed only the golden belt that marked her as one of Tumac's concubines; the Book was with her clothes and weapons in the dungeon far below.

Her brow wrinkled, her mouth creased in a tight-lipped frown and she wondered at the time. The feast hall lights gave no hint of the hour's lateness. Sundown when she rode into the city—how long since then? It was surely night, and the wizard must be seeking the Book with all his night-spawned forces. If he found it . . . she pushed that thought from her mind.

Resolutely, she drained her winecup, tossing the fiery liquid down her throat. Time to find her Chondite friend and leave this wretched city.

And there was only one way to accomplish that.

Her fingers sought the back of Tumac's bony hand and played lightly there for one tantalizing moment. A small, shark-toothed smile flashed on his face, and he gave her hand a squeeze. "You have the most remarkably green eyes," he said, breathily.

Frost swallowed hard, her throat suddenly tight. "I have a number of remarkable attributes," she brazened, "not all of them as assessable as my eyes."

It was not a role that suited her. She was no seductress, and she fought to hide her trembling. But Tumac, his hand on hers, felt her body's quivering, misinterpreted it, and uttered a wry comment over the rim of his cup.

She averted her eyes in calculated coyness. "Shouldn't a maiden tremble with such a man as you?"

The winecup hesitated at his lips; Tumac's eyes rolled over the edge. Slowly, never removing his gaze, he set the cup aside. "Maiden?"

Again, she looked away, wondering if she could force a blush. She settled for a shy nod.

The shark-toothed smile returned, and Zondu's governor licked his lips with sudden desire. He stroked her arm from shoulder to wrist, his palm damp with perspiration. "If you're lying, it will go hard with you," he warned.

She let a little grin slip over her face and toyed with a bite of roasted fowl. "Will it not, in any case?"

Tumac threw back his head and roared. "Well said!" he bellowed, shaking the table with his belly, startling his guests into puzzled muteness. "Well said, indeed!" He beckoned for more wine, and a servant replenished his cup. He downed it with a single, long gulp. Another draught, then he rose pulling Frost with him, her hand locked firmly in his.

"Good friends," he called, and all gave their full attention. "I thank you for your company and pray you continue the revels. I've given orders to the servants that you should want for nothing, be it food, drink or . . ." he grinned, fixing his view unsubtly on her breasts, "or anything else. But, being a weary governor I will seek my bed now. So, I wish you a good night."

Her hand imprisoned in Tumac's sweaty paw, Frost waded through sly remarks and coarse laughter close to the governor's side, blushing hotly as he led her like a helpless child.

A guard fell in behind as they passed through the great wooden doors and down a dim corridor. Soon, she was again lost in a maze of passages, some lit and some not, and she was beginning to despair of ever finding her way out when Tumac stopped at another door. The room beyond was dark; the guard crowded past them to light tapers with a lamp taken from a niche in the hall. That done, he stepped out and closed the door after.

She let go a worried breath and looked around the chamber Silken drapes and tapestries, all of transparent thinness, descended from the ceiling to the plushly carpeted floor. The corners were piled high with rich cushions, but the only piece of real furniture was an immense, carved bed deep with feather mattresses and more cushions.

Tumac led her to it.

There was nothing she could use as a weapon—not a comb or pin of any kind, nothing that would serve as a club or bludgeon. The candlesticks were mounted on the walls, not detachable. It seemed the room had been deliberately stripped of anything that could cause harm.

Tumac released her hand, a hungry leer spreading on his face. Slowly, he began to remove his garments, swaying in a grotesquely sensuous dance as a woman might to seduce a man. Piece by piece he cast aside his clothes until he was completely naked. His eyes raked her form; a low growl rumbled in his throat.

She turned away, disgusted, fighting a growing fear. Cold hands touched her, slithered over her shoulders, questing for her secret parts. An obese body pressed against her, and despite an iron resolve not to, she shivered uncontrollably. Wrapped in his arms, she let herself be turned. The smell of his breath—of his flesh—filled her senses. His own chest hung thick and bulbous as a woman's, and between his thighs a mammoth organ stirred. He buried his face in the softness of her neck; his lips began to nibble.

It was not going as she planned. There should have been something to convert to a weapon, a chance to win her escape. Tumac's hot breath scorched her skin; his fingers fumbled with the golden cincture at her waist. No man had ever touched her in such a manner, nor had such a fear ever gripped her. If she had considered bedding the fat governor to gain her freedom and Kregan's, the plan was too repulsive to carry out.

His touch burned her skin as his hands slid under her thin vestment. Abandoning the belt's complicated catch, he eased the material over her shoulder, exposing her breasts. He was almost drooling as he cupped one ivory mound in his palm. But he wanted her totally naked, and his other hand began to work once more at the stubborn ornament.

And a sudden thrill surged through her, chasing away her fears. It took an effort not to laugh, so great was her relief. She peered at the door, measuring the distance to it, remembering the maze of corridors beyond it, wondering at her chances of finding the dungeon and Kregan without being discovered.

For there was one weapon, after all.

Gently, she pushed Tumac away, smiling promises with her eyes. "Let me," she whispered, taking his hands from the golden belt. The gems that dangled from it glittered on gilt threads in the faint amber light as she unfastened the catch and held it up like a veil between them, secretly testing its strength, assuring herself the links would not break.

She opened wide her arms, and Tumac took the invitation, closing his eyes as he rolled in her embrace. With a calm, irrepressible satisfaction she wrapped the chain around his fat throat and jerked.

His eyes popped open in pain and surprise. With all her strength she jerked again, and yet the governor managed to wriggle a hand beneath the links, preventing the ever-tightening band from crushing his windpipe.

Frost cursed, fighting anew the panic that tried to overwhelm her. The chain disappeared in the flesh of his neck and still the man would not die. His face purpled, a vein bulged in his temple until she could see it throb—yet he lived!

Time was short, and she feared someone might pass in the hall and hear the struggle. She had to end this.

A knee smashed Tumac's unprotected groin. A loud animal grunt, and the governor slumped forward. Savagely, she kicked his feet from under him. His head twisted dangerously, eyes swelling as his entire weight suspended from the jeweled garrote. A pink tongue forced itself between discoloring lips.

But still he clung to life. She put her foot on his neck.

A furious pounding at the door, then it burst open. Two guards rushed in, swords sprouting from their fists. At a glance she recognized the one who had escorted her with Tumac.

She released one end of the chain, and Tumac crumpled on the carpet. Only her uncanny speed saved her from a quick death as the first guard charged. A blade whistled past her ear. She swung the chain, and her attacker screamed as its pendulant gems stung his eyes. A foot sank into his belly; a fist crashed with startling power into the back of his head.

She made damn sure he fell before she stopped hitting. Then, the second guard lunged. A desperate dodge, whirl and tug, and one of the veils that hung from the ceiling swirled down, tangling the man in its folds.

But the first guard had found his feet again, groggy, yet still dangerous with his sword. He swung clumsily, and she danced back. Then her foot caught, slipped on something soft— Tumac's discarded pantaloons.

She fell hard, cracking her head on the floor. The blade rushed up, descended. She rolled, evading death by a hair's breath. But something pulsed in the top of her skull, and her ears were full with a loud ringing. That carelessly strewn bit of silk had been her undoing.

Through blurred vision she watched three more sentries rush into the bedchamber. The fight was over, a useless effort. She held up her hands in surrender, just staying a death-thrust from the first guard.

Tumac was not dead. He tottered on shaky legs toward her, supported on either side by two men. Deep, mottled welts of crimson showed lividly around his neck where the links of chain had bitten. Pain glazed his tiny eyes.

His hand came down against her cheek, but there was no strength in the blow, and she forced a perverse smile.

His voice was a harsh raspy whisper. "You wretched, foolish woman!" A quivering finger pointed high along the wall. Concealed in the upper shadows was a narrow slit. No light showed through, but she guessed its purpose. "I'm never without my personal guard! Even with a woman I am watched and protected!"

The fat little man who had come so close to death glowered, seeming to expect a reply. She considered a number of mocking insults, but decided to hold her tongue. She was in enough trouble already.

"I should have given you to young Telric," he croaked when she plainly had nothing to say. He motioned to the guards. "Take the thankless, ungrateful bitch back to her cell, and never let me set eyes on her again."

Chapter Six

SHE FELL IN A HEAP ON THE STRAW-COVERED FLOOR, AND the cell door slammed shut. The laughter of the guards lingered long after their footsteps faded.

She was back where she started—naked, bound and weaponless. A large bump where her head had met the floor in Tumac's room ached mercilessly, but she ignored the pain as best she could and worked at the chain that held her wrists. Though the numbness in her fingers made the knotted links difficult to manipulate after long minutes she was free. Circulation returned with tingling slowness, and she licked the raw, red bands that chaffed her skin.

She felt only slightly less impotent. Rising, she paced the cell. No furniture—not even the little stool she had tripped over before. Nothing to break up and use as a weapon. She tried her weight against the door; it was thick, solid, betraying not the least sign of weakness. The bars in the small window were set deep in the wood, quite immovable.

She cursed, smashed a fist on the door.

A sound, a shuffle in the corridor, and Frost sidled back into the darkness out of the faint torchlight that filtered into her cell. The shuffling stopped; Orgolio, the jailor, peered through the bars. She crouched in a corner, holding her breath, making no sound.

"You all right, little woman?"

She kept still. Orgolio could not see where she hid; maybe he would come inside to find her.

"Oh, so you not talk to Orgolio, heh? Well, that all right. Lots of people don't talk to Orgolio, but he not mind much."

She was almost touched by the loneliness in his voice, but the bruises on her breast were reminders of his potential for cruelty. No pity, then, for this simple-minded brute. If he opened the door she had to hit him hard and run, and pray it worked better than the last time.

Orgolio sighed. "Well, you be a good little woman, and pretty soon Orgolio come play with you nice."

The face withdrew from the window. She cursed again to herself and shuddered. *Play nice,* indeed. She crept silently to the bars, watched the ponderous jailor drop into a chair a few paces down the corridor beside the table that bore her clothes and weapons. He appeared to fall asleep almost at once.

As she observed him a dangerous plan took shape in her mind. She had to get free and find Kregan if he still lived, then get the Book of the Last Battle away from Zondu. The hour must be very late, and she felt in her soul that Zarad-Krul would attack before dawn. Still, her plan bordered on madness; she shivered at the prospect of failure.

Well, there was no more time to think. She pressed her face to the bars and called.

The jailor's eyelids fluttered. "Eh? Who calls Orgolio?"

"Wake up." Her voice was silken, tempting, she hoped.

He looked, but did not get up. "Is it you, little woman? Don't be impatient—Orgolio come play with you soon."

"Open the door, Orgolio. I'll come play with you out there."

The jailor's smile disappeared. "Dumb woman." He spat on the opposite wall. "You think I open door and let you out. You think Orgolio stupid like everybody else. Well, dumb woman, Orgolio never let you out. But you not be unhappy cause Orgolio will play with you lots. Uh huh, you be plenty happy woman, soon." He settled back in his chair and fell asleep again.

She licked her lips, wiped the sweat from her palms, then called his name yet another time.

"What now, dumb woman?"

This was it. No turning back now. "If you set me free I'll give you something very beautiful, very valuable."

He snorted, rubbed his enormous nose. "Little woman have nothing for Orgolio. Guards take everything away from you."

She gripped the cold bars tightly. "It lies among my clothes right there beside you. I can see it from here. It's yours if you let me go."

He sat up, interested. His sleepy eyes fluttered like nervous birds. "Well, what is it, dumb woman?"

"A dagger," she whispered tensely, feeling weak in her stomach for what she dared. "Of purest silver."

The fat jailor wiped the corners of his mouth, stared at the pile on the table, considering.

"Go on," she urged. "Look at it."

Orgolio rummaged through her belongings and found Demonfang. The belt gleamed in the amber light. As he examined it, turning the sheath slowly, a broad smile split his thick-jowled face.

Then, a new sound startled her—the rasp of her own quick breathing. She forced herself to be calm. "Look closely," she said. "Look at the blade."

Orgolio leered, showing broken, yellow teeth. "Dumb woman thinks Orgolio will let her free now. Uh huh, no. He will keep pretty dagger and not let you go."

She banged her head on the bars, nearly screaming her frustration. "Look at the blade, you stupid cow's ass!" She hadn't meant to hiss. The jailor stared back with a stone expression that made her fear she had angered him. Quickly, smoothly she lied, "It is cunningly wrought by the most skilled craftsmen in Esgaria." Her voice dropped a note, gently insistent. "Look at the blade."

He grinned suddenly and seized the dagger's hilt. Perhaps it was some instinct that made him hesitate, and Frost squeezed the cell bars until her knuckles were white. *Look at it,* she willed, *look at it.*

She clenched her eyes tight, hearing the faint scrape of the blade's edge as it moved on the inside of the sheath.

And Demonfang came alive. The shrill screech of its hunger

rattled the dungeon stones. The jailor's grin turned to terror as the unholy sound shook the roots of his dull soul.

In fearful awe she watched the transformation that came on Orgolio. Fear flashed over his face; the need to kill burned in his small black eyes. The two emotions—terror and bloodlust —warred for possession of his body, a battle reflected in his contorting expressions.

Then, he rose from the chair, gripped in the dagger's irresistible power. Unwilling, he took the keys from a peg on the wall and shambled toward her cell, fighting with every step the force that compelled him.

A key grated in the lock.

It must taste blood—either your enemy's or your own. She gambled her life on that curse, steeled for a fight, and begged aid from all her gods.

The cell door swung back. Orgolio stood silhouetted blackly in the dim light, and Demonfang shone in his fist like fire from Hell's deepest level and screamed like the souls imprisoned there.

Warily, she backed to the center of the cell, allowing room to fight. The jailor was a giant, more than twice her size with a frighteningly long reach. She'd already lost one fight to him this night. She dared not lose this one. She took a breath, unconsciously held it and watched the eerie emotional changes that rippled on her opponent's face: confusion, terror, madness.

A deep-throated cry joined with the dagger's shrieking as the giant lunged. She moved, a swift blur, leaped aside and chopped at the hand clutching Demonfang. The arcane blade screamed angrily as it clattered on the floor.

Better than she had hoped, to disarm him so easily. She dived for the weapon, but Orgolio's massive weight smashed into her, sending her sprawling, the breath rushing from her lungs. Clambering to her feet, she whirled, prepared for attack —and froze.

Demonfang gleamed once more in that huge fist.

That infernal screaming intensified, resonated in the dungeon's confining places, assaulted her senses like a tangible foe. No one would hear it so far beneath the palace, or if someone did—well, it was a dungeon, after all; who would care if Orgolio played noisily?

The cold wall pressed her back. The possessed jailor leered, extended his apish arms in a wide, menacing semicircle as he advanced. Run, dodge or leap—she would never make it past those grasping limbs The blade's insistent, thirsty cries rang in her ears until she feared for her sanity.

His right arm dropped; the dagger swung upward. A desperate cry—reflexively, she caught the driving wrist in both hands, halting death's point mere inches from her vitals.

A short moment they pitted strength against strength, but Frost had the advantage of leverage. The jailor roared; with his free hand he swung viciously at her face, and the force of the blow made her head ring. Still, she would not release the captured wrist. She anticipated his next swing, ducked it, kicked him in the groin with all her might. In the fat sockets his eyes rolled wide with pain that doubled him over. She sidestepped, grabbing his neck, the belt of his trousers, and the stone wall fairly shivered as she smashed him headlong into it. Not stopping to judge the result, she sped into the corridor, slamming the door.

The key was not in the lock. Possibly Orgolio had carried it into the cell. Frantically, she glanced through the barred window. Her opponent staggered to his feet, Demonfang still in his hand. It screamed and screamed; Frost choked back a bitter sob. The giant's eyes met hers, and he came.

It must taste blood—either your enemy's or your own.

That was her hope and her despair. With no way to lock the door she braced her feet on the narrow corridor's opposite wall, shoulders to the hard wood, making her body a living wedge. Orgolio pushed. The door gave an inch. She strained, steeled herself furiously for what she knew would follow.

The shock of his first kick nearly shattered her spine. He threw his weight against the door until one hinge bent, threatened to break. A cracking sound in the old timber. With fist and foot and shoulder Orgolio battered the door, and she squeezed her eyes shut and prayed her own strength would last long enough.

Demonfang wailed.

A scratching made her look up. Fat fingers wriggled through the bars, clawed the wood. A hand pushed impossibly through and a little of an arm; the fist flexed and opened, seeking. She remembered how that hand had grabbed her hair before, and feared.

Then suddenly, a new vehement note slashed her ears as Demonfang's shrieking strained, altered, turned vengeful. Orgolio's frenzied smashing at the door weakened, ceased. Three heartbeats of silence—then a scuffling at the cell's farthest side.

A morbid curiosity possessed her. Rising quickly, seizing a torch from a wall sconce, she peered through the bars and caught her breath.

On his knees, the jailor moaned in despondent terror. His left hand struggled to peel the fingers of his right from the dagger's hilt. The muscles in his arm knotted as he fought to hold the point at bay. But the famished blade screeched, and Orgolio's resistance crumbled. Pale, sweating, he gaped at glittering death.

The right arm jerked, twitched, raised high and plunged down. The point shattered breast-bone with a crunching noise, straight to the blood-filled heart. The screams stopped, the blade's need sated. Then, Orgolio's mouth opened, and those same screams sounded in his human throat. Frost covered her ears, leaned her head on the door until they stopped.

Quiet seeped back into the dungeon. No other sound but her own uneven breathing. Opening the door, she stared from the threshold, afraid to enter, pondering what she had witnessed. Demonfang sprouted like an evil flower from the dead jailor's chest. She was loath to touch it. And yet, the dagger had saved her life; without the blade's strange curse she might have rotted in that cell, a thing for Orgolio's gross pleasure. Reluctantly and with trembling fingers, she plucked it from his body, cleaned the edge on a handful of straw. The belt and sheath lay where he had cast them, and she expelled a heavy sigh when the weapon was finally cased.

Only then did she remember Kregan—and Zarad-Krul.

Her garments were close at hand. She pulled on trousers and boots, then reached for her tunic.

Her flesh prickled. She shook the tunic, swept up her cloak and shook that. A cold dread coursed through her veins. She searched the floor on her knees. Nothing under the table or chair.

Her sword was there. But the Book of the Last Battle was gone.

She threw on the rest of her clothes cursing, and buckled on her weapons. She *had* to find Kregan now. Maybe he knew something about the Book's fate. If not, she needed his advice. But which way to go? The right-hand way led to the upper levels of the palace; the few cells in that direction were dark and soundless when she passed them with her guards. Still, the Chondite might have been bound as she was, maybe gagged, too, or worse. The left-hand way was a mystery. More cells as far as she could see in the light of the torches and lamps. Any of them might hold her friend. An ugly frown flashed over her face. Indecision was not her nature, yet she hesitated, uncertain. A wrong choice meant valuable time wasted—and there was still the threat of Zarad-Krul.

A footstep in the darkness. She slid into the welcome shadow of a niche, sword drawn, not daring to breathe. A light tread. One person, she decided, listening. Closer came the footsteps. A pool of amber, a whiff of burning oil, a hand bearing a lamp. Someone passed her hiding place, unaware.

Swift and silent she reached out, clamping her hand hard over a mouth to prevent a scream. The edge of her sword went to a throat and paused at the jugular. Her prisoner stiffened, but offered no resistance.

Zarabeth.

Frost recognized first the perfume, then the garment and gold-linked, jewel-spangled cincture, recalling that of all Tumac's seraglio only the old whore-keeper was free to roam the palace. "If you make a sound it will be your last," she whispered coldly, and the woman nodded as best she could in the tight grip. Frost released her then, and Zarabeth turned with her lamp held high. Aged, painted eyes twinkled with surprise.

"You're more resourceful than I thought."

Frost shrugged. "What are you doing down here?"

The mistress of concubines held a bottle of wine in her other hand. "I was bringing this to you. Tumac made a public pro- nouncement of your attempt to murder him and swore you would never again see the light of day, that you'd rot in your cell, a plaything for his guards. I couldn't let any woman suffer that." Her tone softened somewhat, but she met the younger woman's gaze evenly. "This is poisoned drink."

"Thanks for the thought," she acknowledged sarcastically, "but why should you care?"

Zarabeth's turn to shrug. "There's little time, and since you're free we must contrive to get you away from Zondu. Suffice it to say that in my own youth I was a lot like you: spirited, rebellious, even skilled with a weapon or two." Then, in the lamplight her features hardened, a fire rose in her eyes. "And I would do anything to rob Tumac of his little pleasures —even poison a young woman he would like very much to remember rotting for having spurned him."

She stared long and hard at the old concubine, taking her measure. "You hate him very much, don't you?"

Zarabeth's face was hard steel, her voice cold. "I was only one of his women, never his wife, but Tumac's father loved me, and I loved him." Bitterness in her words, and grief. "But Tumac was eager to become Zondu's governor, a post as hereditary as kingship in Rholaroth, and one night while his father and I slept in each other's arms, he crept in. With a single sword-stroke he made a headless corpse of his father." She held her hands wide, filled with lamp and bottle, and stared with a strange madness. "His blood spewed over me, and I woke screaming."

Frost offered no response, lost in a memory that was nightmare. She saw her own father at her feet—anger, then death on his face. A sword pierced his body, his life-fluid flowing, staining her boots. And she was the cause.

She held her hand to the light, wondering at its false, unblemished fairness.

"Some night," continued Zarabeth, two tears trailing on her cheeks, "some night I'll repay Tumac in like manner." A moment of unplanned silence hung between them as each grieved for the dead, for the past.

"But that has to wait," the old woman said suddenly. "Now we've got to get you away. Orgolio must be somewhere close. He scuttles through these passages like a fat rat."

"Orgolio is dead," Frost answered. "And I can't leave yet." She silenced Zarabeth's protests with a stern look. "I've got to find two things first: a book with a very unusual binding, and the Chondite sorcerer who was captured with me."

"Forget the book," Zarabeth advised. "That's gone. I can show you where the Chondite is, though why you travel with such *slime* I can't imagine."

She whirled threateningly on the old woman who took a startled, unconscious step back. "What do you mean gone!" she hissed. "Gone where?"

Zarabeth trembled at the fury in those words. "Young Telric took it," she managed. "I saw him with it in his quarters just before he left. I even spoke to him. He wanted proof for his father that you were here, and he thought it might be a diary or journal."

"Where is he now?"

"Gone," Zarabeth answered. "You saw how angry he was with Tumac."

"How long ago did he leave?"

"Nearly two hours."

Frost cursed, then cursed again. So close to Chondos, so damned close. Telric would carry the Book back into Rholaroth, the stupid fool. Unless she could find him and reclaim the fateful tome the world she knew was finished. But was there time? Would Zarad-Krul give her time, or would the mad wizard find Telric first?

"All right, take me to Kregan."

"Who?"

"The Chondite, damn it, and hurry." She gave Zarabeth a little shove to impress her with the urgency of her demand. But Zarabeth slapped the hand away, drew herself up.

"No one pushes me," she said icily. There was a tense moment, a hint of the other Zarabeth who kicked guards and bullied thick-witted jailors. That passed, and the older woman abruptly melted. "Now, just show a little courtesy and I'll lead you."

Kregan was two levels below. Frost heard the guards outside his cell before Zarabeth's small light was detected and quickly extinguished it. Wrapped in the dark where no torches burned, she signalled Zarabeth to wait while she eased slowly forward. Edging around the last corner, she flattened against the wall.

Three guards. In the light of lamps they sat around a table playing *bones* and gambling. One had his back to her; the other would spot her if she moved.

" . . . and this one guy wouldn't go in. Hell, the best brothel in town and we couldn't even *drag* 'im in. Must have been afraid it was habit-forming, haw!"

"Those Traffybanians are so dumb a half-blind camel could beat 'em at *bones.*"

"They fertilize their crops with horse dung, you know."

She listened to this idle banter, sizing them up, estimating her chances. Two were hefty, well built. The third was smaller, but all wore sword and mercy-dagger. Three pikes leaned against the wall near at hand. The passage was narrow, so movement as a unit would be restricted. The lamps were the problem; the light would give her away before she could reach them, and there were no niches or alcoves for her to hide in, making stealth impossible.

Zarabeth touched her arm as she ducked back into the darker passage. "Well?" she whispered.

Frost motioned her companion farther down the way before she spoke. "Three guards with pikes, swords and daggers." She described the setup in detail. "The pikes are next to useless in the confining space. No chance to surprise them, though."

Zarabeth thought. "I could lure them away one at a time. Claim it was Tumac's orders."

"Too suspicious," she answered. "But I can't risk an open fight, either. This has to be quick." She considered for a moment. "How about this?"

The sentries looked up at the sound of footsteps, and three mouths fell open. Zarabeth, whore-keeper, strode boldly into the light. Behind came another woman, head bowed in subservience, completely naked but for a silver circlet which swept back her hair. As she walked her hips swayed enticingly, and her bare feet made soft padding sounds on the stone floor. All three rose and came around the table to see better. There was an unmistakable gleam in their eyes.

"Tumac sends you some entertainment to reward your faithful watch-keeping," Zarabeth proclaimed. Frost floated up to them daintily, delicately, her glance demure and inviting. "And he sends you wine—not enough to make you drunk, but good wine nonetheless. I selected it myself, and I promise you'll never taste its like again."

They seized the bottle, grinning, and Frost began to dance, teasing with her shoulders and taunting with a shift of bare hips, a shivering of thighs and breasts. As they watched the first sentry drank deeply, pouring the liqueur down with greedy gulps; the second and third drank as deeply, wiping lips with dirty hands, jovial and full of mirth.

Until the poison began its work.

A potent medicine, the guards clutched their stomachs,

throats, each other. Their eyes rolled up. First one, then the others cried out, doubled in pain, heaving, coughing, gasping for breath that wouldn't come. The smaller guard glared accusingly at his killers and reached for his sword, but the poison brought him to his knees before he could unsheathe it. His comrades were already down, tongues lolling between blue lips, faces filled with the terror of death.

When it was over she turned to Zarabeth. "Bring my clothes and weapons, please." The old woman hurried back down the corridor as Frost gave her attention to Kregan's cell door. It worried her that no sound issued from it. The noise of the guards' dying should have roused him. She called his name. No answer. Her frantic fingers searched the sentries' bodies until she found the key. Then, shoving it into the lock she twisted and pulled back the door.

At first, she thought him dead. He sprawled on the straw, his hands cruelly bound behind him and his eyes covered with a thick, black cloth. Another rag was stuffed in his mouth. All to prevent his uttering any spell or making gestures or doing any kind of sorcery, she reasoned angrily. Her sword's edge made easy work of the ropes, then she removed the gag and blindfold.

And still the Chondite did not stir. She put an ear apprehensively to his chest. The heartbeat was faint, but definite.

Drugged then.

Zarabeth came through the door carrying Frost's things. Seeing Kregan, she spat and dropped her burden, made warding signs in the air. Frost could barely control the contempt in her voice, for all that the old woman had helped her.

"Stifle your fear. Can't you see he's unconscious?"

The whore-keeper looked doubtful, distrusting. But at last she crept forward, looking with every step as if she would turn and run away if the sorcerer batted an eyelash. Yet, when it was clear that he would not move she knelt down beside the warrior woman, and the fear faded from her.

"I've never been this close to a Chondite," she confided. "I don't like the smell of him." Surprisingly then, she bent over the sorcerer, listened to his heart and grunted. Next, she sniffed his breath. "Chulim," she announced. "A fairly common drug. I'd have used stronger if I were fool enough to capture such a man alive."

Zarabeth slapped his cheeks several times in quick succession and briskly rubbed his limbs. In the corridor Frost found the guards' water supply and dragged the heavy bucket into the cell. She sprinkled a handful of drops on Kregan's eyelids. Zarabeth made a rude noise, rose and motioned her aside. Half the contents splashed on the Chondite as she tilted the container, and when he still did not move she spilled the other half.

A moan bubbled on his lips. Eyes fluttered open.

"Help me get him on his feet," Zarabeth ordered, pulling him to a sitting position alone. Frost took an arm and they heaved him up. On either side they paced him back and forth until his own limbs regained a little strength and he could stand shakily by himself.

Kregan rubbed his temples. "What happened?"

"Too much has happened," Frost answered. For a minute it seemed her friend would collapse again, but she caught him, dealt him a vicious slap. "Come out of it, Kregan. I need you now."

Kregan opened his eyes with effort, but this time they were clearer than before. "All right," he said, "all right."

"The Book is gone," she whispered urgently, "and I've got to go after it."

"What?"

"No time for the full story—it took long enough to find you. It's gone, that's all."

"We've got to get it back," he mumbled.

She shook her head. "Not *we*. Me. I'm going alone. You've got another task."

"I want to help . . ."

"Shut up and just listen, damn it! I've thought this through." She heard Zarabeth's startled gasp as she grabbed the sorcerer and shook him, an act of unthinkable madness to Rholarothans who feared Chondites. "Kregan," her face hovered close to his. "Zarad-Krul doesn't know we've lost it, and he mustn't suspect. He believes we're headed for Chondos, and all his power will bend that way to find us. I'm sure of it. And he's got to keep thinking that if I'm to have any chance of regaining the Book."

"What do you want me to do?"

"Go to Chondos. Tell your brotherhood and any other sorcerer who'll listen what's at stake. Prepare them for war if

85

you can, but do whatever you must to keep Zarad-Krul's attention entirely on Chondos. Otherwise he'll find Telric before I do. Then we're lost.''

Kregan hesitated.

"I can move a lot faster without you," she went on, permitting no argument. "You haven't even got a horse now."

"Neri will be somewhere near."

She waved an angry hand. "She didn't get out through the gate, and even if you could find her she'll never keep up with Ashur the way I intend to travel. You know that."

Kregan nodded slowly, plainly unhappy, but when he spoke again there was a familiar edge to his voice; the last traces of *chulim* were gone. He drew himself up proudly.

"All right, I'll be your decoy," he said, "and I'll raise such turmoil that Zarad-Krul won't dare look away from Chondos. But how will you know where to search for Rholf's son?"

Zarabeth interrupted. "Rholf determined your direction, but not your destination. Telric came here; another son rode to *Tsagah,* the capital. Rholf, himself, is in *Kamaera.*"

"Telric will go to his father," said Frost. "I'll have to catch him before he gets there."

"Kamaera lies west of the Creel Mountains." He scratched his chin. "On reconsideration, it's a madman's plan."

"Have you a better one?"

He frowned at that.

Zarabeth led them out of the dungeon through dark corridors and secret ways until they reached the palace courtyard. So late was the hour they encountered no one, not even a guard, and by the low wall they said their goodbyes. Kregan was brusque, his words reflecting his mood, but he laid a hasty kiss on her cheek before melting into the shadows.

She traced the spot where his lips had touched her, surprised, not a little confused at the way her skin tingled. But there was Zarabeth to bid farewell yet, and she took the old woman's hands.

"I can't thank you adequately with words," she said, "nor even tell you how important a part you've played in this terrible adventure." She touched the circlet with its moonstone gem, started to remove it.

Zarabeth caught her arm. "No, keep it. I gave it freely to you." Her old eyes were suddenly grave, mouth softened. "I don't know what lies before you, child, but I wish you all luck. Be careful—and think of an old woman now and then."

Frost smiled and glanced skyward. This night seemed to last forever. But in the north where Shardaha lay the blackness seemed more than night. Clouds gathered there—dark and evil clouds. She suppressed a shiver as she watched them advance.

Zarabeth looked strangely at her. "What is it, child?"

"Probably nothing," she answered distantly. Then, a fear rose in her; she laid hands on Zarabeth's shoulders and spoke with passion. "If you would carry out your revenge on Tumac, do it now—tonight."

She felt as if her soul were open to this old woman's gaze. How like her mother Zarabeth seemed: strong and daring, gentle, warm, so many mixtures of kindness and cruelty. How like her mother who died cursing her.

"Good fortune, warrior." Zarabeth reached up, kissed her cheek as Kregan had done. "The gods keep you."

She returned the kiss shyly and moved through the garden gate into the silent, empty streets. Only a dog's barking and the low grunt of a pig in a refuse-laden alley disturbed the quiet. Soldiers who patrolled the city had long since turned in for the night, but still she clung to the dark places and kept her sword loose in the sheath.

At last, the city gates loomed. To her dismay they were barred fast with a great wooden beam. Above in a high watch-tower a solitary guard kept vigil over the mechanism that moved the beam and the huge doors. Stealthily, she made for the tower, clambered up the convenient ladder, grateful the city was not designed to resist attackers from the inside. Drawing out her sword she knocked boldly on the closed trap door.

"Who is it?" the sentry called.

She pitched her voice low. "Relief."

Footsteps on the boards, but the door did not open. "You're not due for another hour."

"Have it your way then, damn you. I'll go back to my warm bed and you can rot up here."

"Wait." The door flung back; a hand reached down to help her up. She took it with her right; with her left she shoved her blade through the sentry's gut.

The gate mechanism was an arrangement of chains and balanced weight controlled by one wheel to move the bar and another to open the gate. She turned them, praying no one heard the awful creaking, sped down the ladder and through.

The Zondaur stretched before, lifeless and vast with no moonlight to illuminate the eerie expanse. She set fingers to her lips and gave a low whistle.

Far away a familiar sound, a welcome trumpeting cry that was Ashur. No sight of him in the darkness, but she heard the tempest those ebon hooves raised as they beat across the plain. Then two pools of flickering amber shone in the night racing toward her.

The unicorn reared, stamped the earth, stopping a few paces away. Where eyes should have been those peculiar flames burned with crackling intensity. Only once before had she seen them so bright.

She whirled in sudden alarm, remembering Zarad-Krul. The clouds she had spotted in the north were much closer, a creeping darkness that swallowed stars in its path, full of menace.

A dreadful urgency possessed her as she mounted. Ashur needed no encouragement to speed; she felt the sharp bite of wind on her face and leaned close to the animal's sleek neck. Her heart thundered in her breast.

A low crest rose on her right and she rode for it. At its summit she halted, dismounting. The air was heavy, stifling. Zondu's walls were still visible and she could just see the shadowy tops of the taller buildings.

The clouds came on, and now she noticed the strange shape of them and prayed to all her gods.

The hand of Zarad-Krul hung blackly over the sleeping city —wispy fingers of doom. Frost trembled in her hiding place, chilled to her soul, watching in horrified fascination, fearful that such a hand should ever hold the Book of the Last Battle.

A twinkling in the black palm—sparks of hellish brightness and evil colors sprang into the sky, splintering into more sparks. The hand blazed with scintillant fury as each of the tiny splinters pulsed, burst, filling the sky and staining the city with intense hues, sending shadows racing like bolts of dark lightning from rooftop to rooftop. Then, like a dewy, vibrant rain the deadly sparks plummeted earthward, trailing brilliant fire.

All this Frost saw from the hillside, wondering what she could not see beyond the city walls.

Roused from sleep by the strange light the citizens of Zondu gathered in the streets or leaned from balcony windows to see what was happening. Children clapped their hands and pointed, laughing. Lovers held each other close, thinking it some miracle. Drunks and beggars stumbled from the alleys to beg a few coins from the spectators. Only a few of the older, wiser citizens looked up and tasted acrid fear.

Then, the rain began, and the screaming.

Wherever a spark touched flames sprang up. Fire lines formed, young and old pitching in, but water would not douse the blazes. Faster, thicker fell the sparkling rain amid cries and painful shrieking. Panic spread rapidly through the city, and very few took note that nothing burned save living flesh. Men and women died in beds that were not even scorched. Children perished clinging hopelessly to toys that were left unmarked Slaves and servants ran into the streets seeking safe shelter— there was none.

The magical flames of Zarad-Krul spread everywhere, enveloped everyone.

Frost knew by the flickering light and screaming voices that Zondu was afire. Her mouth went dry as dust, her knuckles white as fingers dug in the barren earth. *Because of me,* she cursed bitterly, *and that thrice-damned Book.*

She watched until the flickering died and the screaming ceased, wishing that the gates would swing open and some of the townspeople yet escape to the Zondaur, but she knew with dreadful certainty that Zarad-Krul's power held the gates fast.

The pungent odor of smoking flesh filled the air.

Then, the fingers of the malevolent cloud streamed downward, black vaporous tendrils. They groped obscenely over the higher rooftops, into granaries and over the battlements of the walls, into windows and doorways.

Though she could not see more, she imagined them crawling along the streets, through houses and taverns, the palace itself, searching for the Book of the Last Battle.

That brought a spiteful smile.

A blast of demonic thunder rocked the countryside, and

three bolts of lightning stabbed, leaving gaping craters where the palace once had stood. The fingers of the cloud curled back, made a grotesque fist, and the black hand of Zarad-Krul shook in anger and frustration. It turned ponderously, uncloud-like, toward Chondos: another thunderblast, and the fist shook again, full of challenge and menace. Then, the cloud began to dissipate, deserted by the arcane force that created it.

She touched the moonstone that hung like a third eye in the center of her brow, remembering the giver, and swore a vengeance against the Wizard of Shardaha.

Chapter Seven

THE CREEL MOUNTAINS LOOMED RED AND MENACING IN the tainted light of sunset. Age sat upon the smoothly worn peaks whispering of mysteries older than the earth they were part of. A wind rolled down, touched her face. The mountains seemed to murmur among themselves. The wind came again, a mellow moan. Far along the horizon the southernmost mountain, Mount Drood, cast a dark and evil shadow.

Frost dismounted, better to examine Telric's trail, cursing the young lord's foolish judgment. It led through the Creel, not around by the usual caravan routes. So eager to reach his father in Kamaera, he apparently chose to ignore the tales told of those wild peaks. A wiser man would not have. Too often superstitions were based on dangerous fact.

She rubbed her aching thighs and shook the stiffness from her joints. Without a saddle the long hard ride was taking a toll, and not on her alone. Ashur's endurance was supernatural. Even so, the unicorn was lathered and shaking with fatigue. All through the night and most of the day he ran with very little rest. She gave the creature an affectionate stroke and a hug, then mounted again.

Ghouls in the Creel, ghosts and demons—she had heard stories even in far-off Esgaria around the fires of her mother's coven. She dreaded going there, but where the Book went she had to follow.

Upward the trail led along a narrow, rocky path. Evidence of Telric's passage quickly disappeared in the steep, harsh ground, but the terrain dictated the only course. A sheer wall rose on the path's right side; a deep, mist-filled gorge yawned on the left. She dropped from the unicorn's back and proceeded on foot wishing the night to delay its coming a little longer. Ticklish business, wandering a ledge in the dark.

As the last light faded the path began to descend. The wall and gorge were left behind and the trail opened into a wide pass through a forest into a low valley. Too dark to find tracks in the softer earth, she followed the easiest way through the woods, knowing Telric would do the same. He did not know he was pursued, had no reason to be devious. With luck she might find a campfire up ahead and a young nobleman waiting. She hoped.

As she rode she searched with eyes and ears. The mountains, so red in the sunset, were black and gloomy. The trees grew thicker as she descended the valley; they swayed like grotesque spirits in a wind that swept eternally from the peaks. The *Breath of Creel,* men called that wind. It stirred her hair.

She stopped suddenly. Was that a sound? The leaves rustled; the wind wailed long and lonely. She forced a smile and chided herself. Such mountain woods were full of night-time noises.

But it came again, a scrambling in the limbs overhead. She froze, listening, while the hair prickled on her neck—a faint shivering of leaves that came when the wind was not blowing.

Her left hand closed over the sword's hilt. Her instincts screamed to draw the weapon, yet she hesitated. If it was an animal that stalked her it might turn aside for smaller, easier prey. But if it was a man—no need yet to risk an arrow or spear in the back. If it were something else . . .

A noose dropped silently from the branches and slipped around her shoulders. Her own startled cry blended with another as she gripped the rope and yanked with all her strength. Someone fell, grasping the limp end. A crunch of bone, a whimper. A man wiggled in the dirt and died, neck broken.

She tugged her sword free as another rope sailed through the air. Reflexively she swung, knocking that noose aside. A third looped over her head, pinning the upper part of her arm. She hacked at the taut line, failing to cut it. A fourth snapped around her throat. A fifth caught her sword hand, and a sixth ensnared her shoulders. Struggling caused the ropes to tighten, and she gave that up, gambling that someone meant to capture, not kill her. The sword fell to the ground, a sign of surrender. Time enough later to fight when the damned ropes were looser.

Her captors came out of the brush between the trees, careful to prevent any slack in the lines. Five pale men with tangled hair and wild, rugged features grinned triumphantly. None were as tall as Frost. They gibbered a strange tongue full of guttural clicks, sibilants and animal-like screeches. She had never heard its like.

Five pairs of smallish hands reached to touch her, and she cringed.

Until now, Ashur had made no move. As hands groped for his mistress he gave an unearthly cry. That black spike dipped, scored. With an angry shake of his great head he tossed a corpse into the bushes. A second died bleeding from the eyes, his skull crushed by the unicorn's hooves. The others dropped their ropes and fled shouting for the safety of the forest.

Shrugging off the entwining coils, she slid down and embraced the unicorn gratefully. Ashur nuzzled her hand, and a shower of blood from the horn embued dark crimson sprinkled her sleeve. Before she could gather grass to clean it there came new shouting and a mad trampling in the woods.

A horde of the same pale men surrounded her, more than she could count in the darkness. She snatched her sword from the dirt and gripped the hilt with both hands. They came no closer, and the ropes they each carried remained looped on their belts. They bore no other weapons she could see. Still, she kept her blade ready and Ashur at her back.

Then, to her great surprise a little girl stepped through the circle and abased herself at Frost's feet.

Why have you come among us, most revered and feared Goddess of Death?

The woman-warrior recoiled in alarm. That voice, soft and so youthfully sweet, was an acid pain inside her head.

You have claimed three of us already. Will you claim more?

After the initial shock the discomfort of psychic contact subsided. Frost glared mistrustfully, not knowing the limits of the child's faculty. Yet, the little girl called her goddess. That might be an indication.

"How deeply can you see into my mind?"

It is a vast pool, and I can see only the surface. I see what you let me see, Goddess. The child abased herself again, stretching full length in the dirt. *I have the strongest power, and I speak for my people with the voice of Dasur.*

"I'm searching for a man not of your people," she explained darkly. Her voice seemed a rude intrusion on the quiet that fell over the forest as she described Telric in detail. Even the wind stopped blowing. "He has stolen something from me, and I'll have it back."

But Goddess, came the voice in her head, *if it is an outsider you seek, why have you and your death-creature taken three of my people?* The child pointed to Ashur.

With a puzzled frown she realized all these primitive folk perceived the unicorn's true form. She understood then why they addressed her as *Goddess.* A woman who bore steel with such a creature at her side—how could she seem less to such a simple and superstitious lot? It was plainly to her advantage to play the part.

"They sought to detain me and have paid a harsh price for that foolishness." She indicated disdainfully the ropes on the ground. "I must find the man I seek."

If it is only the outsider you want, Goddess, then let us bring him to you as an offering.

She hid her surprise. "Do you have him?"

This forest and these mountains are ours, given to us by Dasur who strides through the trees. We are the Children of Dasur. We serve him according to the Covenant and all that is here he has given us in return. The words were a litany in Frost's brain. *Outsiders who do not keep Dasur's Covenant and who dare to trespass in our land must be punished. It is Dasur's law. It is our law.*

A subtle change crept into the little girl's tone. She drew courage from her belief in Dasur. Her words were bold, almost challenging. Were they a veiled threat? A restlessness spread through the ring of watchers, and Frost knew she had to regain the upper hand.

She leaned on her sword, towering over the child in a calculated pose. To survive among these people she must be the Death-Goddess. She took that tender face in an iron grip; her eyes bored into the child's.

"I am no mere outsider, youngling." She forced an icy chill into her voice for effect. "I have been with you always, though you may not know this body I have chosen to wear for the moment. Three of your people dared attack me, and have paid with their lives. Do not repeat that folly." She took her hand away. Finger marks showed livid on the youthful chin.

The little girl crumpled to her knees, hung her head and did not look up. *Death comes where your shadow falls. Do not be angry with us, Goddess. I beg you for the sake of my people.*

"Then, stand up little priestess of Dasur. I have no wish to harm any of you. But be truthful and tell me if you have the man I seek."

Not yet, Goddess, but our watchers follow him even now as he passes through our forest. We were curious why he would brave our mountains at night and decided to observe him awhile. Now we know he flees your wrath, and desperation makes him travel forbidden lands. By morning we will deliver him to you.

"Do it," Frost agreed. These people were familiar with the woods at night. They would find Telric a lot faster than she could.

The child-priestess shouted words in that strange guttural tongue. The ring of watchers dissolved into the darkness, moving in utter silence. The little girl faced her again.

The outsider will be our gift to you, Goddess. Will you wait with me until he is brought?

She nodded, sheathed her blade and followed. At her side Ashur nuzzled her shoulder and followed, too. The child shrank away from the unicorn, fear in her small eyes.

Must you bring the demon-beast?

"We will not be parted." She laid a hand on Ashur's shoulder.

The child shivered and led the way into the forest depths, casting frequent, fearful glances at the unicorn. Down the path they went into the heart of the valley. The night-sounds of the wood rose all around: the chirping of insects, the low growl of a stalking beast, the wind in the leaves.

"Have you a name?" she asked her small guide.

I am called Ali.

"How is it, Ali, that one so young speaks for all her people?"

Only the children of Dasur's Children can speak the silent language that needs no tongue. As we grow older we lose the skill.

"The adults have another language?"

The language of the leaves. A secret tongue that Dasur teaches. Only his children can speak it. Not even the other gods and goddesses know its meaning. Ali stopped and looked up at her, peering suspiciously. *You do not understand it, do you, Goddess?*

"No," she admitted.

Even in the gloom she could see Ali's smile.

So it is the children of the people who intercede with the other gods and goddesses of this world—and with men who trespass in our land.

Frost recalled her own childhood and long hours in dank caverns around sputtering coven fires. She remembered the chanting, the difficult names of power, her first conjurations. How, even then, she longed to be out in the sunlight and clean air.

"You're too young to be a priestess," she said to Ali. "Children should be free to play and find happiness."

Ali shrugged. *I find happiness in Dasur's arms.*

Some day she would feel differently, thought Frost. There was little joy in religious fervor—only duty and hard, unrewarded work. A sadness born of her own memories settled on her, and the rest of the journey passed in silence.

At the bottom of the valley a dozen watchfires shone through the trees. The village of Dasur's Children. Women and children, a few old men stared aghast as she and Ashur strode into the camp beside Ali. The tremulous thoughts of the smaller children faintly touched her mind, but they shrank away from the outsider-goddess and the creature that followed her. The adults bowed their heads reverently, chittering in the language of the leaves.

They had been warned of her coming, she was sure, but their faces reflected fear. She studied them by the dim firelight, again wondering why these primitive people could perceive

Ashur's true form when more civilized men saw only a horse, though a large and wild one. What power had they retained that other men had lost?

The chittering grew until Ali held up a hand for silence. Then, in the language of the leaves, she spoke. To her surprise, the words were clear in her mind as well. The little priestess calmed their fears, admonished her people to treat the Death-Goddess with respect and reverence, commanded them to make her welcome.

But their suspicions were not allayed. Eyes flickered distrustfully from the unicorn to her. Somewhere, a child began to cry; a trembling mother tried desperately to hush it.

Forgive them, I beg you, Goddess. But they are afraid of you and your monster. How can I calm them when even the gods fear your touch?

"I understand," she answered. "Perhaps there is another place we can wait without distressing your people?"

Ali thought. *I will take you to the High Place where Dasur swims and dances in the moonlight, where he makes music in the leaves. There, we may rest and talk, and in the morning you will have your man.*

Frost nodded. With Ashur in close tow she followed Ali away from the village, stopping once before a mud-thatched hut. Ali disappeared inside, then emerged with a rope at her waist.

It is both tool and weapon, Ali explained. *We seldom go deep into the forest without one.*

A well-trod path pointed toward a shadowed mountain peak just visible against the star-sprinkled sky. Surely, that was the High Place Ali referred to. She watched it until the trees blocked her view.

Not far from the camp they passed what appeared to be a well: a low wall of piled rocks ringing a dark pit. Without slowing, she glanced over the rim. The scant moonlight reflected with a dull gleam on the water. Strange, she thought, to dig wells where clear streams were so plentiful and sweet.

A little further along, a second well stood beside the path. Ali ignored it as she had the first, but this time Frost paused to peer over the edge. The trees had thickened, and no moonlight showed the bottom. Snatching a pebble, she dropped it down the well. No splash, but a brittle snapping.

Whatever was down there, it wasn't water.

Beyond the second was a third. Here, the trees were thinner and a little light spilled into the well betraying the same dull gleam as the first. She leaned over and dropped another pebble. *Pop, crack, silence.*

She sucked her lip and played with the mystery. What else could a well hold but water? She dared not ask Ali for fear of displaying her ignorance. After all, how much was a goddess supposed to know?

All the while, Ali continued, unnoticing, never looking back. The little girl never looked away from the direction of the peak. Soon the path began to climb, becoming steep and rocky. Loose stones slipped beneath her boots; safe footing was an elusive thing in the dark.

"Ali, I'll go no farther," she announced, breaking the silence for the first time since leaving the village. "The ground is too treacherous for Ashur, and I'll not be separated from him."

It is only a little higher to a place where the earth is flat and secure. We can rest there in Dasur's sacred place. Please, Goddess, urge your demon-creature just a little farther.

Frost hesitated. Where could there be level ground at this height? The stony trail grew more hazardous with every step. Soon, it would be too narrow, and Ashur would be unable to follow.

Please, Goddess.

There was pleading in the small voice. Ali's round eyes looked into her own. "A little farther, then," she agreed reluctantly.

Indeed, the path did not go much farther. It ended abruptly at the base of a sheer rock wall. Frost muttered under her breath and cursed, fearing a trap.

Ali had disappeared.

Her sword slid quietly from its sheath, while she craned her neck, peering back down the trail. If it was an ambush, someone had planned poorly. The ledge was too narrow for more than one attacker at a time to come at her, and they would have to get past Ashur as well. That made her shiver; a large number of men might press the unicorn over the side. She looked down. Not an abyss, but the steep fall would be as deadly.

Goddess, why do you not follow?

She spun. Ali stood beside her again. When the little priestess spied the blade in the woman-warrior's hand, her jaw dropped and she turned wide eyes on Frost.

Is it my time, Goddess?

The innocent fear in those words made her smile as she sheathed her weapon and drew a deep breath. Then, on impulse she rumpled Ali's long hair. "No, little one," she laughed. "It's not your time yet; you deserve a long life. But show me where you went."

A wide crack split the rock face, concealed in shadows, a tunnel wide and high enough even for Ashur. Ali led the way and the unicorn went after, his peculiar eyes casting pools of dim light on the cavern floor. Frost tangled her hand in his mane, for he could see the way where she could not.

His eyes are the most frightening thing about him, confided Ali, *for they are not eyes at all. If I were tall enough to touch them, I believe their fire would burn me.*

The cave made a sudden turn, then they emerged into paradise. Sweet fragrances of fruit blossoms filled the air. Gentle, constant winds teased her hair, played in the folds of her cloak. Nearby, she heard the bubbling song of a spring. Tiny, white-headed flowers bloomed abundantly in the thick carpet of grass, and unhampered by obscuring trees, the light of a full moon lent everything a frosty, opalescent glow.

An unbroken ring of towering walls, jagged as an old man's teeth, loomed over the garden with protective menace, shutting out the world beyond.

This is the High Place; it is sacred to Dasur, Ali intoned with ritual solemnity. *He is here now, dancing on the leaves, making music in the branches. You can feel his breath on your skin, hear him laughing in the water.*

The little priestess opened her arms, threw back her head. *Dasur, Father of the People, we greet you.*

At the center of the grove lay a pool of water whose surface sparkled and rippled as the wind blew upon it. Removing her scant clothing, Ali paused on its bank, then waded into the cool depths and immersed herself, disappearing completely from view. Frost had begun to fear some mishap when she finally broke the surface again.

A strange gleam shone in her eyes.

Sensuously, shamelessly the little girl began to rub her body. Waist-deep in the pool, she moved like a woman in the arms of her lover. Those small hands caressed tender, childish breasts with a lustful hunger and longing that brought a flush of heat to Frost's cheeks. Ali's bony little hips made gyrating motions that churned the water, and she tossed her head from side to side, emitting a low moan of pleasure from moist, glistening lips.

This is Dasur's place. Ali's voice was a rich melody in her mind. *Come, Goddess, and cleanse yourself. Dasur finds you pleasing.*

The wind whirled around Frost, plucked at her clothes, tugged her hair. Sudden, stiff gusts blew against her back, urging her closer to the water's edge. Without knowing why, her heart beat faster. She sucked an uneasy breath.

Dasur invites you, Goddess. The voice purred inside her head. Small hands beckoned innocently, entreating. Something called her to the water.

Tremulously, her fingers touched the fastenings of her cloak; weapons fell to the ground, boots, then tunic and breeches. It was foolishness. And yet, the pool called her.

She moved forward, and the water licked her toes. It rippled over her thighs, around her waist, between her breasts. The pool engulfed her, swallowed her. As she sank into its shadowed, bottomless depths a warm wetness invaded her being, streamed into her soul, filling her with sensations. At first, she resisted them, but the clasping, gently insistent waters dissolved her will until she fought no more. Sensation rose, swelled, too intense for bearing, yet she could not cry out or do anything to prevent the beautiful, bizarre fantasies that swam in her mind. Something touched her thoughts . . . and she reached with her own to embrace it.

When it was over, she opened her eyes and brushed away the droplets that clung to her lashes. She quivered all over, and it was several moments before she trusted herself to move. At last, she waded carefully ashore.

Ali sat hugging her knees to her chest, smiling. *It was so beautiful,* she sighed. *Dasur, the Breath of Life together that way with a Goddess of Death.*

Frost said nothing. A fog of confused impressions settled upon her. Unsure of what had transpired, she bit her lip and sank to the grass. It felt different—smooth as richest velvet on her bare skin. And the moon seemed brighter than she remembered. Smells were sharper. The wind moaned loud in her ears.

Was that Dasur's voice? She felt between her thighs and wondered, feared. Sleep came after awhile, laden with queer dreams.

The sky was still dark when she woke, but the moon perched on the west rim of the cratered walls. Close by, Ali sat cross-legged, watching her, and the little girl smiled as she yawned and sat up, surprisingly refreshed.

You are so lovely, said Ali. *I no longer fear you. Even your demon-creature has an air of tranquillity about him.*

Across the grove the unicorn munched fruit blossoms and jasmine-scented leaves, a figure of pastoral serenity. The fire-eyes were subdued, telling his contentment as he wandered lazily among the trees.

Ali jumped up and scampered to another tree, seeming more a child than ever before. Her laughter tinkled in the garden stillness as she ran, and when she returned to the pool's edge she carried two plump red fruits. She offered one to Frost.

The woman-warrior looked strangely at it. She had never seen its like, but Ali bit deeply into hers and swallowed, so she did the same. The soft pulp had a sweet, nectarous flavor, and she ate slowly, savoring every bite. When nothing remained except a large pit, Ali held out her hand for it and pushed both pits into holes dug with her fingers, then covered them with dirt. Going to the pool, she cupped water in her hands and poured it on the mounds.

They will grow and bear more fruit for Dasur.

That name brought a chill as she remembered her experience in the pool. She drew her feet under her, hugging her knees, and looked thoughtfully at the rippling, moonbright surface. For a thousand days she would wonder what truly occurred in that water, and the memory, the fantasies and the sensations would haunt her for a thousand restless nights.

In the first rays of morning, Frost and Ali put on their clothes and said goodbye to Dasur's garden. Frost gave it a final look before stepping into the cave that led back to the mountain pass and down into the valley. Her time in the grove had been restful—very likely, the last peace she would know for a long while.

The journey through the cavern was made in silence broken only by Ashur's hooves on the hard stone. As she walked, she laid hands on her weapons, Demonfang on the left hip and her sword on her right. Bitter reminders of her unfinished task. As they emerged once more into the sunlight, she gazed down into the waiting valley.

A thick, early morning mist hung in the low places. The lush woodland sparkled with fresh dew. Gone were the ominous and frightening shadows of the night before.

And yet, there was still something, an aura of foreboding that sunlight could not chase away.

My people will have the man you seek when we arrive, said Ali walking ahead of her. *We do not know why you want him or what exactly it is that you require of him, but if you will permit, Dasur's law decrees a ritual punishment for trespassers. We would not cheat you, Goddess.* She added, *It will effectively hasten him to your realm of the dead.*

Frost shivered that such a request could be couched in so tender a voice. The laughing child who scampered through the moonlit garden was suddenly gone. On this side of the cave Ali was once more a priestess of her people: dignified and cold and very unchild-like.

An ugly world, she decided, where children moved in the dark limbo between gods and men. She drew a heavy, deep breath.

"The man has taken something I must have back," she answered carefully. "When I have it again, he is yours."

By daylight the trail proved easier going. They descended quickly and headed for the village.

Not far along she spied one of the strange wells that had so piqued her curiosity in the night. It stood washed in a circle of sunshine at the path's edge, and though she thought at first to pass it by and speed on to the village and young Telric, the memory and mystery of it was too great. A few quick strides brought her peering over the stone rim.

A cold hand clutched her heart. Not a well—a pit. Skulls with empty eye-sockets glared up at her. Bones gleamed. Human bones, she realized, cracked, chewed and gnawed clean. An animal would have cracked them to get the marrow, but these were not. What then?

It dawned on her with a sickening clarity.

Flesh-eaters.

Frost grit her teeth, struggling to hide her sudden revulsion. Bile rose in her throat, threatened to choke her. She gripped the stone wall so hard that a piece of rock came loose and tumbled with a loud clatter into the pit, splintering a brittle jaw-bone.

Trespassers, came the voice in her head. *They violated the sanctity of Dasur's mountains and were punished for it. So shall your man be.*

She spun, glaring at the little priestess, nearly striking her, then thought better of it and chewed her lip, letting that pain smother her real emotions. Wordlessly, she turned from the pit and made for the village, careful to avoid the others and their terrible contents that lay along the way.

The Children of Dasur were true to Ali's word. Telric swung by his wrists between two tall trees, his head lolling on his chest, seeming unconscious. A guard dozed by the dangling feet of the captured noblemen.

There was no movement in the village.

My people sleep, Ali said.

"No matter," she responded, heading for Telric. "My business is with him."

Ali ran before her and kicked the guard to alertness. He bowed respectfully to Frost and took a step back.

Telric came awake before she finished patting his garments. A dull light of pain shone in his eyes as he regarded her, and there was a deep rope-burn around his throat. Ali's people had caught him as they promised, but they hadn't been too kind about it.

Recognition was slow. Telric blinked. "You!" he blurted. "How did . . ."

She slapped his mouth hard to shut him up. It wouldn't do to let him talk too much and possibly betray that she was no goddess at all, but a trespasser like himself. The guard, following her example, lashed him with a coil of rope. The young lord gasped, but refused to cry out though his face was screwed with anguish.

No time though to think about his pain. Telric had something she needed.

Seizing his hair, she bent his face close to hers. "The Book. I must have it back."

Telric stared with hate-filled eyes. Weakly, he tried to spit, but managed only to dribble on his chin. "You murdered my brothers!", he croaked through dry lips.

"They tried to kill me," she answered in Rholarothan, hoping that Ali would not understand her meaning. "But I was quicker. Now tell me what you've done with the Book."

Telric shook his head.

Ali spoke to the guard in the language of the leaves. There was a brief exchange before she turned back to Frost. *All his possessions have been taken to my dwelling. Perhaps, you will find what you seek there.*

She gave her back to Lord Rholf's son and indicated with a nod for Ali to lead.

Ali's dwelling was a crude hut of thatch and mud construction. An animal hide covered the low entrance. As soon as she stepped through the small door she spied the object of her quest. The old Book lay unceremoniously in the dirt of the earthen floor beside a sword and mercy-dagger, a money pouch, saddlebags and bed roll. She recovered it with a relieved sigh.

It is very important to you, observed Ali.

She returned the little girl's stare. "Should the wrong hands hold this Book neither you or I or all the people on the mountain would feel the Breath of Dasur ever again."

Ali's eyes darted from Frost to the Book and back again. Her little smile faded, and she turned pale as ash and thrust her knuckles into her mouth. For a moment, she was a child again, frightened of something she did not understand. She trembled, and Frost was moved to try to calm her fear.

She placed a gentle hand on Ali's shoulder, but the young priestess slipped adroitly away and regarded her from the farthest side of the hut.

There was much celebrating last night when the trespasser was captured. Though her bearing regained its dignity, the fear-light still gleamed in her eyes. *The people will sleep late into the day, and we should rest, too.* She curled up in a corner on a bed of woven grass and turned her face to the wall. But before she fell asleep she spoke one last time. *Now that you have what you came for, no doubt you will soon be leaving. Good night, Goddess.*

Frost settled in another corner, but sleep was far away. Her poor choice of words had scared Ali who was now eager to see her leave. And why not? The Book of the Last Battle was back in her possession, and Kregan was waiting in Chondos, hopefully with an army of sorcerers. The final battle with Zarad-Krul was fast approaching.

Yet, something else nagged her. Her gaze kept straying to the weapons on the floor, and visions of the bone-pits filled her thoughts. Telric would be punished, Ali said, and when the villagers had feasted on his flesh the bones would be cast into the wells for the spiders to gnaw on. She shut her mind to it, but the images would not be banished.

Ali's slow, measured breathing was the only sound she heard. A peek beyond the hide flap told her no one stirred outside, either. She lifted Telric's dagger.

It was foolish. A blood-feud stood between them. Saving him now would not end that, and Telric would threaten her again someday. It made no sense. Let Ali and her people finish him.

She weighed the merits of the idea. Yet, the sight of those pits would not leave her. The Children of Dasur were flesh-eaters, and the very thought made her stomach churn. Whatever danger the man might be later, he deserved a better fate.

Curse me for a fool, she thought, sticking the dagger in her belt and rising.

Silently, she crept from the hut, pleased to see Ashur close by. The camp still slept; not even a cookfire burned. Imperious as the goddess they believed her, she strode through the village to the place where Telric was bound. Flame-eyed, the unicorn walked at her side.

Awake this time, the guard grinned in welcome and made a slight bow at her approach. She returned his smile, then sank her fist with soundless fury into his soft middle. He folded with a grunt, and her elbow sent him sprawling.

Telric watched the short fight with interest. When it ended he started to speak, but her hand clamped tightly on his mouth.

"If you want out of here with your worthless life, then keep it shut." She cut his ropes with the mercy-dagger, and when he was free he held out a hand to take possession of it. She smacked his knuckles with the flat of the blade.

"I may be a fool," she admitted, "but not that big a fool."

The dagger returned to her belt, and she pointed to Ashur. "Now mount up. I want to be far away when everyone discovers their dinner is missing."

"What are you mumbling about?"

"If you're lucky, maybe I won't tell you about it. You'll sleep easier." She swung up to the unicorn's back. "Now get on."

"One horse won't carry us both," he protested. "The mountain trails are too steep, and mine was lost when these damned *dwarves* captured me."

So Telric thought Ashur was just a horse. What did it mean? What rules governed who saw a unicorn and who saw a horse? Who saw truth and who saw illusion?

No time to ponder it now.

"Get on. We'll manage, unless you prefer to stay."

Telric accepted her hand-up and settled himself behind her. "And I warn you," she added, "if you reach for my weapons I'll cut your fingers off and leave you for the dwarves. They have a taste for your company."

She cast a final look around the village murmuring a quiet farewell to Ali and the Children of Dasur. Despite their manners there was something appealing in their primitive existence. Then, she patted the Book of the Last Battle in its now familiar place inside her tunic and turned Ashur.

They took a slow pace until the forest concealed them from the camp, but when the distance was great enough and the trees were thick enough to muffle the sound of their flight, she touched heels to the unicorn's flanks. Late afternoon found them safe at the foot of the Creel Mountains.

"We part company here," Frost announced.

Obediently, Telric slid to the ground. "You killed my brothers," he reminded, but there was no hatred in his voice now.

"And I saved you," she countered. "Tell your father that when next he's a mind to tally scores."

"It will make no difference. There's a blood-feud between you and all my family, and when we meet again I'll kill you."

"You'll try." She tossed the young nobleman's dagger at his feet, making him jump to avoid the point. "No man should be alone and weaponless in this country. Use that well, son of Rholf, if you dream of meeting me again."

Telric retrieved the blade and balanced it in his hand. For a moment, she thought he meant to throw it, and her fingers curled around her sword-hilt. But the dagger slipped into an empty sheath on his hip.

"May I know your name?" he asked. "I've never met a woman like you, and I would honor your memory when you are dead."

There was a time when her name was something soft and pretty on the tongue, but that was long past, and she put the memory behind her. Many things had changed, and murderers did not deserve soft, pretty names.

"Frost."

Telric smiled. "We're about the same age," he observed. "Under better circumstances, I'd enjoy trying to melt you."

She watched from Ashur's back as he walked away. The caravan route would see him safely around the mountains if he had sense enough to stick to it. He might even find a ride with merchants or travelers.

A cool wind blew down from the Creel. A low moan echoed on the peaks. The Breath of Dasur, Ali called it, and the Song of Dasur. From somewhere in the mountains came a cry—an animal probably, sad and low and disappointed.

When the sound faded she turned toward Chondos.

Chapter Eight

A LONG LINE OF DARKNESS CREPT ACROSS THE NORTHERN sky where, for many days, clouds had gathered, turning black, evil looking. Each morning brought that line closer as dark vapors boiled up on the far horizon and blew down from wizard-cursed Shardaha and filled the air with wretched odors.

For three mornings, since her return from the Creel, she watched from the high parapet of Erebus. Today, wild lightnings filled those clouds, streaking the sky with veins of savage crimson. Rolling thunder echoed faintly in the distance.

"They advance swiftly," she said for the hundredth time to Kregan who only nodded. "Already, the sun seems dimmer."

A violent flash rippled through the clouds; thunder boomed. Then, all was quiet again, but only for a moment. Suddenly, the stones trembled beneath her feet, and the ground gave a rumble. The walls shook. A piece of the parapet crumbled, plunged earthward taking with it one of the gigantic sculptures that rose from every battlement in Erebus. She lost her balance, stumbled and grabbed for support.

Then, Kregan cried out. Far beyond the city gates the plain heaved and twisted. When the dust and smoke settled, a gaping fissure rent the land.

The Chondite paled. "Zarad-Krul has successfully conjured a Dark One into this plane."

"No!" she cursed. "How can you be sure?"

"I can sense his presence. A minor god, but a dangerous one: his name is *Nugaril*. From across the infinite void the Dark Gods have been feeding knowledge to Zarad-Krul. Now his lessons will come much faster and be of a more dreadful nature. With Nugaril's aid, other Dark Ones will be summoned, and Chaos will rule the earth." Then, a wry smile flickered on his face as he measured the fissure's length. "He always did have a flair for ostentatious entrances . . . so the grimoires claim."

She grabbed his arm, spun him around to face her. "We have to tell your Council. They've spent too much time examining the Book. Now we have to fight!"

He pressed her hand. "They already know, just as I knew. But how they'll interpret the news," he shrugged, "that, I can't guess. The Brothers of the Black Arrow will fight because I stand with you. As for the others? Well, Chondos is not a united land. Our sorcerous pursuits have made us independent of each other, and though most agree that we must fight there's still a lot of quibbling over the methods."

Before she could answer, slender fingers sealed her lips, a paternal gesture that only increased her growing agitation. "I know," he continued softly, "time is short. Our main hope lies in *Rhadamanthus*. The old man is the only voice of reason amid a hundred bickering fools."

A second thunderous blast shattered the sky; lightning raged. Angry bolts licked the earth like tongues of colossal, unseen serpents. The land smoked. Kregan's hands squeezed her shoulders painfully, turning her toward where he pointed.

Beyond the city's eastern wall the Cocytus River leaped its banks and spilled over the countryside and through the open, unattended gates of dead Zondu. The same rushing waters beat the gates of Erebus, and only sorcery-strengthened walls saved the Chondite city from a similar fate.

"What is it?" she shouted over a second thunderous roll and a sudden wind that tried to force her words back into her throat.

Kregan's eyes clenched in concentration. The corners of his mouth hinted of pain. "Mentes!" he gasped. "His entrance—nearly overwhelmed me." He shook his head to clear it.

"Mentes and Nugaril: two great evils now walk the earth."

Frost slammed a fist against hard stone. With a bitter resolve, she left the Chondite and sought her own quarters a level below. She pushed open the door, kicked it shut. Her weapons hung on wooden pegs above the bed. Her riding boots waited at the foot of it. Casting off the soft velvet slippers her hosts had provided, she began dressing.

"What are you doing?" Kregan stood in the doorway, frowning. She hadn't heard the door open. For that matter, she hadn't heard him knock.

"If I wait for a decision from your damned Council we'll die without ever striking a blow in defense." She stamped her foot into a boot and looked up, meeting his fierce gaze unflinchingly. "For all the vaunted Chondite power and knowledge you're no more than bickering children."

"So you're going to rush out and whip the whole of Zarad-Krul's army single-handedly," he snapped. "After all, what possible hope can a couple of mere gods hold against you and your almighty sword?"

"Well, I'm not going to just sit here on my butt and wring my hands like the rest of you whining old men!"

She knew by his silence how that hurt him. Suddenly, she threw up her hands and sagged onto the bed. "I'm sorry," she admitted and shut her eyes. "You're right—I'm being foolish. I know you've tried, but this waiting wears on my nerves."

A narrow slash of a window shed light into her room; its northern view showed the same sky she had watched from the parapet. Crossing to it, she stared out and measured again the speed of the advancing ridge of darkness.

"The time for talk is past, Kregan. If your Council fails to move against Zarad-Krul, Chondos will be swept away like a leaf in flood-waters. And the world will come soon behind."

"There are many things to consider," Kregan responded.

She shook her head. "No more time for consideration."

The Chondite sank heavily into a chair; deep lines etched his face. "There are things you don't understand," he repeated. "Do you know why I was helpless against the Eye of Zarad-Krul?"

She had wondered. Yet, with all that had occurred since then she had not thought to ask.

His face was grim. "What I'm going to tell you is known

only to the *Krilar*—the master sorcerers of the Brotherhoods—
and to the Elders. If they ever learn that an outsider shares our
secret, they'll kill you. And me, for telling you."

She nodded, moved by his solemnity.

"Beyond the borders of Chondos we have no power."

She blinked, not sure she had heard correctly, but his serious
expression warned that she had. Her mouth fell open, closed.
Then, a deeper gloom seemed to fill the room, and she sagged
under the weight of a terrible understanding. Her lips formed a
slow curse.

"The land itself is the source of our power," he explained.
"There is a place we call *Demonium* . . ."

At the heart of Chondos stretched the Field of Fire, a rocky
plain where every stone and pebble glowed with an eerie
luminescence that set the darkest night ablaze with bizarre
colors. At the heart of that stood *Demonium*. A high, steep
butte rising abruptly from the flat terrain, three towering
monolithic stones loomed on its crest. Rune-carved, pale as
milk they rose in triangle formation, and no man living knew
their age.

" . . . a gate where all astral planes once met," continued
Kregan, "a doorway to worlds beyond imagining. Though it
closed long ago, a trace of otherwordly energy continues to
seep through, a mystic influence that spreads right through the
soil. Chondos is a land alive, pulsing with that power.

"Then, generations ago our ancestors discovered that the
energy followed certain flow-lines. They built a network of
stone triangles at special points to relay and amplify the
emanations from Demonium. Our country became an arcane
well of magic, itself shaped like a natural triangle bordered on
its three sides by three mighty rivers."

He poured two goblets of wine and passed one to her. He
took a long pull before continuing.

Strange creatures wandered freely through Chondos in those
early days, denizens of other worlds who passed to earth when
the gate was open. "Their off-spring are the monsters that
haunt our land today. Usually, they were contained by the
natures of the rivers that surround us: the Cocytus and
Phlegathone Rivers at east and west have special qual-
ities that prevented their crossing, but the Acheron River
in the north between Chondos and Shardaha had no such

power, and a few demons migrated to other lands by that route.''

Frost tilted her cup. Kregan refilled it. "I've heard it said that Chondites are not truly human.'' She sipped her wine, regarded him over the cup's rim. "What of that?''

"It could be true,'' he admitted. "We're not completely sure of our origins.''

She took another drink and wiped her mouth, setting the half-full cup aside. "What all this means is that you can't launch an attack against Shardaha?''

The Chondite's jaw muscles twitched. "If we cross the Acheron we lose our magic. What good then will be all the sorcerers in Chondos? You see why the Council hesitates?''

She rose, then kicked a stool. It shattered gratifyingly against the wall.

"Blood and iron!'' she swore. "I think I hear the gods laughing. To come so far and find no help at the journey's end. My sword is red with the blood of those who barred our way—and all for nothing!''

Kregan came and laid a hand on her shoulder. But though there was comfort in the touch she shook it off.

Beyond the window, the approaching darkness grinned.

"It's not hopeless.''

She whirled, driving a fist into her palm. "Not hopeless? Must you strike bottom before you know you've fallen in a pit? There's a pit yawning now, my friend, and we're all about to tumble in.''

The Chondite dashed his winecup after the broken stool. A deep crimson colored his cheeks. "We're not cowards, woman! The Council knows the dangers we face, and they're working on a plan.''

"Then what's the delay?'' she snapped. "Why don't we move?''

"You still don't see, you silly *child!*'' The table shook under his pounding fist. "To have any hope of victory we must lure Zarad-Krul *into* Chondos. The battle must be fought in the very shadow of Demonium where our powers will be strongest. And even then, we harbor little hope of winning if Nugaril and Mentes take an active role in the fighting.''

"You mean, you'll *let* the wizard invade?

Kregan glowered, leaned heavily on the table. Slowly, his head bobbed.

She arched an eyebrow and sucked her lower lip thoughtfully. "I'm sorry," she confessed. "You're certainly not cowards if that's your plan."

The angry flush left his face, replaced by lines of weariness. "Don't mistake our motives, Frost. Chondites care little for the outside world; but as you observed, we're all standing on the brink of a pit."

A knock, and the door opened. A woman stepped reverently in, bearing a scroll of parchment. Her hair was the color of morning sunlight and her white dress swirled around her ankles when she moved. Her fair blue eyes raked over Frost and Kregan, then lowered shyly.

Natira, Frost recalled her name. There was an oddness about her, especially her azure gaze which was so hard to meet. The woman's presence disturbed her, evoked certain emotions, feelings of grief and loneliness that stirred her own tormenting memories.

Three steps into the room, Natira made a slow half-turn and stopped. Her eyes fastened on Demonfang where it hung on the wall in its silver sheath. She glided toward it, reaching out to grasp the hilt.

Frost caught her hand.

"Wait," whispered Kregan, suddenly excited. "She's taken an interest in nothing at all since I found her wandering on the field near Demonium. And yet, from the moment of your arrival in Erebus that dagger has held an unexplained attraction for her."

"She mustn't draw it! You know the danger."

"I don't think she will," he answered. "Watch."

Natira ran her fingers along the hilt, the sheath and belt. Then, she licked her fingers carefully as if tasting. A faint trace of a smile creased her mouth.

"I've never seen her smile," the Chondite remarked. "If only she could speak . . . I'd like to know what significance that cursed blade has for her."

Finally, Natira turned away from Demonfang, gave the scroll to Kregan and floated from the room. The sorcerer opened and read.

"They want us at Council," he announced.

Rhadamanthus, Minos and Aecus, the eldest members of the three Chondite Brotherhoods, looked down dispassion-

113

ately from high seats. Behind each hung the banners of their respective orders: a black arrow, a golden star, an argent cup. One hundred pairs of eyes peered from dark, concealing hoods at Frost and Kregan as they stood in the center of the chamber.

Rhadamanthus of the Black Arrow spoke first. Though his hair was white with age, his voice was strong and carried to all corners of the hall. He held the Book of the Last Battle.

"Kregan, Brother, a Privileged Council is no place for your outsider friend."

Her companion met the old man's unwavering gaze. "Elder Brother," he answered firmly. "No one has more right to be here; the Book was entrusted to her keeping, and she has brought it safely from the forests of Esgaria despite all Zarad-Krul's efforts to stop her. She has earned the right to know what decision you have reached."

The old man raised a hand for silence, and the Elders conferred briefly. "So be it, then," Rhadamanthus proclaimed, "she may stay. But you must vouch for her behavior."

Kregan nodded.

Aecus leaned forward as he addressed the Council. "All efforts have failed. The Book of the Last Battle remains closed. Its secrets are still secret."

"Only one course remains for us," Minos announced. "We must lure Zarad-Krul to the Field of Fire. At Demonium we may hope for victory over his minions. A little hope, but all we have. This is the decision of the *Krilar* and the Elders."

"Wait," said Frost. All eyes turned to her. On the nearest faces she read surprise, consternation, disapproval. Only Rhadamanthus smiled indulgently. "It's a fundamental axiom that Light must oppose Darkness; any sorcerer or witch knows that." Her gaze swept the chamber. No reaction from the Chondite masters. "Why not call upon the powers of Light to fight this battle?"

"We've tried what you suggest." Minos shook his wizened head sadly. "Though it was against our very natures, we called on the Names of Light, but the conjurations went unheeded."

Rhadamanthus unsteepled his fingers and frowned. "You see, my child, a Chondite sorcerer taps the interplanar energies that seep through the Demonium Gate for most of his machinations. Beyond that, the Krilar learn to manipulate certain symbols and words of power. *But we serve no god.* Why, then, should the Light-Lords answer us?"

Aecus smashed a fist on the arm of his great chair; a fierce determination burned in the black pits of his eyes. "We'll meet the Shardahani alone—our skills pitted against the Dark Ones he serves. It will be hard, but we can win!"

Her own arcane experience made her doubtful. Whatever might the Chondites possessed, two forces were supreme: Light and Dark. Only a very few of the Neutral gods could equal such omnipotence. Her one hope was that Zarad-Krul still controlled the Dark Allies. As long as that remained true the enemy was only a man—and men made mistakes.

Battle plans were detailed, assignments made. Then, Rhadamanthus stepped down from his seat and bowed before Frost. The Book of the Last Battle rested in his outstretched hand. "Our brother has told how you blinded the Eye of Zarad-Krul while he stood helpless in its gaze." He nodded respectfully to Kregan. "Though you are an outsider and only a woman, we ask you to carry this Book awhile longer. Fate seems to have chosen you as its guardian—not a task I envy you, for when the fighting begins you will be the target of every attack."

Despite the solemnity of the occasion, she grinned. "I'm only a woman, of course, but I accept." To her great surprise the old man leaned forward and kissed her cheek. Making another deep bow, he said, "May your gods be with you, then."

A tremendous cheer went up in the chamber. Hooded robes were thrown off; each man revealed himself girt in sword and curiously worked leather armor carved with runes and the devices of their brotherhoods. They streamed from the hall amid tumultuous shouting to rally the brethren and the armies.

When everyone was gone, Kregan took her hand and sighed. "You wanted action," he reminded her. "Well, now it begins." Suddenly, he wrapped her in his arms and held her close.

It felt good, being held. His arms were warm, offering security. No one had hugged her since her mother. And that memory made her stiffen.

That night, her nightmares returned: scenes of blood, fratricide and worse. Her mother reeled, died uttering the curse that stole away her witch-powers. Faces swam; accusing fingers jabbed her. A sword rose, fell with heartless regularity, gripped in her own hand. Screaming, she tried uselessly to pry her fingers from the hilt. Then, when everyone else was dead it turned on her, rising, falling. . . .

She woke with a cry, trembling in a cold sweat and willed her racing heart to calm. Slowly, the terror faded, and she breathed easier. A candle burned low on the table. Yet, hadn't she extinguished it before lying down? Puzzled, she swung her feet over the bed's edge. She froze.

A shadow in the corner.

She rubbed her eyes and looked again.

"Natira . . . ?"

The mute girl sat unmoving on the room's far side, wide-eyed, unblinking, staring. A faint smile parted that pale mouth.

Frost sucked her lip apprehensively. Entrancement. She'd seen it before, knew the signs. She twisted to follow Natira's fixed gaze, half-expecting what she found.

Demonfang.

The candlelight gleamed on its silveriness. Secured in its sheath, the blade still hung on the wall, apparently untouched. Yet, there was no question that the woman had crept in un-invited for some purpose involving the dagger. Natira's queer interest made Frost uneasy, suspicious.

A chill passed through her. At least, she had not tried to draw it. Fear of that and of more nightmares robbed her of further sleep that night. Wrapping a blanket around herself, she sat back on the bed, propped against the wall with feet drawn up to watch Natira and wait for dawn.

But it was a dawn that never came. Kregan knocked lightly and entered, startling her from a reverie of unpleasant memories. His face was grim, and he was fully armored in elaborate leather.

"No sunlight." He ground his teeth; deep lines carved furrows across his brow. "The darkness of Zarad-Krul is upon us."

She accepted the pronouncement morosely, and pointed to her silent guest. The Chondite's eyebrows shot up in surprise when he saw Natira. He went quickly to her side, lifted her hand. It was limp, unresisting in his own. He rubbed her cheek, then, and shook her. But those staring blue eyes never wavered from the dagger.

"Completely entranced," said Frost. "Self-induced as far as I can tell."

Kregan paced between the two women, looking worried. "Look!" he cried suddenly.

Natira stirred; her eyes fluttered, fingers twitched. Slowly, she rose with a wide yawn and smiled, an utterly innocent expression. With a light, graceful step she drifted through the room and out the door, closing it softly behind her.

The look on Kregan's face was pure confusion. Frost threw aside her blanket, got up and went to the window. No trace of the morning sun. Then, she took Demonfang down and buckled it around her waist, resting her hand on it, feeling its weight on her hip.

"What do you know about her?" she asked finally. "In some odd way she scares the hell out of me—more than any man I've ever met."

The Chondite nodded. "Very little, really. She's a mystery I've not had time to solve. You sense her power. Yes, power. I sense much more—a deep sorrow, a soul-wrenching sadness that reaches out from her and grips my heart."

"Are you in love with her?" She tilted her head, wondered why the question brought a lump to her throat.

"No," he answered curtly, "but there's an empathy between us that I can't control. Rhadamanthus has felt it, too, and a few others. You feel it—that's what frightens you."

He was right. There was a sadness about Natira, an almost tangible anguish. It had touched her, sparked sensitive memories that she wanted desperately to forget.

"Most men avoid her for that."

"But not you."

Kregan sank heavily into the chair where Natira had been, and steepled his fingers. She went back to the window, grateful for a breeze that played on her face, and waited for the tale she knew was coming.

"I found her wandering alone on the Field of Fire," he began.

The Brothers of the Black Arrow had gathered at Demonium to celebrate the Feast of Agathone. Everyone except Kregan had retired after the rituals, but restless, he began to walk, lost in private meditations, and after a time drifted away from the camp.

Suddenly, a great screaming fireball lit the night, trailing smoke and flame. It flared once, then a second time so bright it hurt his eyes. A crash of thunder followed each flare; the final blast tumbled him to the ground.

"It must have struck the earth," he continued, "but I heard no explosion, felt no impact, or found any piece of ground disturbed in the slightest."

Such an omen had to be discussed with Rhadamanthus, and Kregan ran back to camp. "But before I had run far I found her. She was naked, unconscious on the stony ground. Tears stained her face. And when I finally managed to wake her, I discovered she couldn't speak a word. I picked her up, then, and carried her back into camp, knowing the elder would have the means to question her—speechless or no."

But the camp was in chaos. Most of the tents had been flattened by the thunderclap; some had caught flame from the campfires. The horses had panicked, bolted and trampled a few men.

"And yet, every eye turned when they saw my peculiar burden. I took her to one of the surviving tents, laid her gently on a cot and called for Rhadamanthus. He went inside alone to examine her."

A long sigh, a wistful look: Kregan folded his hands. "When he emerged a terrible change was on him. All his years seemed to settle on his shoulders, bowing him like a heavy weight. For two days he spoke to nobody, but his expression was filled with the same dreadful grief that I and the other Krilar felt whenever we came near her. Only, he seemed to feel it more intensely, and to this day he refuses to remain in her presence."

Frost nodded. "So you took her under your protection?"

"And named her Natira," he answered, "meaning *starborn,* for I believe in my heart of hearts that is what she is. Something to do with that fireball and thunderclap. Some spirit of the stars, perhaps, trapped in fleshly form, longing to return home."

"But why is she so fascinated by Demonfang?"

"Who knows?" he replied. "There are mysteries within mysteries, and your dagger has not caught her fancy without reason." His dark eyes narrowed grimly. "Forces are gathering on both sides of this last battle with Zarad-Krul, and pieces of the puzzle have yet to find their places—not even a Chondite sorcerer can see the outcome clearly."

All her memories and melancholies rushed back upon her then, and for just a moment the room was full once more of ghosts from her past.

A rough slap on the shoulder by her Chondite friend drove them away.

"No more time for stories, though," he said, brightening. "We ride for Demonium this morning. Look, I've brought you something." He opened the door. Just outside was a large bag he had set there earlier. He displayed the contents on her bed.

Armor fine as his own, rune-carved and worked ever so intricately lay there. "Yours," he indicated the pieces. "A craftsman labored yesterday and all through the night to finish it."

"Without measurements?" she frowned.

"Trust a little Chondite magic," he chided. "It'll fit."

"How soon do we ride?"

"Within the hour, fast and hard. Last night a horde of Shardahanis streamed over the Acheron and burned *Dulaam,* our northernmost city. Now they're on their way to *Indrasad.*"

A knock at the door. Kregan bid three servants enter, bearing a tray of cold meat and fruits with wine and water to drink. More candles were brought to light the gloom while they made a hasty breakfast.

"Does Zarad-Krul accompany them?" she asked, picking up the conversation between bites.

Kregan shook his head. "Nor Mentes or Nugaril. But other things ride with them—shadows without form or substance, wielding solid blades; flying creatures that strike with talons and edged wings sharp as steel. And there are other magicks at work, too. Otherwise, Dulaam would not have fallen while Chondites stood on Chondite soil."

She considered that, chewing a last bit of meat. "Wait." She swallowed suddenly. "I've studied your maps, and Indrasad lies in the wrong direction."

Kregan pushed back from table, rose. "No, it doesn't."

She rose, too. "Indrasad is in the north-central. It's the Book Zarad-Krul wants, and that's here in Erebus."

The Chondite paced before the narrow window, staring out. "And how do you think the wizard knows that? To lure him

119

into Chondos we let him glimpse the Book in his scrying crystals. Only, his power has grown faster than we realized, thanks to the presence of Mentes and Nugaril, and he glimpsed a part of our plan as well.''

A piece of fruit fell, forgotten, from her fingers. She remembered the maps and traced a mental line. "Indrasad lies in a direct line from Dulaam to Demonium."

The Chondite allowed an ironic smile. "That's where he's going. He knows that Demonium holds our only chance of resisting his power, and if he holds Demonium he can come take the Book of the Last Battle at his leisure."

"So that's how the game's to be played, then. Our armies race Zarad-Krul's minions to the Gate—a race we dare not lose."

"The Nine Cities have rallied. Dulaam is down and Indrasad preparing for battle. The rest are marching or about to march."

"Then, it's time to go."

Quickly, she pulled on the new armor. As Kregan swore, each piece seemed molded for her body. It was light-weight and did not restrict her movements as she had feared. She took down her sword and buckled it on. Over all, she threw her own gray riding cloak.

Lastly, she reached beneath her pillow for the Book. It seemed twice as heavy as before when she slipped it into a pouch and slung it over her shoulder.

Their mounts were waiting in the stables. A white charger was ready for Kregan; Neri had never returned. Ashur, too, had been saddled. Nervously, the unicorn trembled, disliking the feel of it on his back. She stroked the animal's sleek throat, whispering calmly to him; then, carefully, she mounted, whispering and stroking until his trembling ceased.

Outside the stables, Natira was waiting. Her azure eyes flickered from Kregan to Frost to Demonfang, and settled finally on the Chondite with a pleading look.

"No, my *Star-born,*" he said softly. "There's no place for you on this adventure. You're no warrior, and I'll have no time to watch out for you."

Tears swelled in those blue eyes, flowed over pale cheeks, but no sound of weeping did she make. Kregan leaned from his saddle and brushed the tears away with a tenderness that was touching. Then, he kissed her brow and spurred his mount, leaving Natira behind.

As they approached the northern gate they slowed once more to a walk. She could not resist teasing her sorcerous friends. "Surely, these are not the cruel, black-hearted Chondites I was taught to fear as a child, and that the world calls *inhuman.*"

Kregan was not amused. "Don't misinterpret my feelings for Natira, woman," he snapped, then added cryptically, "or for you. There are many Chondites beyond that gate, and some may yet teach you the truth behind those tales."

Outside the walls, the warriors of Erebus waited in long mounted lines. In the darkness, she could not guess their number, but those she could see were well armed and armored. Yet, here and there were men bearing no weapons other than great staves of black wood, silver-bound at each end with fine wire.

Krilar, Kregan called them. The master-sorcerers of the Brotherhoods. And they used no other weapon.

Kregan lead her to a place of honor at the army's head. Nine guardians, Brothers of the Black Arrow, rode at her back. One gave to Kregan a scarlet cloak and his own *Krilar* staff.

"I would rather trust a sword," she said with a worried smile.

He answered, "Wait and see."

The city gates opened once more, and the three Elders, all on white steeds, rode out. They passed through the ranks, past Frost and Kregan to a high knoll not far away. A triangle of glowing stones stood at its summit, and dismounting, Rhadamanthus went among them.

"One of the relay gates I spoke of yesterday," Kregan answered her unspoken question. "If two men stand among those stones—though the triangles be at opposite ends of the country—they can know each other's thoughts. That's how we knew when Dulaam fell."

The three rode back after awhile, took up a place in the lead before them. Then, Rhadamanthus faced the assembled troops. "Indrasad holds against the Shardahanis," he called. "There is no sign of the wizard or his Dark Servants. Though all the Nine Cities ride to Demonium, we shall arrive first. Knowing this, a force of Shardahanis have left the siege at

Indrasad to intercept us." A murmur ran through the ranks. "This day we will meet them."

Aecus raised his staff, let it fall. A fierce cry went up from the Chondites as they leaped forward. No orderly march, but a precipitous, head-long race to Demonium and the hope of victory against Zarad-Krul's forces. She grit her teeth and leaned low to the wind as Ashur's muscled form rippled beneath her.

Well, she had begged for action and gotten it, but as she glanced at Kregan's grim countenance as he rode beside her one question began to gnaw at her thoughts: *who would survive?*

Chapter Nine

THE PACE WAS SWIFT, RELENTLESS. THE HORSES SOON were flecked with foam, their manes heavily lathered. Still, the riders bore down, urged their steeds to greater effort. The very earth shook beneath so many pounding hooves.

Only Ashur showed no strain. The magical beast ran and ran, never seeming to tire. His mane lashed his rider and the saddle chafed her thighs; the wind whistled stinging past her ears. Yet, in the numbing rhythms of the ride a strange excitation tingled through her, mixed with bitter dread.

Here was war where thousands died.

War was not for women, her weapons-master claimed even as he drilled her in a new sword technique.

But as a child she was a warrior, fighting her brother, wrestling with sons of servants and slaves, swinging sticks in imitation of the soldiers who trained within her father's castle walls. Weapons had always held a queer fascination for her. Her earliest memories were of her father's shield and wanting to touch it.

How enviously she had watched while her brother grew and drilled with Burdrak, the weapons-master, learning sword, shield and bow while she was taught the ways of witchcraft by her mother. Though she excelled at the art, it was with a secret anger that her hated brother studied that which she most desired.

It was not a conscious determination, at first, to break the law forbidding women to touch men's weapons or learn their use, but each day she watched the soldiers train and she memorized their lessons. Each morning at her father's feet she listened as Burdrak revealed strategies and philosophies of combat to her brother and a few younger boys.

Then, one night with everyone asleep, she shed her dainty gown and felt slippers and crept down into the castle's lowest levels where she had hidden a training sword and a make-shift shield. In secret, she practiced until the light of morning threatened, and every night thereafter, and then she would hasten to her room for a few hours sleep before the next day began—and the next lesson.

So it went for nearly a year until Burdrak discovered her. At first, the old teacher was outraged; yet, as he watched out of sight and saw the skill with which she wielded her wooden sword, his heart softened. Unmarried, childless, Burdrak loved her like his own daughter. Still, it was not Esgaria's way, and he tried through ridicule and pleading to make her give up.

But she would not. Night after night she went to her secret chamber to practice, and each night Burdrak came to watch, keeping silent for the first few nights, then scorning, then offering small corrections, bits of advice until no longer just an observer, he became her teacher in earnest.

And she became his prize pupil.

She gripped the reins tightly, listened to the rush of wind past her face and the cries of men who hurried so desperately to war, forcing away the memories. Burdrak was dead, killed by the sword he had forged for her, and she grieved sorely. It lingered in her mind that if she helped defeat Zarad-Krul the tragic events of her past might be atoned for.

Yet, how could she expect forgiveness when she could not forgive herself?

Up ahead, Aecus signalled to slow the pace. Kregan drew close beside her, his staff slung over his broad shoulders by a thong. He gripped her arm with a gloved hand, shaking his head. Lines of worry creased his face.

"He's mad," Kregan said of Aecus. "Too much of that pace will kill the horses long before we meet the Shardahanis."

"We're all eager for battle," she said.

He glared keenly at her so that she turned away. "Frost, the past is past. What's done can't be undone. I'm on Chondite soil now, and I can see your thoughts."

She jerked her arm from his grip. "Keep out of my mind, Kregan." Her voice was icy cold, full of warning. "If you would be my friend—keep out of my mind."

"This is not a game, now," he rebuked. "You're not fighting shadows in a sub-chamber of your father's castle. Think of the enemy, woman! Of Zarad-Krul's flesh, blood and bone. Turn your attention there." He touched her arm again, gingerly but firmly. "When the fighting begins, there'll be no time for placating ghosts."

She recoiled, stared in mute shame at the Chondite's solemn features. *He knows!* She screamed inside, *He knows everything!* Tears sprang to her eyes; with an effort she fought them back.

His expression softened, but the worry lines remained. He reached for her hand and gripped it so she could not pull away.

"Woman," he started, "there's a trial awaiting you; I've seen it in the scrying bowl. I know the pain that lies behind you," he paused, swallowed, "and some of what's before you." Suddenly, words failed; he looked away.

"What trial?" she urged. "What have you seen?"

He shook his head. "I can't say." Then, he faced her and their eyes locked. "I would help you if I could; any Chondite would help. But it's no monster that swords can cut or magic bind. You have the strength to face it, though—if you will."

A trembling seized her though she steeled against it. A long, slow breath whistled from her parted lips. "This trial," she said, finally, "will I survive it?"

He shifted uncomfortably in the saddle. "There are many possibilities. Pieces of a puzzle are still missing that may affect the outcome of this war. But, this I know—*when your darkest moment comes, you will conquer only if you yield.* It isn't logical, but it is the truth I see."

She surveyed the plain that stretched ahead of them, seeing little in the dark. All around, men leaned wearily on their plodding mounts.

"You know what the trial is, don't you?"

He said nothing.

"Very well, then. When the time comes I'll trust Tak and Skraal to see me through."

"Trust no gods, woman," he advised, squeezing her hand. "But trust yourself." The sorcerer tugged sharply on his reins and rode toward Rhadamanthus. The two fell deep into conversation.

She steered Ashur away from the main body of soldiers, feeling closely the need to be alone. So much had happened in the past days. She had changed. Courage and determination, self-reliance were slipping away. Guilt and doubt replaced them. *Yes,* she admitted, *even fear.*

Her fingers brushed the moonstone circlet that adorned her brow. She had lost a family . . . then found a friend and lost her. Now, gazing at Kregan's back, she wondered if she had found something more and would soon lose that. She spurred the unicorn to the farthest edge of the advancing force and beyond.

She sought solace in self-pity. She grieved for her family, the Stranger in the forest, for Zarabeth and for herself. Then, pity yielded to hate. She hated her brother, and she hated Zarad-Krul, a mad instrument of suffering. Her fingers sought the Book in its pouch at her side. Its weight seemed to increase as she carried it northward, and she could sense the wizard calling it, conjuring it with an evil will; she clamped her hand tightly on the dusty covers. *He'll never have it,* she swore, *by my mother's blood.*

As she rode farther from the main army her dark mood gradually faded, and she rested, grateful for a moment's solitude, watching the Chondites. The men of Erebus moved in near silence; their black uniforms made good advantage of the wizard-spawned night. Like phantoms, they rode over the plain.

Then, something caught her eye. On a high ridge overlooking their course a small point of whiteness moved against the deeper black, then quickly vanished. She stared, waiting for it to return. It did not.

The gleam of a torch or a metal-tipped weapon, she thought. Was it possible that small force of Shardahanis had traveled faster than expected and planned an attack from the rear? It seemed unlikely. Still, Shardahani peasants were notoriously stupid, and *something* was following the Chondites. She urged Ashur to swift motion and rode to find Kregan.

He was still with Rhadamanthus.

"It can't be the Shardahanis," the Elder said. "We would have been warned."

"How?" she asked.

"We have our ways."

Aecus joined them. "A scout just reported the enemy's position. They're approaching the Tekaf Pass."

"Then, it's not the Shardahanis," muttered Frost.

Aecus shot her a stern look. "What's she talking about?"

"She spotted something on that ridge we passed a way back," Kregan answered. "It seems we're followed."

"By what?"

Kregan flushed, taking offense at the Elder's scoffing tone. "We don't know, yet. But if she saw something, then *something's* there."

Rhadamanthus sat with eyes closed during the argument. Now, he opened them and spoke. "There *is* something on the ridge, but I can't perceive its nature clearly. It resists my probing without apparent effort."

"If it's strong enough to resist an elder it could be a threat to us," Kregan advised.

Aecus roared. "Our enemy is to the north, not behind us! Zarad-Krul is the only threat! We have to reach Demonium before him, and there's no time to waste chasing visions."

"I agree that we can't stop to examine this," Rhadamanthus replied calmly. "But I would send two men back to observe it. Whatever waits on that ridge has a certain familiarity to it . . ."

Aecus reddened. "We'll need every man!"

Frost lost patience. "I like to know what stands at my back when I fight. By the Nine Hells, man, if you're too much of a coward, then say so and I'll go myself. Ashur can outdistance any of your broken down fleabags!"

Rhadamanthus raised a hand. "There is no need for dispute. Two men of my brotherhood will investigate; that is my decision." He turned to Kregan. "Brother, choose two from the lower ranks—apprentices will do—and dispatch them with the proper instructions. They should be safe enough. I have no fear of this thing, whatever it is."

Cursing, Aecus resumed his former position at the lead. Kregan rode in the opposite direction. Rhadamanthus leaned from his saddle, his old bones creaking with fatigue, and whispered. "Have patience with my brother of the Argent Cup, child. His home was in Dulaam, and there is no word from any of his household there."

She nodded sudden understanding. "I'm sorry, then. I'll ask his forgiveness."

The old man shrugged. "No need for that. Grief is not a sufficient excuse for foolish behavior."

She reflected on that, finding a message for herself. If Kregan knew her past, did the elders know, too? She searched that wrinkled face for a sign or clue; but the expression was impassive, revealing nothing. Of all the Chondites except Kregan, Rhadamanthus had been kindest to her. Yet, the idea that her past was general knowledge unsettled her.

"A warrior should not spend too much time in thought." Kregan rode up unnoticed on her right, his errand completed. He flashed a wide smile and rolled his eyes, lifted her hand and planted a gallant kiss on the knuckles.

All her misgivings disappeared and she laughed out loud. Kregan had a way of making her smile that puzzled and pleased her. *A bit of Chondite magic,* she concluded. *He knows my darker moods and how to lighten them.*

"Be gay, my Lady." He made a sweeping gesture that took in all the world. "While you still have the chance."

"I thought wizards and sorcerers were glum, brooding creatures," she teased, trying to match his mood. "You are too cheerful."

"And I thought witches had ugly warts on their noses," he countered. "You are too pretty."

She screwed up her face and rolled her eyes as she had often seen him do. "How's this, then?"

His low-noted laugh rang out, making heads turn. Smiles spread on several faces, and the laughter became contagious as sorcerer and sword-woman continued their banter, teasing each other, making light of every dreadful thing that crawled in Hell. Those riding near joined in with stories and jokes until all the host of Erebus was mirthful. Even sour old Aecus.

But up ahead, the Shardahanis waited. Far-sighted Minos spotted them first. Raising his staff, he called out, and all laughter ceased.

A pair of immense cliffs reared above the flat land like the jaws of a gaping mouth, stretching in opposing directions as far as anyone could see. Only the narrow Tekaf Pass cut a way through, and the Shardahanis held that, blocking the way to Demonium.

"Twice our number," Aecus said, surveying the foe.

"We have eyes, my friend," answered Minos.

But Frost wondered. In the dark at such distance she could barely make out the pass itself. How could the elders see the enemy—unless by magical means?

They pushed on at a walk until even she could feel the eyes staring at them out of the dark. At the entrance the Shardahanis had erected a barricade of rocks and boulders, and a line of rag-tag soldiers waited nervously behind.

"Is there any way around?" she inquired hesitantly.

"Avoid the battle?" Aecus spat. "The enemy lies right in front of us."

Rhadamanthus shook his head. "We can't avoid fighting, I fear. *Tekaf* means the Unavoidable Pass. Where those cliffs leave off deep fissures part the earth extending much farther. Traveling around would mean a delay of days, and the battle might still not be avoided. The enemy has horses, too, and would simply come to meet us."

"Then we fight," Kregan said.

The elders nodded one by one.

Word passed quickly through the ranks. Warriors unsheathed their weapons and masters readied staves. They made no sound: not jape, nor complaint, but sat their mounts bravely awaiting the order to charge.

In the front line hasty, last-minute plans were made. Rhadamanthus and Minos would remain behind and observe, being too old for actual combat. Aecus, therefore, would lead the attack. He turned to Frost and gave his first command.

"Woman, you'll remain with the elders."

She barked a short laugh, made an obscene gesture that even a Chondite would understand.

"She goes," Kregan interceded for her, daring what few of his brothers would before one of Aecus' rank.

Rage smouldered in his eyes. "We'll have no time to watch over a woman," he bristled, "and besides, she bears the Book."

"She must go," Rhadamanthus said with finality. "It's her fate. If you'll not have her, then I'll have to take command as the eldest present."

Their gazes locked in a silent contest of wills. Yet, Frost was indifferent to the outcome; whether the elders willed it or not she intended to fight. Not all their power would stop her, and she was on the verge of telling them so when Aecus crumbled.

"Come then and be damned."

The Elder of the Argent Cup raised his staff. In the darkness the silver wire on each end flared suddenly with an eerie brightness.

"Guard the Book," Rhadamanthus whispered.

"And your back," added Minos somberly.

She touched the pouch and nodded. Her sword hissed from the sheath and she stroked Ashur's long neck before wrapping the reins around her right hand. There was a tightness in her stomach. She wet her lips.

The staff fell.

With a mighty cry the men of Erebus thundered toward the barricade, brandishing swords, spears, gleaming pikes, double-edged axes.

Her own battle-shout was lost in the tumult. The unicorn leaped forward, horn flashing and eyes blazing. Swifter, more enduring than mortal steeds his ebon hooves smashed the ground, carrying her ahead of Kregan and past Aecus.

An arrow zipped by her ear, then another. A pair of archers on the boulder fitted new shafts to their bows, but the unicorn charged on. For a sickening moment she thought Ashur meant to ram the barricade, but suddenly she was airborne and hugging the saddle with her knees for fear of falling. Then, she was on the ground again among a howling foe.

She lashed out; her weapon hummed as she swung from side to side, spewing blood and brains. They came screaming at her. She hacked at grasping arms that tried to drag her down. A spearman thrust for her middle, missed and died as Ashur trampled him in the dirt. Blood quickly drenched her arms and thighs.

A familiar, ululating war-cry told that she was no longer alone. Kregan's white steed sailed gloriously over the barrier. In a blur of motion his staff crushed three skulls. Fighting his way to her side, they sang a harmony of death to the servants of Zarad-Krul.

Then, suddenly the barricade itself was consumed in a bluish glow of swelling intensity. A blast of thunder, and the stones exploded in a cloud of powdery dust. The mouth of Tekaf Pass was open.

In rushed Aecus, grim-faced, shouting vengeance for his family and Dulaam. From the silver tips of his staff twin beams of eldritch force cut a bloody swath through the closest Shardahanis. Twice more those smoking beams scored. Then, striking with a strength that denied his age, he swung that baleful weapon, bashing helms and breaking bones.

Behind him came the rest of the Chondites, hot for battle. Swords crashed in ringing fury. Sparks flew from the metal rims of beaten shields. Arrows arched unseen through the wizard-spawned night, hissing like angry winged snakes in their flight. War-cries, shouts of triumph mingled with despondent moans.

The harsh sounds of fighting beat her ears as the barren Chondite soil grew fertile with blood. An uncontrollable shivering seized her as she looked over the pass.

So much blood . . . so many dead men.

She had killed, yes. Seen death, yes. But not like this. Her lips curled back to scream as she raised her hand, incarnadined crimson.

A pikeman charged, and she could see his eyes through the narrow slits of his helm. That broke the spell. Silently, she thanked him even as she twisted, leaned, struck. Her weapons-master had trained her too well and too long to let panic completely rule her in a crisis. The man sank slowly, staring, a curse on his lips as she withdrew her blade.

Snapped from her paralysis she rejoined the fray. Like a fiend from the Nine Hells she struck and vanished, appearing at another part of the battle, striking, dealing death until her arm was weary and her mind numb with fatigue.

And fatigue was nearly her undoing.

Too late, she saw the assassin dive from his crannied perch in the cliff wall. Dodging his sword was easy enough, but not him. His weight tumbled her from the saddle. She struck the earth hard, stunned, expecting quick cold steel in the back. The assassin loomed over her. *If only she had the strength to strike his feet—she knew how—knock his legs out.* But there was no strength left in her. Leering obscenely, he raised the blade.

But the blow never fell.

Riderless, Ashur reared, tossed his great head and lunged. The assassin's eyes bulged; a scream tore his lips as the horn emerged through his middle. Ashur heaved, and the thrashing body sailed through the air, smashed into the towering rock face.

It gave her the time she needed to get her breath. Recovering her sword, she rose to greet more foes. Seven ragged soldiers circled her, and more were coming, seeing her afoot. She took a two-handed grip on her blade and waited.

"Bitch!" cried one. "If you can be unhorsed, then you can be skewered. We'll see how your precious Chondites fare without you to rally them."

Her guts twisted with a grim dread of what she intended, but there was no mercy in her. One hand left her sword and grasped the hilt of Demonfang. She knew the fearful effect of its screaming. That might save her now.

A raw chill touched her soul as the fiendish blade came free. Its wailing note sang over the pass, drowning other battle sounds. She had never heard it so loud as now in the presence of so much blood.

Furiously she shouted at her attackers: "Come on, then, and savor a bitch's charms!"

Terror flamed in her opponents' eyes. She lunged once, twice with the dagger, swung her sword. At first taste of blood the shrieking ceased, but unsheathed, the blade soon found its voice again. It trembled in her grip, insatiable and demanding. Almost of one will, her foes broke and ran. She leaped on the slowest of them; Demonfang fairly writhed in her hand as she opened his throat. The baleful, dripping dagger was still at last. Grimly, she cleaned the edge and sheathed it.

Foeless for the moment, she took a much needed rest. The battle had broken into small skirmishes through the pass; space was clear around her. In the distance, Kregan, Aecus and a handful of Chondites assailed the hardiest resisters.

Everywhere death littered the earth, and the dust drank up the life-fluid. She leaned wearily on her sword and sighed.

It was nearly over when Rhadamanthus and Minos rode cautiously into the pass, picking their way around the bodies. A nervous Ashur waited nearby. Gathering the reins, she waved and went to meet them.

The Book bounced in the pouch against her side, and she clamped a hand on it, reflecting on what she had witnessed— what she had been part of. There was no glory here. No honor. On an impulse, she drew out the Book, considering its value in blood.

"No!"

She looked up to see who called. Minos waved his arms frantically. Rhadamanthus spurred his horse in a mad rush toward her.

Sudden thunder shook the sky. The air crackled; a scorching bolt of alizarine lightning flashed through the night, stitching a serpentine pattern on the darkness. A hoarse cry ripped from her throat as death reached for her with rippling, fiery fingers.

Dimly, she heard an old man's shout. Another blast of lightning, blue and jagged, twisted out of the earth itself, smelling of sulphur as it streaked upward. It met the first bolt in a glaring burst of whiteness. Heat seared her face. A shattering explosion rocked the countryside, and she was lifted head over heels out of the saddle.

Zarad-Krul, she realized bitterly before the ground smashed all awareness from her.

Chapter Ten

SHE WOKE SLOWLY TO THE DRONE OF URGENT VOICES. Someone called her name. Kregan. Fear in that voice. She tried to answer, but a warm languidness filled her limbs, her head. *I should get up,* she thought. Yet, it was so peaceful to lie still and stare into the black abyss of unconsciousness that hovered so near. They would not let her alone, though. Someone kept calling her name until, with an effort, she opened her eyes.

Kregan's face was a mask of pain. "You look terrible," she managed.

A faint smile. "Are you all right?" He cradled her head in one hand, offered her water from a canteen with the other. She took a small sip and pushed the rest away.

"Just get me off these damned rocks; they're biting holes in my spine."

He helped her to sit, then to stand. It seemed the entire Chondite army had gathered to worry over her. Sheepishly, she put off Kregan's assisting hands and balanced precariously on her own feet. Licking her lips, she flashed a triumphant, half-amused grin.

But then, she remembered the Book. It was in her hands—

she must have dropped it when she fell. Frantically, she searched around. They had not moved her from the place where she had fallen, but the Book wasn't in sight. She shot a desperate look at the Chondite faces. *Could one of them have taken it? Or some agent of Zarad-Krul?*

"The Book . . ." she started. And stopped. A familiar weight banged her hip. Inside the pouch she traced the runes carved on the binding. A sigh slipped between her lips. Someone had replaced it while she was unconscious. Rhadamanthus, probably, or Minos. They had been closest.

"You should not have revealed it so carelessly," Aecus admonished her, his voice gruff, face flushed with excitement and anger.

She met his gaze for just a moment and decided to ignore his bad manners. She gave him her back and faced the other two elders.

"One of you saved my life, I think. But how? What happened?"

"As it turns out," answered Minos, "Zarad-Krul was watching the battle from afar through a scrying crystal. At first, he shielded himself so that we couldn't detect his presence, but as the fighting grew more intense and the Shardahanis began to lose, he let his guard slip."

Rhadamanthus picked up the tale. "We sensed him simultaneously, but doubted he had power to take an actual hand in the conflict, not being physically present. Only a partially accurate conclusion, it seems, but we decided to come closer to the fighting just in case."

"He probably would have stayed hidden," Aecus interrupted, "but when you foolishly revealed the Book of the Last Battle the wizard became so enraged he tried to strike you down."

Rhadamanthus smiled patiently. "Fortunately, his bolt was slow and weak, and I was able to disrupt it with my own. Had he been present, though, or his power just a little stronger, I couldn't have moved fast enough to save you."

Aecus sneered. "You'd be dead meat."

"Well, I'm not," she answered somewhat defensively, "and I'll be more careful from now on."

"We ask no more."

"But Elder-brother," Kregan said. "This, and the attack of

135

Zarad-Krul's Eye in Rholaroth prove that the wizard knows her aura. He can strike at her anywhere at any time."

"At Demonium we can take care of that."

She looked at Kregan, curious, suspicious.

"A ceremony," he explained, "but it takes a lot of participants, and we've not time to go into the details. The Field of Fire is still a good ride away."

Aecus scowled agreement, and she resisted an urge to put her sword between his legs. After all, whether she liked the elder or not, they were on the same side. And she'd watched him fight. He was good—damned good.

The battle had been a short one. They mounted up. The dead were left for the land to claim. There were no prisoners—that was not the Chondite way. There was no time to rest, and nobody complained. Across the dark plains and low hills they rode, and with every bounce in the saddle, Frost discovered a new bruise or an ache not realized before.

It was impossible to measure the time that passed. Thicker than viper's blood the darkness hung in the Chondite sky. No sun, no moon, no star shone through. They ate a little as they went, drank water or wine. Alternately, they rode hard and walked, but only once did they dismount. A stone triangle like the one outside the gates of Erebus reared like an awesome sentinel above the landscape, and the elders called for the troops to halt while they rode on to it.

Frost took the opportunity to nap and dreamed of a crackling fire and a soft pallet. Her poor body felt no relief when she was wakened only a short time later.

The elders returned with information. Indrasad had finally fallen to the Shardahani onslaught, but the remnants of its army were waging war-in-retreat to slow the enemy's advance on Demonium. There was no other sign of Zarad-Krul or the Dark Gods, Nugaril and Mentes.

What was it like, she wondered, to stand within those monolithic triangles and touch another mind on the other side of the country? Maybe someday she would find out, but now it was back in the saddle and onward.

The steady drumming of Ashur's hooves were a strong counter-rhythm to her own heartbeat. The blood pounded in her veins. The wind roared in her ears.

And when the horses would run no more, they walked.

Kregan's white charger startled her out of a half-doze, appearing suddenly at her side. Since departing the Tekaf Pass, Kregan had kept company with the Elders and not spoken to her. She gave a feeble smile of greeting and looked askance.

The Chondite chewed a ration of dried meat. "Woman?" he said gently. "Tell me what puts the wrinkle in that lovely brow?"

His soft words struck a chord somewhere deep inside, warmed her in a way she found almost annoying. She had intended to keep silent to pay him back for avoiding her, but when he questioned her again there was a sadness, a kind of weary yearning in his voice that wrung answers from her.

Anything to keep his company for a while, she realized with a start.

"Your apprentice-brothers," she said, gazing back the way the army had come, "they haven't returned yet. I've been wondering what it was I spotted on that ridge."

"Rhadamanthus said he didn't fear it," Kregan reminded. "Is that all that's bothering you?"

"There's that *trial* you mentioned." Their eyes locked, held. "I'm afraid, Kregan. I don't even know what it is, but I'm afraid."

He maneuvered his mount closer until he stirruped foot brushed Ashur's belly. He set a strong arm about her shoulders.

It was what she wanted, had yearned for, to touch him. And though such weakness was an embarrassment and a shame she yielded to an impulse and leaned her head on his chest. She would not give in to tears, though. It was precarious riding, but they continued that way, embracing.

"There's fear enough to share on this journey," he whispered in her ear.

After awhile she sat up, her composure intact once more, and smiled.

As the distance to Demonium shortened the pace increased. Just before a low crest the army broke into full gallop. Frost crouched close to Ashur's neck and nudged the unicorn with her spurs. Kregan did the same, and they passed the elders, easily outdistancing their comrades. Over the flat plain and up, up the crest.

First to reach the summit, she blinked in disbelief, jerking hard on the reins. The unicorn reared in protest and crashed his hooves on the ground, snorting. Kregan halted beside her while the elders, then the army, flowed around and past them like a human wave.

Below, the land burned with a vibrant fire of many colors: deep reds, blues, oranges, hot golds and cold greens, splendid shades of purple and violet. Like tiny stars fallen to earth every stone and pebble glowed in the darkness. Even the bare spots where no stones lay seemed to possess a hazy luminescence.

"The Field of Fire," Kregan said. "At the very center you can just make out . . ."

"Demonium." She made no effort to hide her awe.

A finger of earth and rock jutted from the landscape, a pinnacle balanced between the sky and the ground. She should not have been able to see it in the night, and yet some unnatural source of light showed it plainly. The summit of that bizarre finger was sheered flat, and atop it stood three immense monoliths.

The Demonium Gate.

"What causes the stones to glow?"

"For thousands of centuries the rocks and stones have lain undisturbed, absorbing the interdimensional energy that seeps through the gate. But, being inanimate matter, they can only contain a small portion of that energy; the rest is released harmlessly as colored fire that has no heat. This place is sacred to us."

"It is beautiful and strange," she admitted after a long silence.

He touched her cheek, just a brush of the fingertips. "There's much here that's beautiful."

She met his even gaze and matched the grin that blossomed on his face. "We'd best ride down," she said at last. "At least we've beaten Zarad-Krul here."

The army established camp at the very foot of Demonium, and under Aecus' direction sentries were soon posted and horses tethered, but left saddled and ready.

Frost and her Chondite companion spread blankets together and built a small fire.

"Your eyes are greener than a cat's," Kregan said as they worked, "and bright as this fire or the stones out there."

"You talk too much," she replied curtly. They warmed

strips of their dried meat rations over the flames, ate and settled back on pallets.

But for Kregan there was no rest. Rhadamanthus, Minos and Aecus strode through, gathering the *Krilar* of every brotherhood. Taking up his staff, he rose slowly, but before he went he kissed his own fingers and touched the moonstone in the circlet she wore. It shone with a translucent light in the campfire glow, like a third eye in the middle of her brow.

She brushed his hand briefly before he turned away. No words passed between them, but she rose, forgetting her fatigue, and watched as, one by one, elders and *Krilar* ascended a steep, treacherous path that led to the summit of Demonium. When a turn in the path carried them behind an outcropping of rock, and she could see them no more, she wrapped her cloak close about her and settled back beside the fire's fading warmth.

Though her bones ached with weariness, sleep would not come. The camp was still. The crackling of her tiny fire and the crunch of sentries' boots on the hard earth were the only sounds.

Then, somewhere a drum began to beat softly, low and constant. Only the wind rustling a tent flap, she assured herself, until the sound began to swell in volume and tempo. She sat up. No one else seemed to take any notice. High above on the rim of the pinnacle, something caught her eye: a wild flickering firelight. She could barely see the tips of the flames, but on the smooth-sided monoliths that reared so impossibly high, twisted shadows danced in rhythm to the drum.

A new sound, a chant in an unfamiliar language, joined a second throbbing drum. She grew hot. The air seemed to thicken about her. Sweat beaded on her face as that deep, distant pulse filled her senses. Her heart pounded; blood throbbed in her temples. Shuddering drums reached a fevered peak. Shadows whirled on the ancient stones. The sky seemed alive with crackling fire.

And when she could stand no more, thought she would scream to drown the sound—the drums stopped. Unclenching her eyes, she looked up. The shadows were gone, and the fire was a subdued glow. After awhile, even that faded.

What had it all meant?

Exhausted, she sank back on her pallet. Kregan would

return soon and explain it to her. Meanwhile, her little camp-fire had burned to coals. She stirred it with a stick, glancing up once or twice at the looming monoliths, barely visible against the black sky since the strange firelight had gone out. Why didn't they shine like the other stones and boulders.

Without meaning to, she yawned and drifted into a sleep troubled with nightmares, peopled with ghosts.

She sat up gasping, shivering, a half-uttered scream on her lips. A balled fist struck at something that wasn't there; a hand went to her sword. It was a full moment before she realized the dream was over and remembered where she was.

Warm arms slipped around her. "Are you all right?"

Kregan's eyes were large, dark pools that gleamed in the light of a renewed campfire. His bed roll was undisturbed, though. It occurred to her to wonder just how long he had been sitting watch over her. "Sure," she managed finally. "It was just . . . nothing."

He reached out to hold her, but the sound of galloping horses startled them apart. Both leaped up, and other soldiers did the same as the noise shattered their sleep.

Frost slid her blade half out of its sheath before Kregan stayed her hand. "Only three riders," he said.

She listened, counted and agreed. By now, all the camp was on its feet. Naked steel glimmered in a goodly number of fists, she noted with some satisfaction. Three riders or not, who knew what might be abroad in this cursed darkness.

The sound of hooves traveled far on the flat, still plain, and she strained to follow the riders' approach over the Field of Fire. She could not so much actually *see* them as she noted the winking of the stones as three vague forms eclipsed the glow.

Straight into camp they came, jerking their mounts to a reckless halt, scattering dust and pebbles.

Kregan went pale.

"The last piece of the puzzle," he mumbled. "Of course, why didn't I see it before?"

Between two apprentices, young brothers of the Black Arrow, sat Natira.

Rhadamanthus pushed through the ring of soldiers, Minos and Aecus in close tow. When he saw the woman he stopped short, a curious expression in his old eyes. The apprentices were breathless from the long ride, but Natira seemed unaffected. Though dust covered every part of her and her hair was a mad tangle, her peculiar beauty radiated like a pale beacon in the night.

"So it *was* you I sensed," Rhadamanthus said.

Natira made no answer.

"We found her on the ridge as the Esgarian female warned," an apprentice spoke. "She was following us, and refused to go back even when we tried to take her."

"She talked?" Kregan was incredulous.

"Not a word, but she wouldn't move except to follow the army."

"Our orders were to investigate and report," the second apprentice interrupted gruffly. "Not to drag some demented woman all the way back to Erebus and miss the real action."

"So we finally let her come," continued the first. "You wouldn't know it to look at her, but she rode like one possessed, not bothering to look for tracks. She just seemed to know the way."

Rhadamanthus paced a wide circle around the three. "Why?" he said at last. "Why are you here?" Agitation showed on his aged face. He apparently expected an answer from the voiceless girl to judge by the way he glowered at her, but Natira tilted her delicate head at an odd angle and watched him with expressionless eyes.

"Well," growled Aecus, "what do we do with her?"

"You'll do nothing." Kregan pushed through the crowd. "I'll take care of her."

"Krilar." Aecus used the formal address, his voice harsh, stern. "You have other responsibilities. We're at war, and you are a master sorcerer."

"I said I will care for her." There was no room for argument. He helped his ward from the saddle with deft care. Wearing no cloak, she shivered a little in the night chill, and the Chondite's arm settled naturally about her small shoulders.

Aecus looked as if he would press the issue farther, but Minos caught his arm. "She has been his charge from the first. Leave be, my friend." Aecus' eyes flared hotly as he shook off the gentler elder's restraining hand. With a curse he turned, strode away, shoving aside any who blocked his way.

Frost also turned away to seek her fire and pallet, deeply

troubled. The Elder of the Argent Cup bore watching; his unpredictable moods bordered on madness. Yet, that was not what annoyed her most, though it shamed her to admit it. The look on Kregan's face, his gentleness as he unseated Natira, the easy and oh-so-casual way his arm went around her; these things tormented her. She mocked herself bitterly for fretting over trivialities when greater dangers were afoot.

Still, try as she might, she couldn't set them aside, and when Kregan deposited Natira in his own bedroll next to hers and left, she hissed across the hot coals of the fire.

"Why in the Nine Hells did you have to come?"

Natira sat up, gazed over the flames; a broad smile suddenly creased her lips. With one hand she began to massage her own small breast while with the other she pointed through the fire to Demonfang.

With a gasp, Frost snatched the hand from the flames. Unbelievably, the skin was not burned, not even reddened by the heat. The woman betrayed not the slightest hint of pain, but continued to smile and point at the arcane dagger.

It was unreal, maddening. The hackles rose on her neck, and she clamped her fingers protectively on the slender weapon on her hip, gripped by an unreasoning fear. Leaping up, she fled to the farthest side of camp and beyond, ignoring the guards who called after her. Breathing hard, full of suspicions she could not give voice to, she reached the line of tethered horses and stopped.

Ashur was close by, untethered, and he made a low greeting as she threw her arms around him and rubbed her face in his silken mane. His eyes were soft, muted flames; his breath warmed her skin. From poll to withers she stroked the grateful creature who was, she thought, her only true friend in all this crazy war.

But there was no peace for her among the animals.

Ashur's unnatural eyes flared suddenly, her only warning that something was amiss, and she spun around. A tenuous veil of shifting radiance hovered over the earth near at hand. The light began to flux and coruscate, changing colors rapidly. Then, from the shining nimbus the Stranger emerged, he who had precipitated this adventure, looking exactly as he had in Etai Calan so many days before, naked and beautiful.

"Beware, my child," he warned. "And be strong."

Her sword rasped clear of sheath; one hand pressed to

mouth, muffling her astonished outcry. She stared at the apparition in fear and amazement, remembering the butterflies and a horrible end.

"You're dead!" she managed hoarsely. "Nothing but bones! How can you . . . ?"

But the Stranger was swallowed once more in light and faded, leaving her alone with Ashur and an unanswered question.

Beware and be strong. Those were his words. But what did they mean? She turned slowly, surveying all directions. Nothing to beware of. And no one in camp gave any indication of having shared her vision. In fact, as the minutes passed and the shock wore off, she wondered if she had seen him at all, if he wasn't just a product of her own fatigue and growing self-doubt.

She had almost convinced herself that was the case when the horses went wild.

Incandescent sparks shot from Ashur's eyes, and the air turned sullen, foul with the taint of evil. A second nebulous glow shimmered over the ground, spreading harsh colors on everything it touched. A dark light this, it pulsed blood red, emerald green and purple, orange and blood red again. The horses whinnied pitifully, stamped and tore at the picket, but the line held.

The glow vanished, leaving a young man, tall and darkly bronzed with hair black as the space between the stars. Heavy muscles rippled beneath his skin, and he moved with the subtle grace of a bird in flight. His fingers were laden with rings; about his ankles hung dainty chains of gold and silver. He wore nothing else but a broad belt of glittering pearls, larger than any ever of this world, and a patch over his right eye.

The youth held out a hand. The nails were long and curved, lacquered. "Give back my Book."

"Zarad-Krul!" She swung her blade in a high arc with all her might, but the keen edge passed harmlessly through arm, chest, arm, leaving the wizard unaffected but for the smile it brought to his cruel lips. She cursed, called on Tak and struck again with the same result.

Zarad-Krul laughed. "Your weapon is useless, woman. I am only my master's shadow sent to reclaim the Book of the Last Battle from a common thief."

She heaved her sword again, cleaving neck, chest and thigh

in three mighty sweeps, but the thing had no substance. Could it truly be the wizard's shadow? She stood back, teeth clenched in an ugly grimace, unwilling to lower her sword, however ineffective it proved.

"Give me the Book and my master will spare your miserable life."

She shook her head, not trusting herself to speak lest her voice crack and betray her fear.

"For the third and last time I ask," said the shadow of Zarad-Krul. "Think before you answer. Believe me, woman. I know your most shameful secrets; defy me, and I can make you suffer in ways you'd never imagine." He extended his beringed hand again. "Will you give me the Book of the Last Battle?"

She clutched the leather pouch hanging at her side, hugged it fiercely, feeling the treasured contents. It meant death if she surrendered it, hers and Kregan's and the world's.

"No!"

She struck one more time, passing her blade through the wizard's head to no effect; then she turned and fled toward camp, expecting some unholy doom with every pounding step.

Reaching the first line of tents, she spied Natira hiding, watching from the shadows, but she did not stop to question the mute woman. A new fear gripped her: no one had come running when the horses went crazy, not even a sentry. Surely, someone should have heard her own outcries. Natira was there, but what about the others?

Straight to the tent of the elders she ran, still gripping her sword. She burst in pale and breathless. Kregan, the elders and some men she didn't know gaped in surprise and consternation.

"Zarad-Krul!" she croaked. "Out by the horses!"

Aecus seized his staff and dashed out with Kregan and two others right behind. Dimly, the sound of shouted orders and flying feet came to her as Rhadamanthus helped her to a stool, offered a cup of hot spiced wine which she gulped down.

Kregan and Aecus returned before she lowered the cup. "Nothing out there, now," her friend said. "Are you sure it was the wizard?"

She slammed her sword-point into the ground, jumped up and cursed, stung that he could doubt her.

"Calmly," Minos said, placing himself between them. "Tell your story."

She left nothing out. In fact, she took a perverse joy in watching Kregan's expression as she related how Natira had apparently observed it all and done nothing. She finished the tale with another cup of wine and wiped her lips.

"Well, the sentries didn't hear anything." Aecus rubbed his chin thoughtfully. "And we certainly didn't."

"Zarad-Krul has many new powers at his disposal since the coming of the Dark Ones," Minos said. "Perhaps whatever transpired was meant for you alone."

"The Book is safe?" Rhadamanthus asked. She started to remove it from the pouch to show them, but the elder waved his hand. "No, put it back. Too much danger in casually revealing it. Your word is enough."

"But what of the Stranger? I saw him die days ago."

"And he is dead," Kregan answered. "I've sought him in ways that couldn't fail if he were still among the living."

Rhadamanthus nodded. "It was a ghost that brought you warning, my child."

Minos met her disbelieving gaze. "Stranger things have happened."

"And will happen, yet," Aecus added.

"As for Natira," Rhadamanthus continued, turning to Kregan, "she represents an unknown at a time when we cannot afford unknowns. Watch her closely, Brother. I want to know her every move. She's followed us for some purpose, and none of us dare rest until we know what that purpose is."

General nods all around. Then, a shout and sudden commotion outside brought them all to their feet. An officer in the insignia of the Argent Cup charged into the tent, knelt at his elder's feet. Eyes were wide in the gray pallor of his face, and he trembled visibly.

"Outside . . . !" The words struggled from his throat. "Elder-brother, come look!"

Floating serenely, motionlessly above the Field of Fire Zarad-Krul sat on a throne carved from a single giant amethyst. His strong, youthful face gazed dispassionately down on the Chondite camp. Though it was dark, Frost could see him clearly as if some unnatural light amplified his image.

Then, suddenly a row of stones that gave the field its name

began to glow brighter and brighter until a wall of flame sprang up from the earth. At the wizard's command it roared improbably toward the Chondites, and the soldiers fell back moaning in fearful lamentation. Frost, too, took a step back, but Minos caught her arm.

"Would you run from an illusion?"

She looked uncertainly from him to Rhadamanthus and found reassurance in that elder's calm gaze. But Aecus looked doubtful.

"Are you sure?" he dared ask.

Minos raked him with a stern glare. "Elder," he said, using formal address, "are you so involved in the physical battle and your thirst for vengeance? Remember your Brotherhood and your vows. How shall the Brothers have faith if the Elder disbelieves? Unfetter your senses; free your *true-sight* from the narrow bonds you have placed on it."

Aecus reddened and looked as if he would strike the old man. She braced herself to intercept such a blow if it came, admitting her quiet admiration for the Elder of the Golden Star and for the calm dignity he maintained through every crisis.

But it proved unnecessary. Shame-faced, the hot-tempered Aecus looked upon the fiery wave that threatened to engulf them. He took a deep breath; his tension seemed to melt away. Then, he smiled.

"Not enough to call it a mirage," he declared at last. "We'll have to prove it beyond all doubt before the troops lose heart and flee."

As one, the three started toward the fire, and Frost would have gone with them, trusting their word over the evidence of her eyes, but Kregan held her back.

"You don't have the *true-sight,*" he warned. "In your heart you may believe the elders, but you don't *know* positively that the fire is not real. If there was the smallest doubt in the smallest corner of your mind it would kill you, illusion or not. You would believe yourself dead."

She watched grimly, risking a quick glance at the Chondite soldiers. They no longer cowered away, but watched in fascinated dread as three old men strode unwaveringly across the field into the mouth of Hell.

The flames reared up, crashed down.

She cried out—and knew Kregan had been right. She had doubted, and that doubt would have killed her. But the elders stood unharmed in the heart of the flames. A heartbeat later, the wall vanished.

A mighty cheer rose from the Chondite's camp. Kregan exuberantly pounded her shoulders, and in that unguarded moment when joy swelled up within her she flung her arms around his neck and kissed him.

"A cup of triumph all around," he grinned when she released him. Realizing her brazenness, she whirled away muttering a curse they both knew she didn't mean.

A haughty laugh boomed across the plain.

"Three old men!" roared Zarad-Krul on his amethyst throne. "Is this the best you can send against me?" The intensity of his mirth shook the very stones.

But Rhadamanthus drew himself up. At his fingertips flared a menacing blue light. His shout came clearly. "We have no business with shadows. Begone, Shadow. Send us your master. Tell the unworthy cur we await him with whips and switches."

Frost whispered to her friend. "Shadow?"

"Had you the *true-sight* you would see nothing but a black shadow stretched upon the throne. Watch."

The blue light danced on Rhadamanthus' fingers, swelling and brightening until a small portion of the Field of Fire was illumined as if by the noonday sun. On the throne Zarad-Krul faded in the growing light, but when the elder ended his cantrip and the mystic radiance subsided, the shadow returned.

"That's no real man!" she exclaimed. "But how's it possible?"

"A complex spell," Kregan answered. "A torch is set at the wizard's back, casting a shadow before him. Through certain incantations the shadow can be separated, animated and sent to do the bidding of its master."

Sharp-edged laughter cut him off. The Shadow of Zarad-Krul leaned forward, wagged a chiding finger at the Chondites. "Ha, fools! Even the Shadow of the man you dare oppose has some power. Learn what a mere shadow can do."

He gestured, and a column of wispy vapor descended from his hand, shimmered, coalesced, became a giant that loomed above them.

Frost gasped.

The giant bore a familiar sword and shield. The armor was Esgarian.

The Shadow gestured again, conjuring another giant, taller than the first, armed with similar weapons and no armor. Two more gestures and two more giants. One, a man of noble dress and bearing; the last, a woman, also of fine dress. Cat-green eyes and straight black hair made her a creature of beauty.

The Shadow on the throne barked a deep-throated laugh. His voice thundered. "A little drama for a thief—she who dares keep the Book from me."

With a grand sweep of his arm one last figure was born. Another woman, green-eyed, raven-haired, beautiful as the first, but armed like the men.

Frost felt her knees start to give; the earth spun too fast and someone flung stars in her eyes. She couldn't breathe. Pain throbbed in her temples; ringing in her ears. Then, Kregan's arm was around her, and somehow she found strength to steady herself.

It was like looking into a mirror. The titans all stared back: her weapons-master, brother, father and mother. Monstrous images of her family. With numbing fear she recognized the weapons and clothes, the facial expressions, knowing in the coldest part of her soul what was to come. The giant version of herself regarded her coldly.

The Shadow of Zarad-Krul called her name—the name she had forsaken on that dreadful day.

"I promised you suffering and punishments beyond your meager imagination, did I not? Can you guess why I've conjured these particular figures? Come now, speak up."

She could not bring herself to answer.

"I can spare you this humiliation—*if you give me the Book of the Last Battle.*"

She clutched the pouch with both hands. An uncontrollable trembling seized her as she felt the Book inside. Zarad-Krul's price for keeping her secret. Her fingers closed on the rough binding; one nail traced the ancient runes. He would tell her shame to the world if she refused, reveal the truth that had destroyed her life, damned her.

The Book slipped half out. The metal lock gleamed dully.

Dimly, she heard voices arguing. The elders and Kregan.

They were holding Aecus. He was kicking, cursing. What was Kregan shouting? Something familiar.

A trial.

"Come now, woman. Or would you have everyone know of your disgrace?" The honey-sweet voice of the Shadow droned insistently in her ears. "Give me the Book."

She looked at the partially revealed Book, and at her friends. They stood apart, unable or unwilling to help. Even surly Aecus, so passionately angry a moment before, watched without moving. But on their faces—fear?

Why wouldn't they help her?

"Give me the Book," the Shadow chanted. "Give *me* the Book. *Give me the Book!*"

"No!"

The scream ripped from her throat; tears of anger and dismay, doubt and humiliation streamed suddenly on her face as she pushed the Book of the Last Battle back into the pouch out of sight. "You—soulless filth! No!"

The Shadow and the amethyst throne vanished amid thunderous laughter. Then, the giant figures began to move.

Her knees buckled, and she collapsed in a trembling heap. An arm settled consolately about her shoulders. Kregan's. Try as she might, she could not meet his eyes. Her shame was too great.

She looked away as memories flooded her, guilt and fear. The elders stood by her now, but would the rest of the soldiers when they knew? Would they fight for a murderess and worse?

Rhadamanthus laid a hand on her arm, strange sympathy shining in his eyes. Then, making sure she saw, he covered his face with a corner of his cloak. Minos and Aecus followed his example, and all the Chondite army.

She was too surprised to cry more; her heart swelled with amazement and gratitude. Though she suspected Kregan and the elders already knew of her crimes, they would not shame her by watching Zarad-Krul's vile reenactment. Somehow, she found the strength to rise. Every face was covered; some had even turned their backs.

She, alone, was compelled to watch.

The face of the giant Frost twisted with concentration as she swung her sword in flashing circles. Undaunted, the image of her brother crept closer, on guard, hatred burning in the huge pools of his eyes.

She couldn't help but shiver. The memories were so vivid, the pain too deep to face alone. With a shaky resolve she swept the cloak from Kregan's face.

"Watch with me."

His arm went around her, and she leaned her head in the hollow of his shoulder, glad of his warmth.

She remembered the night her brother had discovered her practicing. There had never been love between them. Each envied the other too much, wanting what the other had: she, the right to learn weapons, and he—she always suspected—the right to follow the mysteries of Tak. He found her that night with steel in her hands, deliberately flaunting the ancient taboo. So it was his right to take her life.

It was his duty.

Steel rang. Two giants clashed, kicking up earth. One pass. Two. The giant Frost sank her blade in her brother's breast.

Exactly as it had happened.

Later, lacking the courage or the will to punish the daughter he loved, her grief-stricken father threw himself on that same blade. A wailing went up through all the house, alerting Burdrak, the weapons-master. Burdrak had loved and trained her, took immense pride in her swift development. But *his* duty was also clear: avenge the lord of the house he was sworn to.

She had thought to throw down her sword and accept the fate she deserved, but as that mortal stroke descended her instincts betrayed her. Pupil fought teacher, though neither had heart for the battle. Still, in the end Burdrak slipped, dropped his guard and died.

The giant Frost cast aside her sword and threw arms around her teacher's lifeless body.

Just as she had done so many days ago.

Then, she recalled how her mother stepped forward, her face resembling nothing human. "You've learned well the ways of men, how to fight and kill." A sorcerous, menacing anger raged in those eyes of dark green. "You've stolen everything I loved—my husband, my son, my dreams for you. No sorceress, my daughter, but a witch with power greater than I have ever seen. But you've thrown that away. Rejected it."

Mother laid warm, shaking hands on her daughter's eyes, thumbs drew gentle circles on her lids. "And I lay this curse on you: that you will follow a path of violence for the rest of your days, pitting your weapon-skill against foe after foe. Remember, a woman who wears a sword is an object of scorn and derision among men, and many will try to take it from you. But you will fight only with the skills that Burdrak—damn his eyes—has given you. No more. You've stolen my family from me. In recompense, I steal your witch-power."

A pain lanced through her head, and she reeled.

The looming image of her mother gingerly lifted her daughter's fallen sword. "Now I've broken law, too." Her gaze seemed far off, unseeing. "Gods of my coven, where is the daughter I raised? I know you not, woman," she cried. "You are a thing of fire and frost."

The exact words. And exactly as before, mother set the point between her breasts, braced the hilt against the wall and sagged forward. Trailing a thick river of blood, she crawled to her husband, squeezed his cold hand and sighed away her last breath.

The sound of weeping floated over the plain as the giants faded. The drama was ended. One by one, the Chondites unmasked and returned to campfires and pallets. In Kregan's arms she watched them go.

"You've been tried," he whispered, "and found guiltless."

She looked out where the giants had been, wistful. "I'm not without blame."

"Blame and guilt are not the same things. You're as much a victim of that tragedy as a perpetrator."

There was no time to ponder it further. The sounds of battle horns drifted through the still air, louder and closer with each blast. Together, they raced back to camp.

Soldiers were scurrying for weapons. Many were already in the saddle. Aecus strode fully armored from his tent, a look of grim joy painted on his face.

A flare of bright blue lit a corner of the plain. A banner was spotted and identified.

Indrasad.

Chapter Eleven

TATTERED AND DIRTY, STAINED WITH BLOOD THEY looked more like madmen than Chondite soldiers as they rode their lathered steeds into camp. Fifty men—all that remained of Indrasad's proud army. The captain tumbled from his saddle; an ugly gash poured crimson down one thigh. A number of lesser cuts scored his arms. Frost and two others caught him as he fell. On his chest was emblazoned a golden star. In one hand he clutched the broken halves of a *Krilar* staff.

Rough hands seized her wrists, and the captain's eyes bored frantically into hers. "Minos!" he croaked. Someone laid a water-soaked cloth on his dried lips, but he pushed it away. "Where's Minos?"

"Here, young Brother." The elder slipped an arm around the captain's waist, taking much of the injured man's weight on himself. "I remember you—your name is Hafid."

A weak nod. "My men . . . some are badly wounded."

"They'll all be cared for," Minos assured him. "Your wounds need tending as well."

With Frost under one arm and Minos the other, they got

him into the elders' tent where Rhadamanthus was already spreading bandages and healing herbs. Hafid was eased into a chair and a cup of wine set at his right hand. He downed it gratefully while Minos unbuckled the man's leg armor and cut away his trouser's leg.

"We're all that's left," Hafid said bitterly. "Our women, children—all butchered when they sacked the city. What was left of the army retreated here, but they hit us twice again along the way. They could have overtaken us a third time and slaughtered all of us."

Aecus regarded him sternly from the entrance. "Why didn't they?"

Minos pressed a hot cloth to the wound, and Hafid winced. "I don't know," he admitted finally. "With only fifty of us, we couldn't have offered much of a fight, but they gave up the chase just before we reached the Field of Fire."

Minos wiped away a fresh stream of blood and began steeping some leaves in a samovar. "You did well, Brother. We need your strength here, now, to guard the Gate."

"They feared we'd hear the battle and ride out to engage." A smug grin spread over Aecus' face, and his black eyes narrowed.

But Rhadamanthus frowned, shook his head. "They wait for Zarad-Krul and reinforcements. They know we won't abandon this ground or risk battle beyond the Field of Fire. They can afford to bide their time."

Kregan poked his head inside the tent. *"Tumiel's* army approaches from the west, and the banners of *Graskod* have been spotted in the south."

"Good," Aecus mumbled. "Our own reinforcements."

Frost experienced a surge of joy. Two more cities to swell the ranks, and others yet to arrive. She offered a silent prayer of thanks to any gods who might be listening.

Hafid patted the new bandage on his thigh and raised a second cup of wine. "The Nine Armies haven't been united for at least five hundred years," he said, smiling.

"Then, maybe we'll learn something from this," Rhadamanthus suggested.

Aecus spat. "If we survive the teaching, you should add. Besides, the Nine Armies are no more! Dulaam and Indrasad are dead, now. There are only seven cities."

Hafid rose shakily to his feet, his face reddening. "In the hearts of fifty good men—Indrasad lives!"

The two locked eyes for unrelenting moments, then the Elder of the Argent Cup threw down his half-full winecup and stormed out.

Frost considered throwing her own goblet after him, but restrained herself. His moods and unreasoning outbursts were starting to worry her, and the expressions of the others told her she wasn't alone. She stayed a little longer, but at first opportunity excused herself.

There was no way to measure the passing time, but she slept on four occasions. One at a time the armies of the major Chondite cities rode into camp. *Graskod* from the south, and *Sagaeshe. Akibus* followed *Tumiel* from the west. From the northwest came *Aluram,* and *Tarmir* from the east. At the foot of Demonium their banners were planted beside those of Erebus and Indrasad.

With the armies came new supplies. Stores of weapons: arrows, spears and axes, sharp swords and round-shields patterned with the leering faces of unnamed demons. From Sagaeshe came a dozen chariots and charioteers, and from Akibus another twelve, for those cities were renowned in that art. Besides weapons, each army brought wagons of food and water to withstand a siege of months.

On the plain just beyond the Field of Fire the Shardahanis set up camp.

Teams of Chondite scouts ventured through the darkness to observe them. Frost and Kregan were one team. Armed only with Demonfang, she crawled belly down over the rough ground, cursing the small, sharp stones that bit her knees and elbows. When they were as close as they dared, they lay side by side taking short breaths, watching, listening, waiting.

It was an effort not to fall asleep. There was so little to observe, nothing to report. The enemy made no preparations at all. They didn't even bother to pitch tents. They ate hand-to-mouth from their saddle-bags and slept wrapped in cloaks on the cold earth, disdaining campfires.

She nudged her comrade and braved a whisper. "Nothing to see here. Let's go back."

"On the contrary," he answered. "We've learned a lot." He motioned for her to follow, and they crawled back toward the Field of Fire. When there was no danger of being over-heard he spoke again. "We know they don't plan to stay long. They haven't bothered to hunt fresh game, and they're still drinking from canteens and waterskins. Without better supplies they'll have to do whatever they're planning soon. And they seem pretty confident. Not a single sentry, did you notice?"

She frowned. Burdrak hadn't taught her everything, it seemed.

They heard a scrambling to the right, their relief team. Exchanging quiet acknowledgments, the new pair advanced to a better vantage. Frost and Kregan hurried back to camp.

But one member of their relief team, back-tracking, over-took them again before they had gone far. Frost heard him first; her hand fell to Demonfang and she waited for a crawling form to resolve into something familiar. Kregan had his own dagger drawn. Both breathed easier when they finally recognized the man.

He had moved as swiftly as possible. His own breathing came in ragged gasps. "A large contingent . . . Shardahanis! They're countless! Just arrived with weapons and supplies."

Kregan calmed him, asked a few more questions, then sent him back to his partner. When he was safely away, Kregan gave her a meaningful glance. She shrugged and whispered, "I was tired of all this skulking anyway." They leaped to their feet and ran the rest of the way.

Rhadamanthus seemed unsurprised by the news. "It's time, then," was all he said.

Minos did not even bother to rise from his chair, but to Kregan he said, "Convene the Krilar."

Kregan nodded. "Within the Gate, Elder?"

"No, all must take part this time. It will inspire the smaller brothers."

She felt a squeeze of her hand before her friend departed. Then, Rhadamanthus came forward and locked his bony fingers in hers. "Give an old man the pleasure of your company for awhile."

She found an odd contentment in wandering through the rows of tents, stockpiles of weapons with the gentle Chondite. In so many ways, Rhadamanthus was like her father: tough and fearsome, but strangely tender, kind, possessed of that ever-present courtesy that a man of power could always afford.

It startled her now that she could think of her father without pain. He was dead, and she was the cause. Nothing had changed. Or had it? She looked at Rhadamanthus, thought of Kregan, surveyed her new world.

Gradually, they wandered back to the center of camp. The Krilar stood waiting in a circle surrounding Minos and Aecus. They watched her as she approached, and their gazes sent tingles up her spine. From among the tents a crowd of warriors materialized and formed a series of rings around the Krilar's ring. She shivered apprehensively at the weight of eyes upon her.

She faltered. Her companion paused with her, and their eyes met.

"I needed the walk to clear my mind," he volunteered. "So did you. You were very tense."

She looked at the faces in the gathering. *Yes, they were waiting for her.* "I'm still tense."

He patted her hand paternally. "No need to be, my child. This is for you."

Rhadamanthus led her inside the circles. The warriors parted to allow her. When she reached the innermost ring the elders and masters made a short bow. She turned slowly, counting. Thirty masters in all of Chondos. She suppressed another shiver, wondering what part she played in all this.

At a signal, the ring of Krilar shifted, became a triangle with ten men on each side. Rhadamanthus took a position before her, the other elders at either side and slightly behind. A triangle within a triangle, and she stood at the center. Every face wore a solemn expression, and she could feel the tension like a sharp-edged sword. Sweat dampened her palms.

"Take out the Book," whispered the Elder of the Black Arrow. "Raise it high for all to see."

She extracted the Book and did as instructed. It felt heavier than she remembered, and the runes shone queerly in the light of campfires. She fingered the metal lock, tested its strength once more to no avail. It would not yield. Such power in her hands, but locked away, useless.

"Behold the Book of the Last Battle!" Rhadamanthus cried suddenly. "The object of Zarad-Krul's lust!"

Somewhere in the mass of warriors a drum began a slow, sensuous beat. The Krilar paced around the inner group, never losing the shape of the triangle, never taking their eyes from the warrior-woman. Beyond the lines of masters the crowd began to sway and hum. The sound filled her head; it frightened her to realize she was the focus of this bizarre rite.

"Behold the woman—the guardian of the Book!" That from Minos.

"Behold she who blinded Zarad-Krul!" Aecus' voice rolled across the camp.

Another, deeper drum sounded. The masters began to dance, whirling, dipping, sweeping low to gather handfuls of earth which they rubbed into arms and faces, careful never to lose the sacred pattern of their dance. And as they moved, each one gave her a new name.

"Sword-woman."

"Witch-warrior."

"Death-maiden."

An unexpected dizziness made her clench her eyes shut. Voices droned in her ears; she tried to sort the words and failed. Suddenly, a wrenching in her gut, a horrible, disconcerting sensation of being in two places at once, then emptiness.

Her mouth opened, but no scream came.

Then, all discomfort faded, replaced by a feeling of lightness and tranquillity. Tremorously, she opened her eyes.

A potent spell, she mused, secure in the peace that pervaded her. *This should scare the Hell out of me, yet I'm not scared at all.*

Below, she could see the camp and the ritual still in progress. She could even see herself, her own body. Her cat-green eyes were wide, but vacant. Raven hair blew in a mild breeze she could no longer feel, held from her face by the shimmering moonstone circlet.

How strange she felt, clutching the Book above her head, rigidly immobile.

She looked away from her own body, surveyed the elders. Their eyes were vacant stares.

We are with you, said a voice in her head.

Three silvery images, the elders' astral forms, appeared beside her. For the first time, she perceived that she, too, wore a new, glistening body, identical to her true form, but without imperfection or fleshly color.

Below, the dancing ceased. The masters took up their staves and began to twirl them until they blurred from the motion. The metal tips of each staff began to glow, softly at first, then with a fire that rivaled the stones that littered the sacred field, and still they continued to twirl. From each spinning wand a pure blue fire shot into the sky. Thirty beacons of brightness that rose and disappeared in the heavens.

Minos touched her with his thoughts. *A cone of power,* he explained. *No evil can touch us while its influence lasts.*

On the ground the twirling staves slowed, stilled, but the cone remained.

Greetings, my love.

She turned to see Kregan and all the Krilar. Each wore a perfect, new body, smooth and gleaming with a sweet light. They came to her, touching, kissing, embracing. She touched back, marvelling at the sensations. They seemed to feed on her, and she on them. Forms merged with hers, flowed through her, separated. Each gave and took something away. A sharing that reminded her of Dasur's grove, but subtly different.

Finally, the cone began to dissolve. One by one, the silver bodies melted. Rhadamanthus was the last; he brushed her lips and was gone. Alone once more, she gazed down on the Chondite camp. Her mortal body had not stirred.

But the Book of the Last Battle, with her pale, human fingers curled around it, burned with an arcane glow. Those undecipherable runes flickered, danced with a magical light on the ancient binding. And the lock—did the voices of incredibly old gods call out through the keyhole?

Then, it was an ordinary book again, and she was seeing it through her own eyes from her true body. Her arms ached; she lowered them and turned to the elders.

They nodded, smiling. The drums stopped.

"Put it away now," Rhadamanthus said. "It's done."

Already the warriors were disbanding, returning to their individual tasks. A few Krilar leaned on their staves; beads of sweat ran down their weary faces. Eventually, they departed, too. Then, Minos made a deep bow to her and headed for the elders' tent with Aecus in close tow.

Kregan moved to her side. His tunic was drenched with perspiration and his hair was disheveled, but he held himself erect.

"What in Tak's name happened?"

"We freed your astral form from your mortal shell. Any sorcerer can release his own spirit, but to free someone else's required the combined talents of our most powerful brothers."

"But to what purpose?"

He looked to Rhadamanthus, silently asking the old man's permission to continue, receiving it with a nod. "Every living thing from the smallest leaf to the mightiest god possesses an aura that is distinctly its own. Of course, you know that—you were a witch."

That earned him a hard look.

He continued, undaunted. "I don't know if Zarad-Krul knew your aura before you left Etai Calan with the Book, but somehow he was able to follow us across Rholaroth. Maybe he found your shield in Shazad and just divined your location; that would be within his power. But, in any case, once his Eye entrapped us on the plain it was certain he knew both our auras. That's how he found you by the horses. In fact, he could find either of us anywhere, anytime."

"Okay, so where's this long-winded explanation heading?"

Rhadamanthus answered. "We can't allow Zarad-Krul to keep such a power once the battle begins. It would be too easy for him to strike at you from a distance or direct his servants to do it for him. By always knowing your location he would know where to concentrate his attacks. So we've made subtle changes in your personal aura by mingling it with elements of our own. That was the ritual's purpose. Now you wear part of each of our auras, and we wear part of yours. Zarad-Krul will be thoroughly confused."

"And there's an added benefit," Kregan said. "Every elder and master is now intimately acquainted with your true aura. If you're captured we can follow you anywhere, even beyond Chondite borders where most of our powers fail. We could attempt a rescue."

His grip tightened on her arm; his eyes bored into her.

She spared him saying it. "Or if I die in the fighting you'll know that, too, and come after the Book."

"If we can," affirmed Rhadamanthus with uncharacteristic bluntness.

She shrugged. "Well, I don't know about you, but I could use some wine."

The old man smiled and took her hand, stepping between her and Kregan. "A supper is being prepared in our tent. You'll have wine and good fare once more before any trouble starts." He looked away toward where the Shardahanis camped out of view. "But it won't be long, now."

A table was set with hot meats, grains and dried fruit. A loaf of bread was split and soaked in honey. The smell of it made her mouth water, but she waited until Minos, who played host, invited her to sit.

Halfway through the meal, Hafid dashed into the tent. "Birds!" he exclaimed. "At least, we think they're birds. They're frightening the horses, and the men are getting jumpy. You'd better come have a look."

Frost grabbed a last bite of meat, a mouthful of wine and followed the Chondites out. The sound of mighty pinions beat the air; the darkness was full of swooping, half-glimpsed shapes. Hollow, bird-like cries echoed in the night.

"The bird-things we saw at Cundalacontir," Kregan shouted excitedly. "I'm sure of it."

She agreed. "But a lot more of them. You were right, then. They're spies for Zarad-Krul. See how they circle like vultures over carrion?"

Then, without warning, Rhadamanthus called out. "To arms! Prepare! The enemy comes!"

The camp came alive with furious activity as soldiers scurried for armor and weapons. Dust and sparks flew as fires were extinguished. Horses whinnied as they were harnessed to the great chariots, or as apprentices led them to waiting masters. Aecus barked orders, and two young men buckled on his greaves. Only then did the scouting team come rushing breathless and gasping into camp to shout the news.

Frost turned to Kregan in all the confusion. "How did Rhadamanthus know?" she cried, "even before the scouts arrived?"

"He's a Chondite elder," he answered as if that explained everything. "Now hurry! Arm yourself or be left behind."

She made her way through the darkness with familiar ease, recalling the days when she had crept through the bowels of her father's castle for a chance to practice with her weapons-master. Well, it wasn't practice now. And nothing Burdrak had taught her could ease the growing tightness in her gut.

To her surprise, she found all her armor laid out neatly on her pallet. Natira sat in the dirt close by. Seeing Frost, she rose with leather vambraces and laces in hand.

She didn't really need any help, for she wore so little armor: vambraces for her arms, thigh protection and greaves, some leather gauntlets and the strangely carved cuirass Kregan had given her in Erebus. But Natira was eager to help. Smiling queerly, she fastened the buckles, and when she looked up from her work her eyes sparkled.

If she had a voice, thought Frost, *I think she'd be singing!*

There was a bronze helm, but she cast it aside. Too heavy, and it seriously restricted her vision. Kregan wouldn't approve, but then he didn't have to fight in it, either. Natira held a roundshield while she slipped her arm through the straps. Then, the unlikely squire belted her sword in place. Frost watched her carefully, for the swordbelt's buckle rested just above Demonfang's hilt, and she had not forgotten Natira's unusual fascination for the dagger. But, though her gaze lingered on it, the woman made no attempt to touch it.

She covered the dagger with a fold of her cloak, and the light seemed to leave Natira's eyes. She made a short curtsey, and without waiting for thanks turned and ran away, disappearing among the tents. Frost watched until she could see her no more, puzzled, biting her lips, fighting the uncomfortable feeling that her fate was somehow bound to the mute woman's.

She would talk to Rhadamanthus about it later. Now, there was no time to waste.

She called Ashur's name, and all the camp heard the unicorn's answering cry as he rushed between the tents, kicking up stones and dust, narrowly avoiding soldiers who ventured into his path. Streamers of flame boiled from his eyes, and the twisted ebony spike of his brow shone in their light. A wild, unholy beast he looked as his mane flayed the air and the ground shook beneath his black hooves.

Like the horses, he was still saddled; the reins hung loosely about his neck. She afforded him a welcoming pat, swung up and rode off to find Kregan.

The Chondite force assembled on the north side of

Demonium. At the fore, Kregan spotted her first and waved. He wore a sword this time, and his staff was slung over his back. In fact, all the Krilar wore steel.

"But this is only half the army!"

"The first line," he explained. "Chariots, mounted archers and cavalry. Aecus commands us. Minos will follow with a second, larger force of footmen."

"And Rhadamanthus?"

Kregan pointed to the top of Demonium. "My elder-brother waits there. He possesses the far-sight; nothing will escape his notice. His power alone makes up our third line of defense."

"All by himself?"

Kregan gave her a sly, reassuring look that didn't quite mask his own concern.

But there was no time for more talk. Aecus rode to the forefront and raised his staff. The silver-bound tips burned with a soft azure radiance. All eyes watched it; every man waited for the signal to charge.

Suddenly, the air above erupted with shrill screeching as the circling bird-things swooped at the army. A few men threw up their arms to guard their faces from razor-sharp talons; some fell clumsily from the saddle in panic. It was a brief attack, however. The creatures rose high and circled thrice more, then flew northward disappearing in the darkness.

Aecus growled a curse, and his staff plunged.

Her bones jerked as Ashur leaped forward with the first line. The shield banged on her arm and against her thigh. The sword slapped her leg. Over the Field of Fire the army raced, churning dust and glowing stones, and Kregan kept pace beside her, sword in hand. With a grim smile she drew her own blade.

Ahead, the Shardahanis waited, a shouting sea of foemen.

At Aecus' signal, the horsemen parted ranks, letting the chariots to the fore. They would be first to engage. Protruding from the axles, great spinning war-blades cut a bloody swath through horseflesh and footmen with equal ease. Men fell like wheat before a scythe, or were trampled by the teams, crushed beneath iron-bound wheels. There was no retreat for the chariots. When the mighty vehicles lost their terrible momentum the drivers whipped out swords and began to hack.

Close behind the chariots, the archer fired two volleys deep into the enemy's ranks, then split to left and right to harry the vulnerable flanks. In the wizard-spawned darkness their shafts were invisible death.

Frost abandoned her reins and hugged the saddle with her knees. Ashur knew what to do. She raised her shield, took a tighter grip on her sword. A horrible battlecry raged suddenly in her throat as the cavalry crashed through Shardaha's broken front line.

Metal clanged on metal. Flesh tore; bone crunched. Battle shouts and death cries mingled in a raucous clamor. Horses screamed in torment, glassy-eyed, beneath luckless riders. Swords and axes whined.

Aided by the momentum of her charge Frost's first blow split a shield. Her second severed the head from its bearer. Something rang on her shield and she looked down into fierce, burning eyes half-masked under a bronze helm. Her sword met his once, twice, then bit deeply beneath his ribs. Knees buckling, he slid free of her blade, his blood gushing on her garments.

Beside her, Kregan leaned from his saddle, swinging furiously, reaping a ripe crop of Shardahani souls with his double-edged sword. For just a moment she dared to watch and found a prayer on her lips for the Chondite's safety.

On left and right she struck at the enemy, and at first the battle favored the Chondites. But for every one she slew three more seemed to take his place. They came at her, a relentless wave of flesh. Her shield was dented, her arm half-numb from warding off the heavy blows of men twice her strength. Though her blade proved quicker again and again she began to fear as her grip weakened.

Suddenly, a familiar horn sounded: *retreat*. With a desperate thrust she dispatched her nearest foe and turned her mount, cursing as the bitter note sounded again. An unwary footman bounced off Ashur's massive shoulder as she spurred the unicorn. Everywhere, she saw the Chondites fleeing, their numbers nearly halved. Ahead, she spotted Aecus, horn raised to his lips for yet another blast.

"Get clear!" he called when she reined up beside him, and he slapped Ashur's rump. "Get away!"

A mighty cheer swelled from the Shardahani ranks, then laughter, filling her heart with shame and anger, but she obeyed the elder's command. "Laugh, you witless pigs!" she heard him bawl. "It isn't over yet!"

They didn't run far before Aecus' horn sounded a new note. The Chondites regrouped. Frost surveyed them grimly. The superior numbers of the enemy told a heavy tale. Four chariots survived that first onslaught of the original twenty-four. The survival rate was only a little better for the rest of the force.

"Where in the Nine Hells is Minos?" she shouted as Aecus rode past her.

"Get down, and take a tight rein on that beast of yours!"

His tone brooked no argument, but before she could obey Kregan jerked his mount to a stop beside her and swung from the saddle. "What? Where's Minos? We can't engage that number again without help!"

"Get down, damn it!" He nearly pulled her from Ashur's back.

Cursing, she slapped his hands away and straightened herself. No one, not even Kregan, manhandled her. But, looking around she saw everyone had dismounted.

"Stupid, god-cursed way to fight a war . . . !"

"We don't need Minos yet," Kregan shouted. "Just watch!"

A rumbling grew deep in the earth.

"Rhadamanthus?" she whispered, incredulous.

He nodded, pointing.

Far across the field, the Shardahanis wild cheers turned to shouts of fear and confusion as the ground shivered and splintered beneath them. Warriors tumbled helplessly, unable to keep their footing. Horses reared in fright, throwing hapless riders. Then, in their very midst, a great gaping fissure opened; from that dark crack slithered three monstrous gray worms, thick as houses, many times longer than the fissure itself. With serpentine swiftness they moved among the astonished enemy, crushing entire companies with their horrible girth. Hundreds more were swallowed up in the hideous black maws that sucked up anything within reach.

Frost watched with sickening fascination as a few pitifully brave men attacked the things with spear and sword and died for the effort. She had not considered that Shardahanis might possess such a thing as courage. A sobering realization to know that her foes were as human as she with all the human failings and all the human virtues.

"What are those things?"

"Vile creatures from the bowels of the world," Kregan answered. "Rhadamanthus summoned them when he saw we were losing. But the effort will leave him weak. See, even now he yields control."

It was true. Without the old man's guiding will the grisly worms crawled back to the fissure that spawned them and plunged into its black recess. When they were gone the earth trembled once more and the mighty crack sealed itself.

But the enemy force was in chaos. Aecus was quick to seize the advantage. With a wave of his staff the Chondites charged over the distance, screaming at their foes. "Laugh, you whoreson pigs!" she heard the elder call. "Laugh now!"

With sword, axe and lance they assailed the confused and frightened Shardahanis, spilling blood and brains. Bodies dotted the plain. A crimson wake followed the remaining chariots as they pushed deep into the enemy's heart. Men died, pumping life-fluid into the uncaring dust.

Frost's sword was a singing messenger of doom as it whistled through the air, killing men on either side of her. No fatigue now, but a red haze settled over her eyes as she did swift, deadly work.

But when the Shardahanis finally rallied and began to fight back the tide turned once more against the Chondites. The mournful blast from Aecus' horn shocked her from her battle frenzy. She looked around; a black sea of enemy warriors stretched before, and her heart sank. Her comrades were in full rout. The horn blew again. Nothing to do but flee.

This time, though, the enemy gave chase. Shouting warcries they came hot on the Chondites' heels. Frost cast fearful glances over her shoulder and bent low to Ashur's neck, urging him to greater speed.

Then, her mouth twitched in a grim smile. Far ahead, something rippled over the shining stones: Minos and the advancing second line. Now, by Tak, they could fight with renewed strength. Fresh troops might yet make a difference. A horn sounded the order to regroup. She turned, sword ready, prepared to meet the enemy's rush.

But instead, a cry tore from her lips, and she threw up an

arm to guard her eyes. A hot wind scorched her face and hands as a roaring wall of flame shot up from the bare earth. Screams of pain and anguish, the sickly odor of burned flesh rose with the crackling fire.

Slowly, realization dawned on her. Not the Chondites, but the Shardahanis were caught in that inferno. She twisted in the saddle. In the far distance a faint azure glow marked the peak of Demonium; Rhadamanthus had interceded again. As she watched the glow began to fade, and the heat from the fiery wall lessened. She wet her lips and swallowed. A horrible way to die, by fire.

But was there a good way to die?

No time to ponder that. As suddenly as they sprang up the flames vanished, leaving a wide, blackened patch of earth littered with the charred, smoking remains of men and horses. Aecus' staff came down again; she grit her teeth and charged.

The enemy ranks were in turmoil, thrown off-balance by the magical power of a Chondite elder. Frost spurred her steed into the thickest part and went to work. It was butchery. Again and again her sword fell on men too stunned to defend themselves. Strike hard and fast, without mercy, that was the plan. She shut her ears to the death-cries and struck until her arm was too weary to lift her blade, and she pulled back from the battle to rest.

A grim scene greeted her. The second line brought new, angry life to the Chondite side. Archers sent their shafts into the deepest part of the Wizard-lord's army; when the arrows were gone they drew swords and joined the melee. Pikemen advanced with juggernaut precision in phalanx formation, slaying with ruthless efficiency. A hundred slingmen hurled smooth stones with deadly accuracy; when their missile pouches were empty they used the rocks that gave the Field of Fire its name, and if the rougher missiles were not as accurate they took a greater toll on the enemy's courage as they streaked across the dark sky.

Chondite fighting skill and Chondite sorcery. Together, they shattered the Shardahanis' confidence until numbers no longer mattered. The dead strewed the field. The minions of Zarad-Krul were ripe wheat beneath the swords and mystic staves of Chondos.

A chorus of voices swelled over the din of fighting as the Chondites began to sing. The tunes were eerie, haunting, full of counter-balanced harmonies that made her shiver. They sang of Hell and death and terror, of their brotherhoods and elders, of the guardian of the Book. Yes, they sang of her.

Death-maiden, the songs named her, Reaper of Souls. The sword trembled in her hand; crimson droplets ran down its length and were sucked up by the ground. A sudden numbing fear gripped her heart as she saw what her own future held. Sweat beaded on her brow. She wiped it away with a blood-soaked sleeve, making a red smear.

"You fool! Why in the Nine Hells did you sound the recall? We could have chased the dogs all the way back to Shardaha!"

Frost stared at the ground, the ceiling, the four walls of the tent, determined to stay out of the argument. But as she listened to Aecus rage at Minos she clenched her fists.

"We had them beaten!" The Elder of the Argent Cup bellowed. "We could have crushed Zarad-Krul's army to the man and finished this thing here and now!"

Minos' eyes went cold. "We are not in the business of slaughter, and this is not a stockyard for your personal pleasure. Our immediate concern is to guard the sacred Gate."

Rhadamanthus sank wearily onto a stool. "We have to hold our line here, friends." He stressed the last word, attempting to bring peace to a tense situation. "We haven't enough men to guard Demonium *and* pursue stray Shardahanis across the countryside."

"Zarad-Krul will show himself soon enough," Minos said. "To face him will require all our united strength."

Hafid stirred from his place beside Kregan. "Then we're a living wall between Demonium and Shardaha. If the enemy comes no closer we go no farther. That's bitter."

Minos shook his head, frowning. "The Shardahanis are only men. It's not important if they keep their distance. The real enemy is the wizard and the Dark Ones he called into our world. A victory over men means nothing if we lose the greater battle to them."

"I'm sick of this!" Aecus shouted. "Where in damnation is Zarad-Krul?"

"Why should he show himself now?" She barely recognized her own low, carefully restrained voice. "When he can sit back and let us fight among ourselves like this."

Minos folded hands over his stomach, a smug look on his face.

Silent until now, Kregan spoke up. "Elder-brother, I wanted to chase them, too, but now I see Minos was right. Zarad-Krul allowed his forces to be broken. *He allowed it!* He knew that no force of men, no matter how large, could stand long against the elders and Krilar on Chondite soil. Either his presence or one of his Dark Allies might have turned the tide, but he chose not to intervene. I don't know why, but he must have had a reason."

A bowl of liquid rested on a pedestal at Rhadamanthus' right hand. For some time the old man leaned over it, stared into the still water. "It's no use," he announced finally. "I can't see him in the scrying waters. The Dark Ones shield him from my power."

"Maybe you can't see him because he's dead," Aecus snorted. "That's a frequent fate for one who reaches too far beyond the limits of his control. Maybe the Dark Ones killed him."

Frost was openly contemptuous. "How many lives will you bet on it?"

The elder's eyes flashed with anger, but Rhadamanthus interceded before he could respond. "Zarad-Krul lives, make no mistake about that. Though I can't see him in the waters I can feel his presence." He shut his eyes, his lips parted slightly. "Yes, surely you can feel him, too. You're an elder."

Minos nodded.

Aecus kicked the table, spilling wine and utensils. "All I feel is that you are fools! This interminable waiting eats at a man's mind! We should strike now while we have the momentum of a fresh victory. Chase the Shardahanis from our soil and carry this war over the border to Shardaha—to Zarad-Krul's very doorstep!"

A deep silence fell on the tent; all eyes turned on the enraged elder, disbelief on every face. Then, Rhadamanthus rose slowly, pointed a shaky finger. "Your thirst for vengeance has unhinged you, Aecus. Remember who you are! Remember *what* you are!"

Aecus' face screwed in pain and confusion; he clapped the old man's shoulders, his eyes misting. "I've lost my family, friends, my city! I'm a man, Rhadamanthus, a man!"

"I know," Rhadamanthus answered gently, "and it hurts . . ."

"No." There was nothing gentle in Minos' voice. It was cold—cold as edged steel. "You lost all that long ago. Now, you're the eldest of a Chondite brotherhood, and your loyalty is to the men and women who follow you. They look to you for leadership and guidance in the mysteries. I'm beginning to wonder if you can provide it."

She had never seen Minos so stern. What did he mean? What had Aecus lost before? Why didn't somebody end this damnable arguing?

Aecus responded with a torrent of curses. Hafid, then Kregan, tried to calm him, but he insisted on a plan to invade Shardaha. He drew a map on the dirt floor, began to outline strategies. Rhadamanthus patiently tried to point out the flaws. Minos' replies were less polite. The elders bickered in loud voices.

Her own temper began to rise. All the camp could hear the dispute. That wasn't good for morale. Each elder was sole commander of his brotherhood; if they continued bickering how long before dissent rose among their followers? It had to stop. Now.

Her sword hissed out. With any angry curse she plunged it into the center of Aecus' crude map. Startled out of their feuding, the elders jumped back amazed, and turned to glare at her.

"Why not fight it out with steel?" she stormed. "Then someone will die, the other two will repent, mourn, fall tearfully into each other's arms and my ears will be spared anymore of this vile mouth-fencing!"

Kregan, Hafid, the elders looked at each other, too stunned to move or speak.

"You seem confused," she said to Rhadamanthus and Minos. "Your precious Gate isn't the object of Zarad-Krul's quest." She patted the Book of the Last Battle in the pouch at her side. "This is. You chose Demonium as the battleground because you thought you had the best chance of defending it here. But if I rode away with the Book, Zarad-Krul wouldn't look twice at your pathetic pile of stones. He's already proven he needs no Gate to summon the Dark Gods.

"And as for your feeble-minded plan," she drew her foot

through Aecus' map, erasing it, "let me assure you I've no intention of going to Shardaha—with or without the Book. I'd sooner walk naked through a snake-pit than fight Zarad-Krul in his own courtyard. Hell man, let him come to us. We'll be waiting with hot food in our bellies and raw steel in our hands. Why should I exhaust myself chasing him when he has to come to me to get what he wants?"

Aecus trembled visibly with rage. His lips quivered, his hands clenched, unclenched. He tried to meet her unrelenting glare, and when he couldn't he kicked over her sword, muttering, and stalked from the tent.

"This was not foreseen," Minos said.

"I'm deeply worried," Rhadamanthus agreed.

Frost sighed, picked up her blade and wished for a jug of wine. She settled instead for the quiet semi-solitude of her own small camp and a few hours sleep. As always, she dreamed of home and her last days in Esgaria. But this time the memories were gentle and filled her with a dull, soulful ache. She awoke damp with her own soft tears.

Not a nightmare, she admitted, *but in its own way just as bad.*

She stretched, yawned, massaged the stiffness from her limbs and lay back again, staring at the sky. No stars, no moon, nothing but heavy black clouds and darkness.

Then, a bird. Two more birds. Suddenly, the sky was filled with fluttering; a familiar, evil cry shattered the stillness. Zarad-Krul's bird-things!

She leaped up, grabbing her sword-hilt. The black shapes circled and swooped, climbed high in the night, plummeted earthward and climbed again.

A war horn's reverberating blast drowned the birds' shrill screeching. Warriors sprang up from their sleeping pallets, reaching for armor and weapons. The quiet camp became a flurry of activity. She wasted no time, but began buckling on her own armor.

Before she was finished Kregan appeared at her side, breathless. "Shardahanis," he called. "Another army as large as the last."

"Zarad-Krul?"

"No sign of him."

She cursed, completed her armoring and started for the

horses where Ashur would be. Kregan caught her arm before she got far. "Rhadamanthus wants to see you first."

She shrugged, annoyed. "At the tent?"

"There." He pointed to Demonium and a path that led to the summit. "He's waiting at the foot of it."

She ran wondering what the old man could want. Sure enough, he was where Kregan said, but when she called he answered nothing, only beckoned.

Together, they ascended a steep trail that zig-zagged up the almost sheer rock face. In places there was no trail at all, just hand and toe holds carved into the stone. Rhadamanthus, old as he was, mastered them with surprising ease and agility, but her sword and the free-swinging leather pouch which contained the Book hampered her movements. By the time she reached the end her garments were damp with perspiration.

Three ancient stones loomed, the monoliths she had seen only from a distance. She sucked in a breath as she regarded them. Whether natural stones or sculpted, she was unsure; but carved deeply into each were symbols and runes whose meanings she could not even guess at. They sent a chill up her spine. Of course, they were arranged in a triangle. At the center, a flat, triangular-shaped stone lay upon the ground.

An altar.

"Why did you bring me here?" Impatience in her voice. "My place is below with the warriors."

"I don't deny it." Rhadamanthus folded his arms and regarded her with weary eyes. "The brothers have come to rely on you as a rallying figure. I think some would follow you even against an elder's wishes. They respect you; some of the younger apprentices even worship you."

She arched her eyebrows at that. Chondites were an unusually reserved lot. If the common soldiers felt anything for her she hadn't known it. "So?"

"You belong down there, yes. But not the Book—not this time."

She clapped a hand on the pouch, frowning.

The old man made an apologetic motion. "Sometimes we can see the future. When you first brought the Book to us we looked into the scrying waters and foresaw the events of this war until the time when the Dark Gods took an active part. We saw the battle at Tekaf Pass; we saw the battle just fought

171

against the Shardahanis. All in generalities, no details. But we knew you were not fated to fall in either, so we let you carry the Book into the conflicts. Indeed, you were meant to do so."

"So what's different now?" She considered a moment. "Are you telling me I'm going to die?"

Rhadamanthus shook his head, an expression of pain lingering on his face. "I don't know, child. The vision has gone wrong." He folded his hands. When he opened them again a bowl of water rested on his palms. She had seen him use that bowl before, his scrying bowl, but now there was a crack in it, and the water seeped slowly out and ran through his fingers. "The future we foresaw days ago in Erebus is no longer valid. Aecus lost his reason; we didn't foresee that. Nor did we foresee this second engagement with a Shardahani army. We killed too many of them—there should be no such force."

He folded his hands again, and the bowl disappeared. "Now we can see nothing. Too many incalculable factors have entered the fray, powers we didn't even suspect. All our fates are in question now."

"You think the Book is safer here?"

"Every Chondite has pledged to defend Demonium with his soul. Place the Book on the altar stone. That is the very center of our defense. One third of our warriors will remain below to protect this place, and I'll be right here." He laid a reassuring hand on her shoulder. "If Zarad-Krul wants the prize he'll have to fight every step of the way."

She hesitated, but the old man's reasoning was sound. She had carried it for so long, endured so much to safeguard it. It was not easy to entrust it to others. But at last she unslung the pouch and held it out to Rhadamanthus.

He stepped back, averting his eyes. "Take it to the stone. I held it once when it first came to Chondos. I will not touch it again."

A horn-blast made her look out over the field. The troops were moving without her. She bit her lip. Rhadamanthus said no more. The quiet, ominous monoliths waited. The altar stone waited. Steeling herself with a weak smile she stepped inside the great triangle.

The earth didn't open and the sky didn't fall. Slowly, she let go the breath she had held so long and extracted the Book. How heavy it seemed now. She was almost tempted to shove it back in the pouch and flee, but reluctantly she placed it on the altar.

A long sigh shook her, and she felt suddenly relaxed, a state she hadn't known in days. She tossed the leather pouch down beside the Book, gave it one last glance and turned away.

Rhadamanthus stood on the rim, watching below.

She wasted no more time in talking, but descended the path quickly, easily, now that she was familiar with it. Ashur waited patiently at the bottom. Someone, probably Kregan, had hung a new round-shield on the saddle to replace her battered one. Fitting it to her arm, she climbed onto the unicorn's back and set off in pursuit of the army.

Chapter Twelve

SHE CAUGHT UP TO HER COMRADES EASILY. BOTH ARMIES had stopped their charges with some distance remaining between them. The leaders regarded each other across the eerie field. Frost reined up beside Aecus, Minos, Kregan and Hafid.

"How in Gath's Nine Hells could an army that size cross Chondos without your knowing it?" she spat. "They're at least as many as the first force."

Aecus shook his head. "They moved fast. Killed our scouts and collected the bodies of their dead before we knew it."

She had noticed that. The field should have been littered with bodies. The Chondites had gathered their own fallen after the battle, but uncounted Shardahani corpses had been left to rot. They were all gone.

"They're just sitting out there," grumbled Hafid. "What are they waiting for?"

"What are we waiting for?" Aecus muttered. Drawing a deep breath he raised the war horn to his lips. The troops readied their weapons, leaned forward in the saddles, anticipating the attack.

A wall of flame shot up crackling between the two armies. A

scorching wind blew stinking black smoke into the Chondite ranks.

Frost cried out, fought to control her panicked steed. The smoke stung her eyes, filled her nostrils with a fetid odor. A fit of coughing wracked her, and the hot air seared her lungs. She twisted, trying for a glimpse of Demonium, recalling how Rhadamanthus had conjured such a wall before.

But this was not his doing.

The flames died; only a pillar of thick smoke remained, reaching into the sky, and from that came laughter to freeze her soul—deep, maniacal laughter that drowned the astonished shoutings of her allies. She had heard that bitter voice before and knew its owner. A cold hand clutched her heart as the pillar began to dissipate, revealing the man-shape within.

Zarad-Krul!

The wizard threw back his head and laughed again. The jewels and chains that adorned his otherwise naked flesh shook with the intensity of his mirth. He raised his hands in mystic gesture.

A second, more potent wind whipped across the plain at Zarad-Krul's command, raising clouds of choking dust, blowing unwary Chondites from their mounts. Frost cowered behind her shield to avoid the chunks of earth, pebbles and loose material that flew in the gale's wake, clinging to Ashur's back with her knees, one hand tangled in his mane until the wind ceased.

Then, a blast of thunder. Scarlet lightning laced the darkness, lending the land a blood hue. Zarad-Krul pointed to a boulder a short distance away. Bolt after smoking bolt, like angry serpents' tongues, suddenly lashed the stone, beating, hammering until it took on a new shape. In moments, where once was a common boulder stood a thing like a monstrous scorpion carved from solid rock.

Frost stared at the ugly pincers, the three great stinging tails, the dark and horrible maw that gaped with hunger. Her stomach churned, muscles knotted in fear. Yet, she could not tear her eyes from the evil genesis taking place.

The lightning's fury grew, streaking the night with veins of fire. The stone scorpion trembled as eldritch energy flowed into it. The pincers flexed menacingly; the stings curled over its back, black and venomous, long enough to pierce an armored man through. Two dark eyes that shone with ancient evil opened, glared at the Chondites.

Zarad-Krul's laughter filled the night, reminding Frost of stories that the cosmos was created with music. Now, she had a fearful vision that it was the Wizard-lord's mad laughter that gave birth to his Dark Allies.

Kregan sucked in a breath. "Nugaril," he named the creature.

Then, the very fabric of the night began to shift, coalesce in subtle ways. The air turned icy; the clouds swirled. At the other side of the field another creature took shape, man-like, but far greater in stature, a giant. Born of the night itself, it was a shadow without flesh or feature.

"Mentes?" she shouted.

Kregan nodded.

The wizard's laughter reached an insane crescendo that ate away her courage. Alone, she would have fled. Only the presence of her friends and a fear of shaming herself before them made her stay. She gazed on the Dark Gods, Zarad-Krul and his vast army, wondering what Hell on earth was about to unfold.

With a mad cry, Aecus drove spurs into his mount and flew across the field toward Shardaha's master. The Chondite captains looked to Minos for orders to charge, but that elder gave a stern glare, bade them hold their men.

A red rage fell on Frost. She drew her blade. *Damn my fear, then. Better to die with a lone fool than an army of cowards.* But Minos backed his horse, blocking her way. Kregan caught her arm.

"Stay," the elder commanded. "I gave no order to attack."

She stared dumbfounded at the old man's impassive face.

"It's his choice to go alone," Kregan whispered, a glimmer of sorrow in the depths of his dark eyes. "We foresaw his single combat with the wizard before Rhadamanthus' vision went wrong. Only the outcome is in doubt. If he wins then victory is ours without further battle. If not . . ." His voice trailed off, leaving the rest unspoken.

Her sword fell back into its sheath, but Kregan's hand did not leave hers. Together, they watched the lone rider that sped toward Zarad-Krul.

A few scant paces from the Wizard-lord, Aecus leaped from his horse. Free of its burden, the frightened animal raced away, its furious hooves cracking sparks from the glowing stones. Yanking the staff from his back, the Elder of the Argent Cup scratched a hasty circle in the dirt and thumped the ground three times.

A massive bubble of earth and rock swelled around his foe, climbing his form, swallowing, finally burying the wizard before he could utter a sound or make a move.

A mighty cheer tore from a thousand Chondite throats.

Yet, in the space of a heartbeat the mound cracked, turned to ash and dust that was borne swiftly away on an unnatural wind. Unharmed, Zarad-Krul roared with laughter and gestured. In his upraised hand an ebon splinter, a piece of the night itself, solidified. A spear whose barbed point dripped with a foul poison.

Zarad-Krul let fly. Straight for Aecus' heart the evil shaft sped, and the elder made no effort to dodge. At the last fleeting second his staff moved, seemingly of its own will, and deflected the occult lance. At that same instant the Chondite shouted an ancient name.

Roots, brown and twisted, sprang up from the barren soil, entwining the Shardahani in a choking embrace. Twice more the staff struck the earth; the ground turned to mire that sucked the wizard down as the roots strangled the breath from his struggling body.

But somehow, Zarad-Krul freed his hands. A wave, a clap and the earth turned solid once more. One danger averted, he craned his neck and spat a slimy wad of saliva on the roots. They withered and died. He shrugged off the brittle remains.

One summoned wind, but a greater wind countered it. Water quenched fire. Shivering cold fought parching heat. Zarad-Krul sent two of his hellish bird-things screaming for his foe's eyes, and the stones of the field became deadly missiles streaking to the Chondite's defense.

Frost watched it all, fascinated, cheering with the other warriors when Aecus gained an advantage only to see him lose it before the cheer fully left her lips. Still, she found a grim hope, for Zarad-Krul wasted no more energy on laughter. All his power was focussed on the duel.

Incredible forces shook the land, ravaging the terrain as the battle raged. Deep wounds, jagged gashes scarred the country-side. The air stirred nervously, full of dust and strange odors. Sparkling bolts, incandescent fires illumined the darkness, burned briefly, winked out. Then, as if by some unspoken consent, both adversaries ceased their manipulations. Unmoving, their hate-filled eyes locked.

Frost squeezed Kregan's arm. "What's happening?"

"A direct contest of wills." He could not look away from the scene. "One mind against another on the astral plane."

"A rare opportunity," Minos commented with unusual coolness. "We may discover which is the stronger motivating force in the human spirit: the lust for power or the thirst for vengeance."

Frost glared. "Damn your hard heart! The man's your friend."

He returned her gaze with utter detachment. "Yes, he is. And it's not for you to pass judgment on my feelings at this moment, is it."

She saw it then, the pain in his eyes. Fear for the safety of a friend. Or a brother. She nodded apology and understanding.

Interminable minutes dragged by. Neither Aecus nor Zarad-Krul showed a sign of weakening. The silence hung thicker than the obscuring clouds above. Not a sound came from either army: no cry, no clank of weapon or creak of armor. Even the animals kept still, sensing the tension.

Then, Zarad-Krul twitched; his eyebrow arched ever so slightly. A hand went to his temple, and pain flashed over his face. The Chondites went wild. A jubilant shout rose over the plain as the wizard's knees buckled and he collapsed screaming.

Aecus loomed over his foe. His long sword came out of its sheath for the death-stroke.

But suddenly, triumphant cheers turned to cries of anguish and outrage as Nugaril scuttled to the wizard's side on six stony legs.

Frost opened her mouth, but no sound came. Petrified, she watched the Dark God snatch Aecus up in one great claw and squeeze him until the blood gushed out. With casual indifference he dropped the sorcerer's broken body into his yawning maw and swallowed.

No command from Minos could hold the angry Chondites back. They surged forward, crying vengeance.

Astride her unicorn, Frost lunged ahead, that final image of

Aecus' death forever burned in her mind. A length of steel blossomed in her left fist as she steered her mount straight for Zarad-Krul. All that mattered was to spill his blood.

Yet, speed and fury won nothing. Nugaril lifted the black-hearted conjurer from harm's path and rapidly carried him to a rock escarpment a safe distance away.

The Chondites roared.

An opposing roar went up. The army of Shardaha charged.

The two sides met with a clamorous din, no order or strategy to the fighting, but a contest of unbridled savagery. The clang of steel on steel, the whine of arrows in the night, the grunting gasping of luckless warriors, the pitiful whinnies of terrified mounts. Harmony to chill the souls of sane men.

She plunged into it. Her sword sang through flesh and bone as she raced from one part of the battle to another, a remorseless killing machine, bent on single-handedly gutting every Shardahani in sight.

An azure flash caught her eye; she glanced around for the briefest moment and smiled grimly as weapons more potent than steel entered the fray. The staves of the Krilar streaked the night with soul-stealing energy. Men howled, touched by the blue radiance, and died without a mark on their bodies.

Then, a shadow that was more than shadow, Mentes came to the Shardahanis' aid. The dread god swung his foot, scattering men and horses indiscriminately, crunching bones beneath his stride as he waded into the battle.

Frost looked up and screamed a warning that went unheard in the tumult.

In the god's right hand a spear took shape from the fabric of night itself, similar to the one Zarad-Krul had hurled at Aecus, but longer and more viciously barbed. Mentes wielded it with deadly accuracy. One thrust pinned a Chondite wriggling to the earth, and another spear formed in the unholy fist. His aim never failed; no shield could guard against him.

Nor was Nugaril to be forgotten. With Zarad-Krul safe, he darted among the Chondites with an insect's speed, crushing warriors in his horrible claws, swallowing the bodies to appease his ravenous appetite. Worse yet were the monster's thrice-damned stings. With appalling swiftness those venomous tails lashed out, piercing men through, dripping poison that bloated the flesh, turned it sickly green until it ruptured and red blood poured into the dirt.

179

She groaned in disbelieving anguish as Nugaril and Mentes strode through her allies. Minor gods, Kregan called them. Neither steel nor mystic staff had any effect on them. A numbing cold gripped her as her comrades fell like sheep slaughtered by such unopposable power.

Something smashed her shield. She drove the point of her sword through the eye-slits of a challenger's helm.

Rallied by the presence of the Dark Gods, the Shardahani warriors fought with renewed fury. She might slay ten and win a moment's respite, but before she caught a ragged breath ten more were on her again.

The Nine Cities faltered. Though they fought bravely, fighting skill was not enough, and the Krilar, sorely pressed by enemies who saw them as the most serious Chondite threat, had no time to prepare spells more elaborate than the life-devouring light they conjured from their staves.

Where was Rhadamanthus?

Where was the vaunted power of Demonium?

She set her jaw resolutely. The Chondites needed something to rally them—something to pull them back together as a fighting unit. If they could get no help from their own sorcerers there was still one element of magic on their side.

With a savage cry she cast aside her shield, crushing a foeman's face with the metal edge. Demonfang came shrieking free. Leaning from the saddle she plunged it to the hilt in a Shardahani throat.

"Fight!" she urged her comrades, and she held up the dripping blade, braving its banshee note until it shivered in her grip, severing a warrior's spine to slake its thirst. And its thirst was endless. A knot of Shardahanis fell back in fear.

"Show them the color of Chondite steel!"

But suddenly, a cold shadow fell upon her. Ashur bellowed, his eyes flaring with sizzling flame. The unicorn reared, whirled, made an ineffective attempt to block something with his horn. Something huge.

Frost barely stayed in the saddle, aware only of a half-glimpsed shape that looked like a giant claw. She struck reflexively without thought.

Demonfang shrilled, bit deep.

Nugaril roared in pain. A black, foul-smelling ichor poured from the wounded pincer, scorching the earth.

She stared in horror and surprise, too numb at first to

realize her deed: *she had wounded a god!* The dagger twisted wildly in her hand, eager for another taste of gods' blood.

A shout went up from the Chondites as they witnessed Nugaril's distress. Singing her name they swarmed to her side. A dozen men leaped from horses onto the scorpion-god's back, and another dozen joined them. Sword and axe slammed against the monster's body; blades broke on that unyielding skin. Stings and pincers lunged at the fearless warriors, but for each man that died another took his place.

Yet, only she could hurt Zarad-Krul's dark ally. Again and again she darted in, stabbing with all her strength. Demonfang screamed its intense pleasure. Nugaril howled, struck at her with his stings, but the agile unicorn sprang away with his rider before they found a target.

Brackish liquid oozed from a score of wounds.

She studied the waving claws, waiting for another chance to rush in.

"Get back!"

Even over the sounds of fighting she recognized that voice. Kregan drove his steed straight for her, ran down a warrior in his path.

"Sheathe that damned blade!" He called to the other Chondites. "Get away!"

She didn't wait for an explanation. A tremor ran through the ground. *So Rhadamanthus had decided to act.* She stabbed the scorpion-god once more to quiet her shrieking weapon and returned it to the scabbard.

The tremor grew stronger. She pushed Ashur hard, putting distance between herself and Nugaril, riding away from the heart of the battle.

And Kregan stayed beside her.

A ponderous rumbling shook the plain. Warriors on both sides tumbled head over heels, unable to keep their footing. Frightened horses threw their riders and fled aimlessly.

Then, the earth fell away from Nugaril and huge worms, creatures she had seen before, wriggled onto the surface, up and over the Dark One's form.

He struck at them, but his stings had no effect, and when his pincers severed one the halves continued to act independently. Nugaril found himself engaged in a deadly and unexpected duel.

"He took his own sweet time about helping out." Frost held Ashur on a tight rein, grateful for a chance to rest. There was a dull ache in her left shoulder from swinging her sword.

Kregan held his mount similarly. "Rhadamanthus works on his own schedule. We don't question an elder's reasoning." His grim expression melted. Leaning close, he planted a small, pecking kiss on her cheek. "Besides, if he'd acted sooner you wouldn't have introduced Nugaril to that crazy dagger." He rolled his eyes in mock alarm and laughed. "Attacking a god with that tiny thing!"

"It's not the size of the wand that makes the magic work. . . . "

The jape was cut short by a new sound that rose over the din of battle. The thunderous fluttering of thousands of wings—a sound she knew all too well. And the bizarre cries of the bird-things.

If Rhadamanthus was at work, so was Zarad-Krul. In an instant the air was full of butterflies that bit and stung the flesh and screeching vulture-like birds that rent armor, skin and bone with razor talons and gross, misshapen beaks.

So the war raged, steel against steel, sorcery against sorcery: men, birds, butterflies, worms, dark gods. All at odds in a furious dance of death. She watched from a safe distance, catching her breath and resting her arm before charging back into it.

When a hard blow penetrated her leg armor she gave no thought to the pain or the warm fluid that ran into her boot. She struck twice at her attacker. The first blow dented his helm, dazing him; the second split metal and skull. It took all her strength to tug her weapon free.

She looked around for another opponent, and a string of Esgarian curses spilled from her lips.

Forgotten in the excitement, Natira raced among the fighters riding the horse that once had carried Aecus. Her white gowns fluttered like the wings of an insubstantial angel. Her hair streamed behind her. Amazingly, no sword threatened her, no warrior sprang into her path. Straight to Frost she came smiling.

Always smiling. Her eyes settled on Demonfang.

Threats and oaths failed to drive the mute woman away, and Frost could waste no more time on her. A pair of foes rushed side by side. Spurring her mount, she ran between them, kicking one man's shield as she sliced his comrade from gullet to groin. A blade slid ineffectually off her greave. She turned back to the remaining attacker; her unexpected kick momentarily unbalanced him, but now he held his shield close and firm, prepared for her mounted assault.

He never saw the horse that rode him down. His shattered body smacked the earth and stirred no more while his killer regarded him with that sweet, innocent expression.

Frost considered Natira with a frown, trapped between admiration and annoyance. The clean, quick way she had downed the man from behind with no warning.

"When I find your keeper, I going to kick his . . ."

She never finished. An involuntary cry ripped from her as an arrow abruptly sprouted from Natira's left breast.

But the woman made no sound, not even a sigh of pain. Tentatively, slender fingers touched the shaft, explored its length, rumpled the fletchings, traced the painted crest of its maker. Then, with a jerk, she plucked it from her body.

Her smile never faded.

Frost gaped, nearly dropping her sword. No wound, no blood. Yet, the shot had been a fatal one. She had seen the arrow, heard its cruel thud as it struck. The woman should be dead.

Yet, she was unharmed.

Before she could seek an answer a whistling axe brought her mind back to the fighting. She blocked it with a double-handed swing, cutting through the attacker's middle on the return. The mystery of Natira faded further from her thoughts as still another threat bore down on her.

With a shock, she recognized her new challenger.

She shook her head, unwilling to believe. But the evidence was there. The wound in his ribs still gushed crimson, proof of her handiwork, for she had slain him but a little while earlier. A second time she dispatched him, driving her blade straight through his heart. With a sigh, he tumbled to the ground.

But a cold dread fell upon her, a fearful suspicion. With desperate speed she rode away from the battle to gain a better vantage, noting as she went faces and uniforms, weapon-styles, oblivious to Natira who followed at her heels.

She knew now what had become of the Shardahani bodies left to rot after the first battle. And she knew why no elder had detected a second army moving into Chondos.

There was no second army.

Her gaze swept over the battleground, searching for Mentes. No longer did the Dark God expend his energy hurling arcane spears. A more fearful employ occupied his time. Dark waves flowed from his outspread fingers, bathing Shardahani corpses in a necromantic radiance. They rose, still bleeding from wounds, and marched back into the fray.

So the first army had risen from the dead to fight again, to die again and rise again.

She drew a deep breath flavored with despair.

Natira touched her shoulder, pointed. A figure hurried toward them, waving his arms. Wiping away blood that ran from a cut below his helm into his eyes, Kregan brought his mount to a hard stop. A score of cuts laced his thigh where a piece of armor had fallen off. His face twisted with pain and fatigue.

"There!" In the west a bright, burning glow approached the Field of Fire. "I rode back to get a better look. If it's what I think, we've lost the war."

It seemed to grow clearer without getting nearer. Straining against the gloom, she began to make out a shape.

"I can't see for all this damned blood," Kregan shouted, slapping at the crimson stream above his eyes. A barely controlled note of panic quavered in his voice.

Squeezing his hand for reassurance, she described what she saw.

A quadrigae of golden horses with eyes of wildfire pounded the earth. No, not horses at all, but monstrous mockeries of horses. Gleaming, ivory fangs curled between lips and under chins; the manes were stiff, razor edged. Clusters of scaly serpents writhed where tails should have grown. The hooves were cloven, and when the creatures breathed spurts of white-hot fury scorched the rocky ground.

Behind, a chariot carved from a single immense fire opal shimmered with impossible lustre. Fashioned into its working were skulls of bleached bone whose eye-sockets were stuffed with gems and precious stones. The great, grinding wheels were iron-bound, studded and spiked for war.

On the chariot stood a creature, man-like she guessed, but shrouded all in black with a cowl pulled close so the face was swallowed in shadow. Not even the hands showed; the reins disappeared into empty sleeves.

"What in the Nine Hells is it?" She had never seen her friend so pale. In a war of strange and bizarre happenings she had struggled to keep her courage, but Kregan's reaction to this demonic charioteer shook her to the roots of her soul.

"And why can I see him with such detail when he's still so far away?"

"Far and near," the Chondite answered cryptically. "He's not yet fully materialized on this earthly plane. We see him as if through a closed window as he races across the vast distances between dimensions. You see his form, but not his substance. It's only a matter of time, though, before those wheels scatter the dust of this world."

She blinked, not understanding.

"That is Shammuron," he explained. "No minor god like Nugaril or Mentes, but one of the *Raldori,* the triad of Dark Gods who tip the scales of life and death unfairly when Fate is not watching. In our wildest dreams we never suspected Zarad-Krul had power to summon him. Against the lesser two we might have held out. Against Shammuron there is no chance."

Someone tugged her sleeve. Turning, she met Natira's eyes. Something in those blue pools gave her strength, convinced her there could yet be hope against even a Raldor. Impulsively, she gripped Natira's hand, wondering how she could ever have feared such a gentle lady.

Shammuron's image grew distinct, yet she perceived it was no closer to Demonium.

"Well, he hasn't completed the crossing yet. If we can defeat Zarad-Krul before he does, that window will stay closed."

"There isn't time, I tell you!" Kregan beat a fist on his bleeding thigh. "We can't get to Zarad-Krul. We're barely holding his army back from the Gate."

"There may be a way, damn it, if we can get help!"

His voice lost its edge; he stared. "What help?"

She thumped the sheathed dagger on her hip. "If Demonfang can wound a god, maybe its unnatural sharpness can sever the locking strap that seals the Book of the Last Battle."

"We've tried cutting it," he argued.

"Not with Demonfang."

Hope grew slowly in his eyes. "The spells on those pages could turn the tide even against Shammuron."

Before she could say more a coruscating amber light

185

blossomed suddenly in their midst, bringing with it the Stranger from Etai Calan.

"Look to Rhadamanthus!" he warned. "Look to Demonium!"

Then he vanished as disconcertingly as he came.

She whirled to see the distant peak. Sporadic bursts of brilliant fire crowned the summit, illuminating the ancient monoliths, tinting the clouds with flickering hues.

The Book!

She launched across the field, cursing the moment she agreed to leave it behind. Other hoof-beats told her Kregan and Natira followed, but she pushed ahead, driving Ashur furiously.

Straight into camp she rode, scattering campfires and utensils. Silent horror greeted her. Every man—nearly a third of the Chondite host—sprawled dead, gazing into Hell with unseeing eyes.

She leaped from the unicorn's back, scrambled up the path to the Demonium Gate, uttering a desperate prayer to her homeland gods. It seemed an eternity passed as she climbed that steep course, but at last she sprang over the edge. Her sword hissed from the sheath.

Rhadamanthus and Zarad-Krul faced each other with only a short space between them. How the wizard had reached Demonium unnoticed she couldn't guess, but it was clear by the gleam in his one good eye that he recognized her.

"You!" he spat. "The witch who blinded me! I searched for you on the field with my magic, but couldn't find you. I see your aura has somehow changed." He made a sweeping gesture, and a black lance hurtled through the air seeking her heart. A second took form in his fist as he let the first one go. "No matter," he cried. "Die now!"

Quick as thought, Rhadamanthus' staff licked out, knocking aside the first missile. But, even his swift reflexes were helpless to intercept the second.

Pointed death flew at her.

She tensed, ready to spring aside. Then, before she could move Natira leaped in front of her, a living shield. Frost hadn't even seen her come over the path. A despairing crunch as the spear slammed into her chest sent her tumbling.

The warrior-woman held her breath, waiting, hoping. Sure

enough, Natira got to her feet, removed the lance as if it were less than a splinter. It might have been for the harm it did. She cast it down; it melted into its element.

Zarad-Krul stared. Rhadamanthus was no less stunned. Kregan, who had scrambled over the edge right behind Natira, ran to her side.

But Frost saw a chance. Springing at the Wizard-lord, her blade clove a glittering arc. *End it now,* she thought, *his death will stop this insane war.*

Impossibly, the wizard threw himself aside to avoid her stroke: Jagged rocks scraped his golden skin as he rolled to escape her angry slashes. A red flame burned in her brain, making her forget all technique; nothing mattered but to kill savagely, brutally, finally.

Then, a handful of flung dirt doused that flame. She stumbled back, muttering oaths, clutching her eyes.

"I can't fight all of you!" Zarad-Krul rose slowly, painfully, bleeding where the stones had torn his flesh. "Sorcerers and witches! But there's one coming who can! Yes, *one* who can!"

A mocking smile stretched the corners of his mouth. He clapped his hands once; two of his bird-things swooped out of the clouds, seized him by the shoulders and lifted him into the night.

Rhadamanthus collapsed against a monolith, forgetting Zarad-Krul, unable to stand. She ran to his side. He was feverish. A clammy sweat beaded on his ashen face.

What had he endured alone in combat, this eldest of the elders?

His old hand gripped hers, weak with exhaustion, imploring her help. Then, his tired gray eyes closed in sleep.

Without warning an unseen force rocked Demonium. The ground quivered. The monoliths trembled in their foundations.

"Shammuron!"

Desperately, she tried to wake the Elder of the Black Arrow, but nothing stirred him. Kregan called to her. Together, they gazed over the field as the Raldor extended a hand. Near their feet a portion of the edge crumbled as Demonium quaked once more beneath the Dark God's power.

"The transition between planes is complete," the Chondite

shouted. "See how the stones churn under his wheels? He comes for the Book of the Last Battle."

And he did not come alone. Without Rhadamanthus' conscious control the great worms abandoned the struggle with Nugaril and crawled back to the bowels of the earth, leaving that god and Mentes free to turn their attentions toward the sacred Gate.

"Then, by their own names, let's give them a battle."

She found the Book where she left it, snatched it up from the altar stone. But now it seemed nearly too heavy to lift, and it exuded a heat that threatened to burn her fingers. No matter. Straining with all her might, she heaved the volume up, clutched it to her breast and bore it back to the rim.

Kregan was already busy. With his staff he scratched a hasty pattern in the dirt. Angles and lines of amazing complexity took shape as the Chondite began to chant, his voice spiraling to an ever higher pitch. His muscles corded, went taut under the skin. The pattern on the ground began to glow.

She could not wait for him to finish. Shammuron, Nugaril and Mentes were dangerously close, and Kregan's sorcery was taking too long. The Book was their only chance. She fingered the ornate lock and the strap that bound the covers tight. Within lay the power to repel the evil that was almost upon them.

The lock had to be broken or the strap cut. One weapon alone might succeed where mundane steel and magic had not. Her hand closed on Demonfang.

A piercing shriek drowned Kregan's chant, shattered his careful concentration.

Then, another shriek. Frost screamed, realizing her mistake too late.

The dagger quivered, twisted in her hand, demanding its due. But there were no enemies near to slake its lust. In her eagerness to slash the binding she had forgotten the blade's fatal curse: *it must taste blood*. With a look of anguish she turned to Kregan, Natira, sleeping Rhadamanthus. Another shriek split her ears, more urgent than the first, more commanding.

Demonfang required a death, a sacrifice. But who? Which of her friends?

It was impossible to choose.

An odd tugging sucked at her mind. Though she fought the sensation, it grew, began to squeeze her will. Images of suicide assailed her, of hanging, drowning, falling. Monsters dredged up from her nightmares pressed her down, rolled her about, tossed her like a child's plaything until she thought the only escape lay in slitting her veins on their ivory claws. Death, a lusty young man, embraced her. The ghosts of her parents beckoned. Orgolio, the jailor, laughed hysterically, calling her names. She shut her eyes, but the visions continued, all with the same insistent message.

The point turned slowly, screeching, toward her heart.

Suddenly, other hands locked around hers. Fighting the dagger's spell, she snapped open her eyes. With surprising strength Natira forced the point around. An ecstatic smile lit the woman's face as she redirected the fiendish blade, set it to her own heart and lunged.

An orgasmic sigh parted her lips. No other sound from her.

Bright crimson spurted. Frost jerked her hands away in dazed anguish. The dagger went silent, and she waited for Natira's mouth to open and scream with its voice. But no sound came. In a swirl of soft gowns, she sank, eyes glazing swiftly with death.

Frost backed away from the dying woman, suddenly afraid. The Book slipped from her grasp, fell forgotten in the dust. A thick bile rose in her mouth; she shivered uncontrollably, unable to speak as Kregan cradled Natira in his arms. Profuse tears streamed his cheeks as he rocked her back and forth.

Feebly, Natira lifted an arm, beckoned her close.

She responded with a hesitant step, but shame and guilt made her stop. Yet, Natira called again, begged with those fading blue eyes. Frost collapsed at her side.

"I'm . . . sorry!"

But Natira laid a finger on her lips, silencing her. Then, those fingers stroked her cheek, a tender, forgiving touch. With her other hand, Natira eased the dagger from her heart.

The point flashed. A wincing pain stung her palm.

Frost stared disbelieving at the red streak Demonfang had made, too frightened to move.

With the last of her failing strength the small figure in the dirt pressed the wounded palm to the gushing hole above her heart.

A warm tingle crawled up Frost's arm as the two bloods conjoined. Uselessly, she tried to free her hand, but Natira's grip was inhuman. She gazed, horrified, into the smiling face, into azure eyes laced with pain.

Then, a heart gave its last beat.

A scream boiled in her throat; the warm tingle turned to hot, coursing fire that spread all through her, searing right through her soul. Thousands of needles prickled her skin. Molten liquid raced in her veins, bubbled in the sockets of her eyes. Her guts churned, aflame.

For an instant she felt expanded beyond the boundaries of flesh, of mortal memory or conception. The entire cosmos seemed to merge with her.

Then, stillness, a momentary calm. The scratch on her palm stared back at her, a thin scarlet smile. She sucked her lip, knowing and fearing what was to come.

It hit with a rush—a song that grew within her, melodies a human mind could barely contain. A symphony of sheer, raw power.

She understood now what Natira was, perceived the incredible nature of her final legacy. She rose and looked out over the Field of Fire, seeing the battle with perfect clarity unhampered by distance or darkness. She saw from all angles and viewpoints—through the eyes of every participant.

The Dark Ones were very close.

At the core of her being a song began its first note. She gazed on Shammuron, the dreaded Raldor. The song reached for a new note.

Beneath his rumbling chariot the stones exploded in showers of sparks, splintering the wheels, overturning the charging vehicle.

Her cloak and raven tresses lashed the air on a wind of her own creation. With unmerciful savagery she unleashed the music that roared within her, striking with a fury no longer human. The song became a chorus, an orchestra, and the music crescendoed as she blasted her unholy foes. They staggered, but still came on.

But in the middle of her attack, Kregan leaped up, grabbed her shoulders and shook her violently. It was so easy to discern his fear and confusion, to read the love in his heart. Love for her.

He thinks I'm possessed. He doesn't understand the change within me or realize the cause of it. But I have no time for explanations. The Dark Ones still stand.

With no more thought she brushed him aside.

Natira's gift was like a drug. She reveled in the energies at her command. More than magic or sorcery: such power was an extension of her will as natural and easy to use as her arms and legs. She wanted more—and knew how to get it.

In her own mind she found the psychic binding-spell placed there by her sorceress-mother. Simple to remove it and tap her own witchcraft. And there was all the energy of Demonium. Hers to command.

She lashed out again, all the elements her weapons. Shammuron stumbled, fell in a driving rainstorm. Nugaril spread his claws to grip the earth as raging winds strove to push him back. Riding the night like a black, shipless sail, Mentes writhed in the turbulent lightning that wracked his shadow-form.

Yet, they were gods. The Raldor found his footing and turned the rain aside. Hugging the ground, Nugaril pulled himself along with his pincers. Mentes smothered the lightning with a cloud of ebon radiance. Ever closer they came toward Demonium.

And over the plain came a hateful laugh. Standing again on the rock where Nugaril had put him, Zarad-Krul cheered his evil allies.

The true-sight of the great mages was hers now, and no illusion could hide the true appearance of Shardaha's wicked lord. Gone was the golden, muscled youth. Gone were the perfect limbs and beautiful features. Zarad-Krul was knarled and bent with age. Filth matted his thinning, dun-colored hair and beard. Bluish veins floated livid on his puffy, wrinkled flesh, and the teeth were rotten in his lipless mouth.

But the blinded eye was no illusion. Her sword had done that. One socket gaped terribly empty.

Insane glee shone on his mouldy face; he smacked his hands together in joyful malevolence and danced.

Her spirit sang a new song; an arpeggio of power rushed forth. If she could not halt the Dark Ones, she could still aid her battling Chondite friends against the wizard's human minions.

Her music touched a sharp note and cracked open the earth on the armies' right flank. An invisible hand herded the Shardahanis, tumbled them into the yawning abyss screaming in dismay. A few on the farthest edges of the fighting escaped the hand and fled, begging their master for protection.

She looked on them with unforgiving eyes, and the flesh on their bodies burst into fountains of scarlet flame. The smoke and stink rose up around the wizard, filled his nostrils, doubled him with a fit of coughing.

A terrible smile creased her lips, and her thoughts ranged over the field. *Laugh now, little man, as you gag on your pitiful dreams, and know that I can slay you just as easily, just as agonizingly.*

She turned her power on his bird-things and butterflies, perceiving they were not birds or butterflies at all, but ugly fiends disguised in those shapes. They, too, exploded in flame, fell to earth like tiny shooting stars.

Then, another mind touched hers. She reeled with the jolt, nearly bending under its alien strength.

What purpose . . . female . . . to frighten . . . mad mortal? His withered mind . . . no longer important . . . We come . . . for the Book . . . for you.

She straightened, adjusting slowly to the chaos of Shammuron's thought pattern. The Dark Gods were right below, wreaking havoc in the Chondite camp.

Come then, you bastard-spawn of some insignificant bitch-goddess.

The Book of the Last Battle lay by Natira's feet where she had dropped it. She gestured, and the ancient tome trembled, rose, levitated to her open hand. Demonfang, still clutched in the dead woman's hand, wailed a long, hungry note.

Be silent, she commanded.

The dagger obeyed her will, and at a crook of her finger, also levitated.

Laying the gleaming blade next to the leather strap that sealed the Book's covers, she drew it carefully. The strap parted, offering no resistance. The runes began to shimmer, and the Book opened itself.

The pages fluttered, turning rapidly of their own accord, displaying the knowledge written within. She absorbed it all at a glance. A blood-writ spell passed her eyes, the one she sought. An instant later, the Book closed, and the leather strap became one piece again, denying evidence of the dagger's edge.

No matter. She remembered everything.

She shouted words in a language she did not know, and an immense vortex began to whirl with her at its center, sucking dust and stones into itself. It spun with increasing fury, feeding on the power and energy she poured into it. Sweat beaded on her forehead, ran into her eyes as she concentrated.

Far across the plain its force swept warriors off their feet. Zarad-Krul toppled from his rock perch. Even the Dark Gods as they at last achieved Demonium's crest were hurled back to the field by the maelstrom's raging.

Frost felt her knees buckle. The vortex was consuming her power. She sagged to the ground. It swelled, grew stronger. But more was needed, and she had no more to give. Valiantly, she strained, offering her last song.

Sensing her depletion, the vortex lifted, moved away from her. Within the monoliths the altar stone became its new locus.

The Gate had power to feed on—infinite power.

No longer did gale winds buffet the countryside. The monoliths contained that. The tempest reached upward instead, through the sky, swelling at a fantastic rate, drawing energy from the Gate, energy to open it and rip a hole in the space between the planes.

Too weak to stand, Frost waited, praying her spell would work.

Then, out of the vortex sailed a shining creature on pinions of white down feathers. Graceful as a wild swan, it climbed the sky, and she saw that though the wings were those of a bird the body was like a man's. She crawled to the edge of Demonium as it soared over the field.

Silently, Mentes raised his hand; a wave of blackness flowed forth. The swan-being rolled away with confident ease, and a spark of golden fire flashed from a taloned finger. Mentes roared in pain.

One by one, a host of strange creatures emerged from the vortex, flying or walking or slithering, drawn into earth's plane by her last conjuration. With forces no mortal would ever understand they assaulted the Dark Ones. The air tingled with eldritch energies. On the same ground where men fought and died, ancient gods renewed an eternal struggle.

Its work done, the vortex dissipated. Voices on the pathway

caught her attention. Hafid and a few of his comrades clambered over the rim and hurried to her side, their expressions full of awe at the combat they were witness to.

"In Gath's name." Hafid's voice was a taut whisper. "What are those creatures?"

"The Lords of Light," she answered.

"God against God." Hafid made a holy sign and hid his face. "Then, is this truly the Last Battle?"

She had no answer for him.

"Well, that is no god." A warrior whose name she could not recall pointed.

Zarad-Krul had seized a stray horse. Over the field he rode to aid his malevolent allies, hurling spells and long curses that were less than useless against the Gods of Light. Suddenly, his mount stumbled. The wizard slammed the earth hard, one leg bent oddly beneath him. The last vestiges of his sanity crumbled. He beat his fists impotently on the unfeeling rocks.

Nugaril turned cold, gleaming eyes on the whimpering human. His huge claws flexed menacingly; the stings twitched over his back. Leaving Shammuron and Mentes to fight alone, he scuttled over the broken earth to the wizard and snatched him up in one terrible pincer.

Zarad-Krul had a moment to stare into that waiting maw before he fell shrieking into its darkness.

Frost grimaced as the jaws ground shut.

Hafid nodded smugly. "As we were taught, evil feeds on evil."

It was nearly over. No traces remained of Mentes; the shadow-god had faded from the Lords of Light. Though Nugaril fought on, claws and stings were futile weapons against his foes; the glow in his eyes began to dim; he moved sluggishly as if his life force were draining away. Shammuron was under siege; a hole of shining whiteness opened in the air, and the Light Gods forced him ever closer to it.

She wanted to close her eyes and surrender to the exhaustion and fatigue that washed over her. Body and mind ached for the oblivion of sleep. Yet, Hafid shook her suddenly, exclaiming in her ear.

The swan-winged god drifted gently from the sky to stand before them. In a taloned hand he held the Book of the Last Battle.

"I am Shakari." His voice was rich, melodic, full of sweet odors and promises of flowery, sun-drenched meadows, rippling streams of crystal water.

He extended a hand, and she took it tremorously. There was a pleasant warmth to his touch as his fingers closed on hers. All weariness melted away, and pain dissolved as her wounds miraculously healed.

When she attempted a sputtering thanks the being called Shakari only smiled and placed a finger on her lips, an oddly human gesture.

He led her between the monoliths. The Gate appeared undisturbed by the vortex's fury. The looming stones remained erect, unmarked.

On the altar stood the Stranger, grinning broadly. "So my young warrior, you've come far since we met in Etai Calan."

"If I was young then," she answered, "I think I've grown very old since."

"In some ways," Shakari conceded. "Much has happened since your encounter with Almurion. You have changed."

"Almurion?"

The Stranger made a deep bow. "We never had time for a proper introduction, did we?"

"But you should be dead. I saw the butterflies pick your bones."

Almurion lost his smile. "I suffered death as all men must. You see my spirit-form now. I've continued for a time to serve the Lords of Light, for it was granted to me when I stole the Book that I would see the end of this conflict, though I could no longer play an active part. Now, it is finished, and I will soon depart this world forever."

"The Book of the Last Battle is safe." The swan-god stroked the volume as if it were a pet animal. "But a great harm has been done."

"What harm?" She could not help but frown at his chiding tone. "We won, didn't we?"

"There was more at stake then mere victory, child," Almurion said. "I told you once the Lords of Light were not intended to take part in this war. Yet, you summoned them against their wishes with the spell you found in the Book. That has upset delicate cosmic time tables. Now, there can be no foretelling when the *true* Last Battle will take place."

"Worse," Shakari continued. "That summoning spell was designed to call the Dark Ones at a time and place of *our* choosing. Now, they know it can also be used to call us. They heard when you spoke it. And they will remember."

She looked away. The land was quiet now. The battle over. "You have your concerns," she answered evenly, "and I have mine. My world is safe for the time being, and I still have my life and the lives of some of my friends." Her eyes locked with Almurion's. "That was all the reward you offered if I carried out your task."

He responded graciously with another bow and a grin.

"But one thing troubles me. When Natira's power first flowed through me I thought I detected a purpose—some plan to all this."

Shakari fluttered his wings. "Is it not purpose enough that the Book was rescued from the clutches of the Dark Gods?"

Almurion stepped down from the altar-stone and stood close to the swan-god. "Who can say what a purpose is?" He made a sweeping, all-encompassing gesture. "There are gods beyond gods, my child. Even Shakari has someone to worship. And his gods have their gods, hierarchy on hierarchy never ending. Who can say what purpose is fulfilled or whose plan? How could any being know?"

"Do not waste time searching for purposes," Shakari advised. "That is a maze of circles and angles, full of dead ends and locked doors. Full of answers to questions that were never asked."

Wind and dust stirred around her, grew stronger with every heartbeat. A low moaning filled the night, rose to a fever pitch.

Suddenly, she stood at the center of a new vortex. The Lords of Light began to gather.

"We must leave you now, human." The wail of the vortex drowned speech. Shakari's voice was an echo in her mind. "The Dark Ones no longer walk your earth, and we must prepare ourselves for the greater war to come when Light and Darkness meet for the final time—when the universe will die and be reborn in the image of the victor."

The swan-god passed the Book of the Last Battle into Almurion's hands. "Yet, there is one thing left to do." He laid feathered hands on either side of her head and pressed gently, forcing her to meet his gaze. "You have seen the writing in the Book, and though we are grateful for what you have done, you cannot be permitted to keep that knowledge. Soon, you will sleep, and when you wake you will have no memory of what you saw on those timeless pages."

Shakari·stepped back.

Almurion raised a hand in farewell. "Live long, Frost of Esgaria, and remember me."

Then the world blurred and she sank to the ground, the vortex raging loud in her ears. The Lords of Light rose up through its center, spiralling dizzily and disappeared. Shakari and Almurion with the Book were last. In her mind the swangod sang a soft song, and she didn't resist as it lulled her to sleep.

Chapter Thirteen

SHE AWAKENED TO SWEET AIR AND A PLEASING WARMTH on her face, recognizing the walls of her room in Erebus. Had it all been a bad dream, then? Another of her nightmares? Beyond the only window the sun shone brightly in an unblemished sky.

No, not a dream. The livid scar on her palm was real.

She threw back the coverlet and found herself dressed in a soft linen gown. Someone had bathed her, too, and lightly scented her hair with herbs. She swung her feet out of bed, sat up.

Movement in the corridor.

"Kregan?"

A serving girl turned, startled, when she jerked open the door. Then the young, dust-smeared face lit up. The girl made a quick curtsy, muttered "good morning," and sped excitedly off, rattling bottles on her tray.

Frost bit her lip, frowning. The wench could have stayed long enough to answer some questions. Where was everyone? The place was so quiet. Easing the door shut, she went back to her bed, hugged her knees and leaned against the tapestried wall.

Where was everyone?

A knock. Somebody called her name.

Well, whoever it was, she'd welcome the company. If only she'd thought to look for some clothes. But no matter. She called out for them to enter.

Rhadamanthus led a string of servants inside. At his direction they heaped a small wooden table with platters of meats, fruits, raw vegetables and breads. A cheese was set at her right hand, jugs of wine and fresh water at her left.

It hadn't occurred to her that she was hungry, yet when the food was before her she ate ravenously with a relish she had not known for weeks. Dismissing the servants, the Elder of the Black Arrow took a chair opposite her and began carving a plump fruit with a slender dagger. They talked between mouthfuls.

"Natira was a goddess."

Rhadamanthus nodded, sipped his wine. "Yes, a Neutral. I'm not sure when I knew for certain, but I suspected." He set down his dagger, leaned on one elbow. "There was always an aura about her. I feared it at first, but later . . ." His voice trailed off.

"I remember the feeling." She chewed a bite of meat.

Natira's power was gone, expended in the summoning of the Lords of Light, and without it her own witchcraft was dormant again.

"For a moment, when her magic flowed into me, we shared a common mind, one set of memories. But it ended too quickly. When she died I was left with her power and knowledge to use it, but no more."

"And you're still not sure what role she really played in it all?"

Frost nodded. "You called her a Neutral?"

"Some powers are unaligned with either Light or Dark. They'll have no place in a cosmos ruled by one or the other exclusively. For them, the Last Battle means utter oblivion. Yet, their own laws bind them from taking sides or interfering in that final struggle."

"But she did interfere!"

"Not really." The elder picked up his dagger, smeared butter on a piece of bread and washed it down with water, then wine. "She struck no blow against the Dark Gods."

"But she gave me her power!"

The old man's eyes twinkled. "And *you* used it against them. It's a fragile difference, I know. But then, gods can be like that sometimes. That's why we Chondites seldom bother with them. It's easier to draw magic from a pile of stones if you know how. And the stones don't talk back or make unreasonable demands on your morals."

She gazed beyond the window. A flock of birds flew through the sapphire sky. "Does a goddess truly die?"

Rhadamanthus rocked forward, snatching a strip of meat. "She did what she came to do, knowing from the first it meant her death. What other reason for her fascination for Demonfang? She recognized it as the instrument of her death. And to give you her power she had to die."

But a deeper understanding filled her. Rhadamanthus had part of the truth, but not all. "You say that the Last Battle means doom for the Neutral Gods?" Yes, those were his words. She smiled a thin, ironic smile. "Shakari told me that by opening the Book and summoning the Light Lords I caused the time of that Battle to be delayed *beyond all foretelling.*"

Rhadamanthus thought, then nodded appreciatively. "She knew the dagger was her death," he said, "but also that it could open the Book."

"And that delayed the doom of the Neutral Gods beyond all foretelling as well." She set her own eating dagger aside, regarding the wine in the bottom of her cup pensively. "I thought I sensed a purpose to it all."

"Purpose?" Rhadamanthus steepled his fingers. "Who can fathom the purposes of gods?"

"I've heard that before." She tossed down the last of her wine and wiped her mouth. "In any case, it's over and we won."

He shook his head. "A costly victory for Chondos, I'm afraid. Our best young men are dead, our brotherhoods depleted. We'll try to recruit new apprentices from the common populace, but it'll be many years before we can raise another army of quality warriors."

"Cheer up, Elder. Some of the women are already hard at work on that problem. I've instructed a few myself."

Hafid grinned broadly from the doorway, in obvious good spirits despite the sling on his arm. She launched a chunk of meat at his nose.

"This woman might take offense at such quaint humor," she said, matching his grin.

"No offense meant, milady." He made a deep bow. "You've already proved *your* skill with a sword. Now our females have a chance to prove theirs with a similar weapon. If you'd care to learn its use, I'd be pleased to teach you."

She mocked his bow with one of her own. "I prefer a longer blade with a hard, sharp point."

"As do all women who speak truthfully."

He barely ducked another chunk of meat. They laughed together. It was good to hear laughter.

With Indrasad gone, he called Erebus home now. He poured himself wine and grabbed some cheese, hauled up a stool to sit on. For the better part of the day the three of them talked.

Aecus, of course, was dead, and Minos lay near death from a wound received in the earliest part of the second attack. Though the wound had been cauterized against infections and treated with various remedies, his life remained uncertain.

Of the Nine Cities, two had been utterly destroyed.

Slowly, the setting sun stained the sky indigo and crimson. Though she enjoyed the company of her friends, her thoughts wandered more and more to Kregan. *Where was he?* Servants had come and gone all day, smiling, wishing her well, showing courtesy and respect.

Yet, Kregan had not come.

When a woman came to refill the wine jugs, Frost caught her arm.

"If you can find Kregan, tell him I want to see his worthless hide on my threshold before the sun is gone, and if he's late Rhadamanthus will hear how he spent his last night in Zondu."

The woman returned a look of shocked distress, nearly spilling her tray. The elder motioned her quickly out of the room and closed the door.

Frost rose carefully, trying to read the old man's eyes. He turned them to the floor. Hafid became suddenly interested in something beyond the window.

"Has Kregan been hurt?"

No answer.

The table shook under her pounding fist. A bottle overturned. Its crash echoed in the room's silence.

"Tell me!"

The Chondites regarded each other gravely. Then, Rhadamanthus sighed. "Perhaps, it's best to show her." A stricken look flashed on Hafid's face, but the old man could not be dissuaded.

He led the way down a series of corridors and too many flights of stairs to count. The lighted passages were soon left behind; they made their way by the light of a single sconce. Ever downward went the course. The floor turned cold, damp beneath her bare feet. The heavier footsteps of her companions reverberated ominously in the narrow halls, the harsh rasp of her breathing the only other sound.

She was sure they had gone far underground, deeper in the city's bowels than Kregan had ever taken her.

They stopped before a huge door of polished bronze adorned with a heavy ring and the mark of the Black Arrow. Passing the sconce to Hafid the elder seized the ring with both hands and strained.

The door creaked open.

As they entered, an apprentice bowed wordlessly and left the chamber. It was ablaze with candles, lamps, braziers. Clouds of incense floated in the air. Ritual symbols and bizarre geometrical patterns decorated the floor, ceiling and three walls. But on the east wall, in the center of a white triangle, hung an immense horn bow and a quiver of ebon arrows.

She turned, taking it all in, and caught her breath.

Kregan's body reposed on an elaborate stone altar at the room's far end. A soft blue cloth stretched over the top of the altar, and a robe of the same material covered him from the chest down. The fingers of one hand curled loosely around a shaft like the ones in the quiver.

She crept closer, fighting the emotions that swelled within her.

"You must not touch him," Rhadamanthus warned. "It would be disrespectful."

His skin was ashen, the lips had lost all color. An ugly bruise marred the Chondite's brow.

She couldn't hold back the tear that trickled on her cheek. Hafid slid an arm around her, offering support, but she shied away.

"How?" she cried suddenly. "Except for a few cuts he was perfectly well when I summoned the vortex!"

The old man shook his head sadly. "He was standing when the terrible winds began. I was awake by then, but too weak to move, and I watched helplessly as he was lifted by the maelstrom's raging and slammed against a monolith. You see the bruise where he struck his head."

It didn't seem possible he was dead. They had survived too much, vanquished too many foes to be parted this way.

Hafid took a firm grip on her arm, pulled her away. "He would have called it a fair trade. His life for his world. He wouldn't want your grief. Come away, now."

"Not yet."

His grip tightened. "Please."

"Let go!" She knocked his hand away, stepped closer to the altar.

"Stop!"

Ignoring them, she bent over Kregan and planted a gentle, farewell kiss on his lips.

And froze.

What trick was this? There was warmth in those lips, and the nostrils flared ever so slightly. She touched his face. It wasn't cold at all!

"What in the Nine Hells?" she cried. "He's alive!"

Rhadamanthus seized her shoulders and pulled her back. His eyes burned into her. "I asked you not to touch him."

"But you told me he was dead!"

"No, he didn't," Hafid answered. "You assumed it. But the truth is—until four days ago, he was dead."

Confusion, anger flushed her cheeks.

"It's difficult to explain." Rhadamanthus folded his hands, rested his forehead on his fingertips before speaking again. "You're not versed in Chondite ways. Kregan died at Demonium. But for a master sorcerer, a *Krilar*, death is something to experience and conquer. The final test of our art."

"A test very few of us pass," Hafid added.

The old man looked away. "Almost none. Eleven masters died fighting Zarad-Krul. Only Kregan has returned to us." He faced her again, and his voice choked with sudden emotion. "For three days and nights he lay cold, unmoving. But, he was my most apt pupil; I prayed he would succeed where so many others failed. Then, on the morning of the fourth day breath returned to his body and warmth to his limbs. He had wrestled with death and won."

"Then, why don't you move him out of this dark hole to a place where he can be cared for properly?"

"No." A strange light lit up his face. "He has seen the unnamable things that crawl in the Hells, and the sight has numbed his soul. Anywhere else he would be easy prey for any demon or malevolent spirit to possess; but here among the trappings of his brotherhood he remains safe."

"How long will he stay like this?"

The elder shrugged. "We never know. He may awaken in an hour or a day, a week. Maybe not for years. That's happened before."

Hafid leaned close. "And when he does awake our work will begin. At first, he'll have no memory. We'll have to teach him and retrain him."

"But this time, Kregan will do more than just absorb our teachings." Rhadamanthus turned a fatherly gaze on his still pupil. "This time he will know intuitively the truths that bind the universe together. And that will give him power."

"The power of an elder," Hafid said. "And he'll found his own brotherhood."

She repeated that slowly, letting its meaning sink in. She faced Rhadamanthus, then, and a tingle ran up her spine. "Then, you've died and returned to life."

"A number of times." The old man regarded her evenly. "But each time is harder than the last. No man can cheat death forever."

Her voice quivered. "How old are you?"

"Do you know the story of Tordesh and the building of the causeway?"

She nodded.

He indicated the bow and quiver on the east wall. "I killed his horse with that weapon and shamed him back to Zondu. That was in my first incarnation."

She had lots of questions, but he would speak no more of the past. "You still haven't explained why you wanted me to think Kregan was dead."

The elder frowned, rubbed his temple. "If I wanted that I would have told you his body was lost on the field and never brought you down here. But because I knew you cared for him I wanted to give you a last chance to see him before you left."

"But I'm not leaving."

"I'm afraid you must." He wore a sad, but unyielding face. "If you have any love for Kregan or friendship for me, then you must leave Chondos."

Suspicion, resentment flared. She clenched her fists stubbornly. "Why do you want to get rid of me now?"

Her quick temper triggered all her senses. Hafid made a furtive movement behind her, the faint rustle of his garments betraying his position. One hand felt for the sword she wasn't wearing. Curse her for not dressing when she had the chance.

"I can't explain everything," the old man said with genuine anguish. "But you *can't* stay." His cheeks went scarlet with embarrassment. "Forgive us, but you haven't any choice."

She glared. "What if I refuse?"

Hafid caught her arm, a grip that meant business.

All her anger and frustration exploded. Her eyes narrowed, lips curled in a feral expression. Child's play to break Hafid's grasp. Seizing his injured arm she flung him against the wall. Her open hand cracked twice on his face. That wasn't enough to satisfy her. Dazed, he tried to back away; she kicked him in the stomach, ripping right through the light gown she wore. As he fell forward her knuckles beat his head, and when he didn't move she kicked him twice more for good measure.

He hadn't had a chance to even groan.

She spun on Rhadamanthus, trembling with unabated fury. "Now," she hissed through a tight throat, "I'll go before I forget just how old you are!"

Obediently, he led her from the chamber, directing the apprentice who waited just beyond the great bronze portal to see to Hafid.

When they were back in her room, Rhadamanthus was conciliatory. "You needn't leave right away. In the morning I'll have provisions prepared, and Ashur will be waiting. Your garments are in that chest by the bed, and your weapons, too."

He paused, forlorn. "You didn't have to beat him," meaning Hafid. "His arm was in a sling."

"So was my heart."

He departed sadly. She kicked the door shut behind him and paced the floor until the last vestiges of her anger faded, leaving only the hurt.

She didn't want to leave Kregan. What she felt for the

Chondite wasn't love, exactly. But it could be someday. She was sure he loved her.

What was the reason for Rhadamanthus' unexpected rudeness? He was right about one thing; she shouldn't have beaten poor Hafid.

She collapsed on the bed, utterly confused. Sleep stole upon her, bringing the old dreams of her family and new nightmares of the war. She tossed and turned, scattering the covers. She relived it all. Every moment, every bloody death.

Then, she screamed. Wide awake and shivering, she sat up, stared into the darkness beyond the window, a night speckled with stars.

When Rhadamanthus knocked the next morning he found her dressed, armed, ready to leave. She refused breakfast. If provisions were adequate she might eat something along the way.

"You're not angry anymore," the elder observed. "You have every right to be."

"I had a dream last night," she confessed. "More than a dream, really." She hesitated, gathering strength to say the words. "I killed Kregan, didn't I?"

He eyed her closely, and finally nodded. "You would not have learned that from any Chondite. It wasn't your fault. Kregan knew better than to interfere while you were waging mystic combat with strange and untested powers."

She bit her lip, hoping that pain would hide the deeper grief she felt. "He was concerned for me. I saw that in his mind, but I pushed him away. Only not with my hands. The magic did it. It hurled him headlong into that monolith. I wasn't aware; I didn't give him another thought."

Rhadamanthus didn't answer.

"And that's why you want me to leave. Because I killed him."

"If you are responsible for his death, then you are responsible for his elevation. No, child. You're not condemned for that. But Kregan knew better than to interfere, and he did so anyway. He loves you. That's why you have to go."

A glimmer of understanding came, but she kept silent.

"With Aecus dead and Minos' life uncertain, Chondos will need a new elder to continue the teachings."

She interrupted. "But won't they return to life?"

"Aecus has no body to come back to, and Minos is a doubtful case; his last incarnation was especially difficult. In fact, I doubt if either of us will achieve another incarnation. And without elders to continue the brotherhoods our way of life would be lost."

"But how does my staying threaten your ways?"

"Like Aecus and Minos, I fear my time will soon be up. But I don't fear death so long as Kregan lives to carry on. Yet, he loves you. That's why he tried to prevent your duel with the Dark Ones. Child, love is something a sorcerer can ill-afford, and a Chondite elder can't afford it at all. It distorted his judgment once. I can't let it interfere with his duties to his people."

She regarded him blank-eyed, not quite convinced.

"The real problem," he continued, "is that you're just not the kind of woman to be content with household chores and children. Something pulls your spirit, calls you to wander. You've just tasted adventure, and I can see in your eyes that you like it. Sooner or later, you would leave, and Kregan would follow without a thought for Chondos." He drew a deep breath and met her gaze with complete calm. "I can't allow that. So you must leave before his memory wakens."

Her heart leaped. "He won't remember me?"

A subtle smile flickered on his lips. "How could any man forget you?" He made a short bow. "But by the time he does remember I hope the weight of his obligations will be too strong a bond to let him pursue you.

"For you see, despite everything I've just said, I *have* permitted myself to love. I love Chondos. And Chondos needs Kregan more than you do."

At last, she understood.

The Elder of the Black Arrow walked her down to the courtyard. Ashur stood waiting, laden with provisions and a saddlebag full of gold coins. The unicorn trumpeted a greeting. "Well, I've gained something from all this," she said stroking the proud beast from crest to withers, touching Demonfang where it rode on her hip.

Rhadamanthus pushed her hand from the dagger. "Listen to an old man's warning, I beg you. Ashur is yours as long as he'll stay with you. But that *thing's* work is done. Get rid of it at your first opportunity. It means trouble if you keep it."

She glanced at the arcane blade, then at the scar its edge had left on her palm. "I'll consider it, my friend."

An odd contentment settled on her as she swung up into the

saddle. It was a fair morning made for riding. A light breeze stirred; the sun was not too hot.

The elder accompanied her to the city's western gate, but he wore a disconsolate silence.

"How is Hafid," she asked abruptly. "I meant to see him before I left. I wanted to apologize."

"A little bruised," he admitted, "but otherwise all right. The worst damage was to his pride."

The streets were nearly empty at this hour of the morning. They arrived at the gates, passing only a few merchants on their way to set up shop in the great square. Amid the clank of chains and gears the gates ponderously opened.

"Where will you go?"

She shrugged. "Korkyra maybe. It's said the forests there are thick as Esgaria's, and the Calendi Sea at its storm-tossed wildest. Of all the things in my homeland, I think I've missed the sea and forest most."

Rhadamanthus reached for her hand, pressed it to his lips, then held it a lingering moment. A tremor passed through him, and like a spark it communicated to her.

She leaned down, kissed his cheek. "You know," she whispered, "it's just as well this way."